Christmas at Conwenna Cove

D0299802

DARCIE BOLEYN

Christmas
at
Conwenna Cove

CANELO

First published in the United Kingdom in 2017 by Canelo

This edition published in the United Kingdom in 2019 by

Canelo Digital Publishing Limited
57 Shepherds Lane
Beaconsfield, Bucks HP9 2DU
United Kingdom

Copyright © Darcie Boleyn, 2017

The moral right of Darcie Boleyn to be identified as the author of this work
has been asserted in accordance with the Copyright, Designs and Patents
Act, 1988.

All rights reserved. No part of this publication may be reproduced or
transmitted in any form or by any means, electronic or mechanical,
including photocopy, recording, or any information storage and retrieval
system, without permission in writing from the publisher.

A CIP catalogue record for this book is available from the British Library.

Print ISBN 978 1 78863 573 8
Ebook ISBN 978 1 911591 44 3

This book is a work of fiction. Names, characters, businesses, organizations,
places and events are either the product of the author's imagination or are
used fictitiously. Any resemblance to actual persons, living or dead, events
or locales is entirely coincidental.

Look for more great books at www.canelo.co

Printed and bound in Great Britain by Clays Ltd, Elcograf S.p.A.

For my husband, with love always. XXX

Chapter 1

'What on earth is that?' Grace Phillips peered over her mother's shoulder into the musty smelling shed.

'I have no idea, and it smells like something's been living in here. Possibly cats.'

'It is a bit stinky, but how would a cat get in?'

'There's a hole in the floor just there,' Louise Phillips pointed at the corner where there was a space large enough for a cat to squeeze through, 'and the door wasn't locked.'

'Poor thing. It's hardly luxury accommodation.'

'No, but it's warm and dry.'

Louise Phillips tucked her wavy red hair behind her ears then approached the object that had roused their curiosity: a bulging sack that was propped up against the workbench. She glanced back at Grace, who nodded – after all, it couldn't be anything terrible – then reached out and poked the sack.

'It's probably just tools or something...'

'Probably.'

'Here, let me do it, Mum.'

Grace leant over and released the thin rope that held the sack closed, then opened it.

'What's inside—'

'Ahhhh!'

Grace threw the bag and ran out of the shed, her mother hot on her heels.

'What're we going to do, Mum?'

Louise shook her head. 'I don't know. What did you see?'

'Something awful.'

They stood in the doorway, clinging to each other, their eyes wide and their hearts pounding.

'Was it what I thought it was?' Grace asked.

'I don't know. You haven't told me what you saw. I need to take a look.'

'Really?'

Louise nodded.

They crept back into the shed; Louise kicked at the sack but nothing happened, so she took hold of the bottom and shook its contents over the floor.

Grace gave a squeal then raced out of the shed again.

'Grace!'

'Mum?'

'It's okay. Come back.'

Louise was folded over laughing as she pointed at the pile on the floor.

'They're legs.' Grace wrinkled her nose.

'Yes they are. False legs.'

'Wearing shoes.'

Louise nodded again, and Grace noticed that she had tears running down her cheeks.

'That was so funny, Grace.'

'No it wasn't. I just saw shoes and legs. They could easily have been real legs. I mean look... there's one wearing a trainer, one wearing a dress shoe, one wearing a sandal and even one wearing a Croc!'

Her mother was still laughing, and Grace felt her own mouth curving into a smile in spite of her embarrassment.

Louise moved some of the limbs and held one up. 'Look at this.'

'It's wearing an ice-skate.'

'And the skate is all chipped... like someone's used it to chop wood or something.'

Grace prodded the flesh-coloured plastic of the limb tentatively, as if it might spring into life at any moment.

'What're they doing in there?'

'I have no idea, but according to the estate agent, the old guy who used to live here discovered the Internet in the year before he left, and he used to buy all sorts of things if they were on offer. So we were warned that we might well find a few unusual collections lying around.'

Grace wrinkled her nose. 'You're telling me. What was he going to do with them all? Did he even have a false leg himself?'

'Who knows? Poor man, being left here all on his own.' Louise's cornflower blue eyes, identical to Grace's, shone as she met her daughter's gaze.

'He probably wasn't alone,' Grace said, keen to stop her mother's compassionate mode kicking in. Her mother had a heart of gold and more empathy than anyone Grace had ever met. 'I mean, you told me this is a lovely village. So I bet he had lots of friends here.'

'I hope so.' Louise nodded, the silver in amongst the red of her thick hair catching the winter light as they went back out to the garden. 'Is it time for a cuppa yet, love?'

'I could certainly use a warm drink to help me calm down. My heart's still thundering.'

'You go on in and I'll join you soon. I just want to see if I can make enough space in there for our bikes.'

'Okay, Mum. But… what are you going to do with the legs?'

'Get them outside first then have a chat with your father about it. I'm sure he'll think of something.'

Grace and her parents had arrived in the Cornish village of Conwenna Cove, the previous evening, as dusk fell. The wind had been howling around the yard, skittering brittle leaves across the patio slabs, and rattling the old windows of the cottage her parents had bought. Grace had been dismayed to enter the property for the first time. She'd only seen photographs of the exterior on the estate agent's website, and had taken her mother's word for it that the cottage was 'exactly what she'd always wanted', and that it was 'so cute and cosy' inside. The reality, as Grace had discovered last evening, was that Rosehip Cottage had been empty for five years and those years had not been kind.

The previous owner's daughter had moved him to a care home in Kent, and the cottage had been locked up, and then basically abandoned. It hadn't been put on the market until recently, in the hope that the value would increase, and indeed it had. This was unfortunate for Grace's parents, as there was a lot of work to be done in order to make the cottage inhabitable. Grace suspected that repairs and renovations wouldn't be cheap. And, with it being late November, a lot of the major work would likely have to wait until spring when the weather improved. But her parents hadn't wanted to wait to make the move, so Grace had decided to tag along to give them what would be a much-needed hand.

The morning was chilly but, in the sunlight, she had to admit that the old stone cottage looked better than it had in the dark. With the ivy climbing around the window frames and the red wood pergola at the side of the cottage, that she suspected would be fragrant with the sweet scents of roses and honeysuckle in the summer, the cottage could have come straight out of a fairy tale. But the best thing about the cottage was that out front, if the hedge was properly trimmed, there would be a beautiful view of the sea.

Grace let herself in through the back door. The kitchen was warm when she entered, and her mouth watered at the aromas of cakes and pastries baking.

'Hi, Dad, it smells amazing in here. What're you making?'

'Thought you and your mother might appreciate some scones and jam tarts. I managed to figure out how to work the Aga, so the rest of the cottage will soon warm up, and the bonus is that I can get back to baking regularly. I've missed having the time to do it over recent weeks, because we were so busy packing and dealing with paperwork from the bank, the solicitor and the estate agent.'

Grace located three mugs and some teabags then switched the kettle on. As she waited for the water to boil, she thought about what this move meant for her parents. They'd had a tough time of it over recent years, with the passing of her paternal grandfather and her mother being encouraged to take early retirement. Louise hadn't been keen on the idea of retiring initially, wanting to continue to work as a receptionist at the dentist surgery – where she'd been for the past twenty-five years – at least until she was sixty, but Grace and Simon had encouraged her to accept the generous severance package on offer. It was one of those once-in-a-lifetime deals that wouldn't be available again and it was too good to refuse.

Apart from Grace, her parents had no other remaining ties in the Welsh capital, so they'd decided the time was right to move to the Cornish village they'd fallen in love with on their honeymoon thirty-four years ago. Grace was happy for them, but had no intention of staying in Conwenna herself. She was considering seeing out the lease on her rental flat in Cardiff, then possibly travelling for a year or more. After all, she'd resigned herself to the knowledge that the more traditional route of wife and mother wasn't something she could ever entertain, so why not take advantage of her freedom once her parents were settled, and see some of the world? At least that was the plan she'd considered, but the reality of it was quite daunting and she knew she'd really miss her mum and dad.

'What's your mother doing now?' Simon Phillips peered through the smudged windowpane.

'She found some legs in the shed, so she's getting them out to make room for the bikes.'

'Legs? Not real ones I hope.'

Grace giggled.

'No, Dad, they're prosthetic ones and quite old-fashioned models too.'

'Thank goodness for that. I'd hate to have our little Cornish idyll ruined by some macabre discovery. Well, I hope she can get the bikes in there, because I don't think we're going to get much use out of them this side of Christmas.'

'I don't think you will.'

'Still, something to look forward to in the spring and summer next year.'

Grace loved how her parents still made time for each other, even after thirty-four years of marriage. They cooked together, exercised together and even did the crossword together. She knew that they had a special bond, and sometimes wondered whether it was so strong because of what they'd been through. Would they have stayed so close if things hadn't happened the way they had? She just couldn't imagine them being any other way, and the idea of one having to cope without the other was too awful to contemplate.

Conwenna Cove was a new start for them and they deserved to be happy. Her mother had always told her that life had its ups and downs, but it was important to grab happiness whenever one had the chance. Grace tried to follow that advice, although sometimes her head overruled her heart. Which was one reason why she was probably still single, having turned down a marriage proposal just last year – much to her parents' dismay. They'd told her that they just wanted to see her happy and she'd insisted that she was; as happy as she expected to be anyway. She didn't need a man, especially one like Marcus, to make her feel fulfilled.

She'd known Marcus since school but not had much to do with him at all, then she'd bumped into him in a café the summer before last and he'd been all over her. She'd thought it strange at the time but also been flattered by his attention, although when she thought about it now, his interest had increased when he'd stopped talking about himself and his woes for five minutes to ask what she did. When she admitted that she was a successful author, he'd wanted to know more and insisted they trade numbers. He'd taken her out about six times after that, and come to her flat for dinner and coffee, but for Grace there had been no spark. That was why, when he'd proposed, she'd been completely shocked. She'd let him down as gently as she could, but he'd been quite rude and left her reeling with a barrage of insults and a few unpleasant text messages. Then two weeks later, as she'd been queuing in Costa, he walked past with another woman, his arm wrapped possessively around her shoulders, and Grace had known that she'd had a very lucky escape.

Before Marcus, she'd had lovers: men she'd met through acquaintances and a few through dating apps, but none of the love affairs had developed into anything more serious. Grace had always found a reason not to commit, and sometimes the men had too, thereby, saving her the trouble of ending their flings.

She poured boiling water onto tea bags, then went to get the milk from the rickety old fridge that stood in the corner of the kitchen. Her parents' own fridge was currently in the hallway, left to settle after the long journey in the removal van. As Grace bent over to open the fridge, something shot out from underneath, causing her to yelp.

'Grace?' Her father rushed to her side. 'What's wrong?'

'Something just ran across the floor.' She pointed in the direction of the hallway that led off the kitchen.

'What was it?'

'I don't know. A mouse, maybe? Not big enough to be a rat. At least, I don't think so anyway.'

Simon shook his head. 'Think we might need to consider getting a cat. What with the woods and all those fields behind, I bet there'll be plenty more where that came from.'

'Dad, you don't want your house littered with dead rodents.'

'I didn't mean I want a cat to kill them, Grace. Just as a deterrent.'

Grace smiled. Her father had such a big heart that he wouldn't even kill a fly, just usher it rather politely out of the house.

'Although I have to admit that your mother and I still hope to have a dog now that she's retired. We were just holding off until we'd moved, but I can't see what's stopping us now.'

'Well, if you do get one, go to a rescue centre. There are so many dogs needing homes.'

'Of course. Adopt don't shop, right?'

'I'll just see if that mouse, or whatever it was, is lurking in the hallway.'

They both peered into the cool darkness of the hallway, but with the large boxes, the fridge and a pile of books that belonged to Grace's parents in the way, it was highly likely that the small rodent had already found itself a new hideaway.

'I guess we'll have to look for it later.' Simon shivered. 'Hope the poor thing isn't too scared.'

They returned to the bright warmth of the kitchen.

'So do you think you'll be able to manage the work that needs doing round here, Dad?'

Simon ran a hand through his grey hair. 'It seems worse than it is.'

'Really?'

His brown eyes lit up as he looked around him, full of excitement about his new home. 'It's all superficial and nothing I can't handle. This is a good solid stone cottage. It's been here for years and will be long after we're all gone. I should be able to fix it up no problem, but if there's someone local who can lend a hand with some of the external work, then I'll be able to do it quicker. Although, most of it will have to wait until the spring. Which is fine… as long as we're warm and dry, I can cope with a few chipped window frames and walls in need of painting.'

'And that bathroom needs replacing.'

'Yes, it certainly does. A green bath is not to your mother's taste.'

'I think it's the ingrained scum line around the rim that's more of a worry than the colour of the bath itself.'

A timer on the worktop pinged; Simon grabbed the oven gloves and opened the Aga door. He removed two trays and set them on the cooling rack on the worktop. The fluffy scones had risen perfectly and the buttery pastry of the jam tarts was crisp and golden. Grace's mouth watered because she knew how good her father's baking would taste.

She was relieved that he didn't think there was that much to do to the cottage. He should know, after all. Simon was a gifted carpenter and had run his own building business for many years. He'd sold it on two years ago, to a man who'd started as one of his apprentices, after deciding that climbing around on roofs wasn't what he wanted to be doing as he entered his sixties. He was nearly as fit as he'd been at thirty, and he had the same energy levels, but that he didn't want to be grafting so hard any more. He said that he wanted to enjoy his retirement and spend more time with his wife and daughter.

'Right I'd better take that tea out to your mother. She's probably decided to pick the shed up and move it somewhere else knowing her.'

'Probably,' Grace laughed.

'Help yourself to a scone.'

'Thanks, Dad!'

And as Grace sat at the oak kitchen table with a steaming mug of tea and a freshly baked scone smothered in butter and strawberry jam, she felt her concerns about the cottage start to slip away. Perhaps her parents really would be happy here. Perhaps moving to Cornwall was the best decision they could have made.

Perhaps, Conwenna Cove wouldn't be such a bad place for them to live after all.

Chapter 2

'Good morning, Pamela.' Oliver Davenport entered the small reception of his veterinary practice that was based in the cottage adjoining his own.

His grey-haired receptionist smiled at him.

'Morning, Oli. Cold enough out for you?'

He nodded. 'Freezing. Hope I don't have many call outs today.'

'None so far.' Pamela gestured at the computer monitor on her desk. 'Just a few cats, dogs and rabbits coming in.'

'Righty-ho. I'll go on through then.'

'Oli… there was one thing.' Pamela held up a yellow post-it note, and peered at him from behind the small square glasses that magnified her hazel eyes.

'Yes?' He approached the desk.

'There was a call about five minutes ago. Edward Millar found a cat under the slide in the children's park. He was walking past and he heard mewling so he investigated. Looks like she's just got a young litter. He said he'll bring them in.'

'Oh, okay.' He rubbed the back of his neck.

'Oli? Are you all right?'

He nodded. 'It's just…'

'I know. Why don't people get their animals neutered?'

'Exactly. It infuriates me.'

'Well, it's too late for this little female, but hopefully she's not in too bad shape.'

'I hope so, it's hardly the best time of year for kittens to be outside. Poor girl, and poor kittens. Okay, well let me know when Edward arrives.'

Oli went through the door that led into his main consulting room and through to the small adjoining room that served as a cloakroom and storage space. He removed his coat and hung it up, then opened the door to the recovery room where the animals staying overnight, or for a longer term, were kept.

'Hello, Maxine.'

The veterinary nurse peered up at him from her position kneeling beside a crate. A stray strand of the chestnut brown hair that had slipped out of her ponytail was tucked behind her ear, and in the bright strip lighting Maxine's freckles, that made her look a lot younger than her fifty-five years, appeared darker.

'Morning, Oli.'

'And how's the patient this morning?'

'Signs are good. Honey is a lucky girl.'

Oli knelt next to Maxine, and rubbed the ears of the golden retriever that was in one of the larger crates under the window. The dog licked his hand in response.

'Yes, she is. No more trying to jump over barbed wire fences for you, Honey. Mrs Turner will be in to collect you later.'

'Yes, she should be ready to go home, but make sure Mrs Turner has the cone to stop Honey chewing at those stitches.'

'Of course I will.' Maxine shook her head.

'Sorry... telling you how to do your job again.'

'It's all right, Oli. It's more a case of you thinking out loud.'

He straightened up and peered out of the window that overlooked the rear car park.

'Pamela said we've got kittens coming in.'

'So I believe.'

'I just hope we'll be able to find homes for them. If they make it after being outside in this weather, that is. I wouldn't be surprised if they're suffering from exposure.'

'There is that,' Maxine said, as she wrote on Honey's chart, then clipped the notes to the front of the crate.

'When will people learn?' he tutted.

Maxine patted him on the shoulder. 'I don't think they ever will. That's why we're here, Oli.'

'True.'

'Your father get the children off to school in time?'

'As always. I don't know what I'd do without him.'

'Me neither.' Maxine's cheeks flushed. 'He's such a good man. Right, shall we have a cup of tea before the morning rush begins?'

'Great plan.'

Maxine went to make tea and Oli crouched down in front of Honey again. The dog gazed at him with her big brown eyes. 'You know, Honey, she's made my dad happier than he's been in years. Think I should tell her?'

The dog licked its nose.

'Ok, will do. As soon as I've had a cuppa. After all, everyone deserves to know when they make someone else happy, right?'

-

An hour later, Oli had checked each of the three kittens over and Maxine had settled them, along with their mother, into one of the eye-level crates on a soft blanket. The mother had eaten a good meal and was currently feeding her offspring. Oli had estimated their age to be around three and a half weeks as they were walking, but still wobbly on their little legs.

Oli was standing in the reception area with Edward Millar and Pamela.

'So you've no idea who they might belong to?' Oli asked the older man.

'None at all. Could be someone from the village or further afield. Possibly someone travelling through and the cat escaped from their vehicle, or she could have just wandered here from one of the local farms or nearby villages.'

'Well apart from being hungry and a bit cold, she's in pretty good condition. But it's lucky you heard her when you did. Too long outside and the kittens could've suffered from exposure.'

'Perhaps she's come down from Foxglove?' Pamela referred to the local farm. 'You know… to get some peace.'

'Give Neil a ring and find out if he's missing a cat.'

'Will do.' Pamela nodded and picked up the phone.

'We'll need to find some homes if they don't belong to Neil.'

'Are you hinting there, Oli?' Edward smiled.

'Well… I know Mary has a fondness for waifs and strays.'

'She does that. Took in Jack and Eve and, of course, me,' he laughed. 'Heart of an angel that woman.'

Oli smiled. Mary Carpenter, now Millar, was known for having a huge heart. She'd taken in Jack Adams, an ex-marine, when he'd arrived in Conwenna. Jack now lived in one of Mary's cottages with her niece, Eve, and their young baby son who'd arrived in October. The two had fallen in love over a summer when Eve had come to visit. Like many who came to Conwenna Cove, Eve had come for a break and ended up staying. The Cove just had that effect upon some people. As for Mary herself, after years of singledom, she'd fallen in love with fisherman Edward, and Oli didn't think he'd ever seen a happier couple.

Pamela put the phone down.

'Oli, I spoke to Elena up at the farm and she said they're not missing any cats and she also said to tell you, that as you well know, they get their pets neutered.' Pamela winked at him. 'She says they've enough to deal with up there without a litter of kittens.'

'That's true,' Oli replied, thinking about the greyhound rescue sanctuary that Neil and Elena Burton ran up at their farm. 'They are responsible pet owners. So it's back to the drawing board.'

'I'll send out an email,' Pamela said.

'And I'll ask around in the village,' Edward added. 'I'm sure we'll find out whose cat it is. Unless it's someone who doesn't want to be found out.'

The door to the surgery opened and Mrs Turner, Honey's owner, entered.

'Good morning!' Pamela sang. 'You're early.'

'I couldn't bear to be apart from her for another minute. How's she doing, Oli?' Mrs Turner asked, her face haggard with concern.

And for Oli, another busy day was well underway.

Grace wandered along the pretty cobbled street, admiring the different shops that Conwenna Cove had to offer. She paused and peered in through the window of the gift shop, Pebbles, eyeing the pretty wares on sale. Her gaze fell on a picture made entirely of shells. It showed a couple standing on a rock, their arms around each other, their faces turned towards the sun. It was very pretty and very clever. Then she sighed. It was also soppy and romantic and she had no time for all that nonsense.

She walked a bit further along the main street, and passed a surf shop called Riding the Wave and an ice cream parlour called Scoops and Sprinkles. Even though the ice creams looked amazing, she was way too cold to have one. However, there was a café across the street and the idea of a hot chocolate was very tempting.

After a morning spent clearing out one of the bedrooms in her parents' cottage, she'd been in need of a walk and some fresh air, so she'd pulled on her warm padded coat with the faux fur trim around the hood and her sturdy walking boots, and set off to the main street where the shops were. She'd left her parents debating over whether to keep an antique chair they'd found; a debate that would likely go on for quite some time, but that, no doubt, her mother would eventually win. The artificial limbs had already been packed up and her father was going to deliver them to a local hospital later that week to see if they could find a use for them.

She crossed the road and went into the café, appreciating the warm air as it greeted her. Instantly, her fingers and nose began to tingle.

'Morning.' The handsome man behind the counter offered a warm smile. 'Take a seat and I'll be right over.'

Grace chose a table by the window, removed her coat and sat down. She'd quickly changed into clean jeans and a baggy jumper before leaving, not wanting to go out in her dusty dungarees, but having seen the hunk behind the counter, she was now wishing she'd chosen something a bit more flattering.

'Right, what can I get you?' He'd arrived at her table and Grace tried not to blush as he smiled at her, his piercing blue eyes twinkling in what happened to be a face that could have got him into Hollywood.

'Uh... I'll have a hot chocolate, please.'

'And something to eat?'

'No thanks... uh... I'm...'

Hurry up and say something.

'We do have an amazing chocolate fudge cake. Why not have a slice of that?' He smiled, dazzling her again with his whiter than white teeth.

'Okay, but don't do this every time I come in here will you or I'll end up huge.'

'What?' He leaned back and eyed her. 'You're gorgeous. No chance of that happening.'

Grace's cheeks now burned furiously and she felt like she was fourteen again.

'Are you on holiday then?'

'No. My parents just bought a cottage here so I'm staying with them while they settle in.'

'Fabulous! Is it Rosehip Cottage by any chance?'

'That's the one.' Grace pulled her sleeves over her fingers then realized what she was doing and pushed her sleeves back up.

'Lovely cottage that one. Bit neglected, but with some TLC it'll soon be back to its best. I'm Nate Bryson by the way. My aunt and uncle own this café.'

'Pleased to meet you. I'm Grace… Grace Phillips.'

'From Wales by the sound of that lovely musical accent?'

'Yes. Cardiff actually.'

'Oh, I love Cardiff. Went there years ago to see the castle and a rugby match too. Brilliant place, so many great cafés and pubs.'

'Yes, I guess it is. When you live somewhere you don't always appreciate it as much. I mean… I like the shopping there, but I haven't been inside the castle in years.'

'Well, when you go home check it out again. Unless, of course, Conwenna works its magic and you decide to stay.' He winked.

'There'll be no chance of that happening. Not that it's not lovely here… but I've things I want to do. Need to do, actually.'

'Ah I see. Loving boyfriend back there waiting for you?'

'No!' Grace realized she'd snapped. 'Sorry… I meant, no, there's no boyfriend but I have plans now that my parents have moved. That's all.'

'Well, I'll get your drink and cake, and seeing as how it's quiet, you can tell me all about them. If you don't mind me joining you, that is?'

'Right. Okay. No, of course not. That would be lovely.'

As Nate walked away, Grace swallowed hard. She couldn't believe that she'd blushed like a teenager just because a good-looking man had spoken to her. Granted, she didn't have much interaction with the opposite sex, but there was no need to become flustered because one of them had paid her some attention. And Nate was probably just being friendly. No doubt he was like that with every customer who came in here. Besides, he looked like he was probably a surfer or a rugby player, which might mean that he was good fun to be around but that he didn't take life too seriously. Or was she stereotyping? She didn't know anything about him other than he seemed nice and he was gorgeous. She had no idea how seriously he took life or what he'd been through in his time. And as she knew well, people carried pain around with them that others often knew nothing about.

Come to think of it, perhaps this was just what she needed – a new friend who knew how to laugh and live in the moment. Someone different to chat to and to enjoy being with. It wasn't often that Grace got the chance to spend time with a handsome stranger after all.

So when he returned to the table with two hot chocolates and two slices of cake, Grace vowed to try to be friendly and not to give him the cold shoulder that she knew she often gave men, all men, whatever kind of interest they showed in her. She wouldn't be staying in Conwenna for long, so she could afford to let down her guard, even if just a little bit.

An hour later, Grace's face was aching from smiling. Nate was one of the funniest people she'd spoken to in ages. In between serving customers, he told Grace about himself. It turned out that he was a surfer, three years older than her at thirty-four, and he'd been in Conwenna for five years. He had a very easy way about him and he made Grace feel relaxed too. Interestingly though, as she'd got to know him, she'd realized that she didn't fancy him. Sure, he was handsome in that tattooed, blonde-haired surfer way, with his leather wristbands, faded jeans and muscles bulging under his t-shirt, but he wasn't her type at all. Not that she had a type, of course.

Grace just wasn't interested in relationships; not now, and not ever.

The bell above the café door tinkled, and Nate turned, then raised a hand, as a tall man entered, his collar pulled up against the cold. Nate went to the counter.

'I'll go serve Oli then get us another drink, shall I?' Nate asked as he picked up the plates and cutlery.

'Lovely, thanks.' Grace nodded.

She realized that Nate had forgotten her mug, so she picked it up and followed him to the counter. She put the mug down then turned to the new arrival, expecting another friendly greeting.

'Hello.' She smiled.

The tall man Nate had referred to as Oli just stared blankly at her, his striking blue-green eyes almost luminous, as if he could see right through her.

'I'm Grace Phillips. My parents have just moved into Rosehip Cottage.'

She held out her hand, but Oli didn't take it. There was an awkward pause. So she dusted her hand off, as if to suggest she hadn't been waiting for him to shake it, then tucked it into her jeans' pocket.

'Oli Davenport, this is Grace Phillips. Grace, this is our local vet, Oli. Grace is staying in Conwenna for a while.'

'Ah, right. Very good.' Oli frowned as if remembering something. 'You haven't lost a cat have you?'

'No. We don't own one.'

'Right. Never mind.' He accepted a cake box from Nate then handed over some cash. 'Nate, we're looking for the owners of a small black cat. She's had a litter… about three and a half weeks old they are. Edward Millar found her in the park and brought her to the surgery. Appreciate it if you'd ask around, perhaps put up a sign?'

'No problem at all.' Nate gave Oli his change.

'If we can't find out whose it is, we'll be looking for homes for the mother and the kittens.'

'They'll need homes?' Grace asked, having to tilt her head to look up at him. He had to be over six foot and he had incredibly broad shoulders.

Oli turned his blue-green eyes on her again and she almost winced. They were assessing her, making her feel uneasy, completely unlike Nate's teasing azure ones.

'Yes. Of course.' He shook his head impatiently. 'Thanks for this, Nate. See you tomorrow.'

Oli turned and walked out of the café, leaving a cold gust of air in his wake and a very confused Grace.

'Is he always like that?'

'Awkward, you mean?' Nate laughed. 'He can be when he's busy. And he's probably got a lot on his mind. He gets furious about animal neglect and is probably on the war path about someone not having their cat spayed, or neutered, or whatever it is that stops them breeding. He's really nice when you get to know him.'

'I'll take your word for it,' Grace replied, although inside she knew that she had absolutely no intention of even trying to get to know the very rude vet. In fact, she was wondering as she returned to the table and sat down, exactly who the hell Oli Davenport thought he was.

Oli headed down the main street, his head bowed against the chilly wind, but it still managed to creep under his collar and around his neck like clammy icy fingers. It was coming in from the Atlantic Ocean, so not only was it cold, it was also damp and he shivered. Conwenna Cove was a beautiful place to live, but in the winter it certainly left its inhabitants exposed to the elements and the prevailing south-westerly winds. It was a good job Edward found that cat when he had or she could have lost all her kittens and perhaps perished herself.

Linda would have hated that, to know that a cat had lost her kittens. She'd probably have cried about it and would have wanted to home all the litter. But that was Linda. His heart started thudding as he thought about his wife's compassion for people and animals. She'd been so kind, so generous, so...

Oh what did it matter? She was gone and therefore had no say in what happened to the damned cats. Not that he didn't like cats, because he did, but whenever he thought about his wife, he had an ache in his chest that made him almost angry. It was natural, the grief counsellor had told him, to experience anger and frustration after losing your partner so young, but it would pass... eventually, and until then he should allow himself to feel, not try to stifle his emotions. Apparently, it was all about acceptance. But though he managed his feelings the majority of the time, he still had flashes of resentment that he'd lost his wife, the woman he'd loved and the mother of his children.

But he had to go on. However dark some of his days had been, Oli had to go on for his children. And he would. Because he loved them and he was all they had.

23

He really had no choice other than to put one foot in front of the other and to keep moving forwards. As much he sometimes wanted to close the curtains, get into bed and never get up again.

When he reached the harbour, in spite of the late November chill, he decided to take a seat on one of the benches that looked out to sea. He often found comfort in gazing out at the skyline because the sea appeared to be endless, as if it went on and on and on. A bit like he imagined Linda did. In his heart and mind at least. He placed the cake box on the bench next to him and tucked his hands into his pockets to try to thaw out his fingers. He couldn't afford to get frostbite, not when his hands were his livelihood. If he couldn't operate on the animals that came in and needed his expertise, then what good would he be as a vet?

Today, the sky was gun-metal grey and the horizon hazy, as the late morning sunlight pierced holes in the low-lying winter clouds. The sunbeams shone through like lasers, highlighting areas of the sea. He loved the variety of horizons that Conwenna Cove boasted, whatever time of the year it was, but this one today, sombre and dark with flashes of light here and there, matched his mood.

However, this wasn't about Linda or the cat; something else was bothering him this morning.

He had been quite positive when he'd set off for a late morning walk to the café to pick up cakes for his staff and for the children's tea. Oli was pretty confident they'd find homes for the cat and her litter; there were a great many animal lovers in Conwenna. But then he'd walked past the Conwenna Café window, and he'd seen the most striking woman he'd ever set eyes on. Linda had been beautiful, yes, with her pale skin, brown eyes and light blonde hair. But Grace Phillips… she was a head turner, reminding him of a painting he'd once seen of a mermaid who'd walked right up out of the sea. And even the fact that he'd thought about her beauty had left him consumed with guilt, because he shouldn't be noticing other women in any way, shape or form. It just wasn't right; it was a betrayal of his wife and of the love they'd shared.

But Grace's red hair had caught his eye first, like wavy flames in the café window, and as he'd passed, to enter the café, she'd thrown back her head and laughed at something Nate had said. It was then that Oli had seen her face: heart-shaped, perfect little white teeth in a rosebud mouth and a smile that had lifted his heart. Or would have had it fallen on him. But she hadn't been smiling for Oli, it had been for Nate.

Of course it had been. And Oli really liked Nate. He was a happy-go-lucky kind of guy with his surfer good looks and his apparent devil-may-care attitude. And that was what bugged Oli the most about this. Nate could have had his pick of the local women; whether it was high summer or the dead of winter, he always had a pretty woman laughing at his jokes. He just seemed to have a gift for relaxing them and always seemed totally relaxed himself. It must feel amazing to be that comfortable around the opposite sex. And now it seemed that Nate had the interest of beautiful Grace too, and Oli wondered if she had any idea what she was getting into.

He shrugged, then released a deep sigh. It was none of his business anyway. It wasn't as if he was going to try to form any sort of connection with Grace, or any other woman for that matter. One broken heart in a lifetime was enough and in the two years since Linda had died, Oli had steered clear of women altogether. And that was how it would stay. He knew for certain that his damaged heart wouldn't survive another loss, or even another bump in the road. He was barely holding on as it was.

He stood and picked up the cake box, and started walking; he passed the art gallery called A Pretty Picture, and Café Paris, before walking along the coastal path that took him back towards the surgery and his home. Hopefully, Pamela would have the kettle on and he could enjoy a cake and a cup of tea, because that was about as much excitement as Oli wanted from life right now.

Chapter 3

The delicious aromas of roast dinner and woodsmoke met Grace's nostrils as she entered The Conwenna Arms that Sunday morning. She'd decided to take a walk along the harbour – before making her way up to the pub that Nate had told her opened on Sunday mornings to serve brunch – and been delighted at how pretty it was, even in December. Small boats bobbed on the water, their windows glinting in the morning sunlight, and the sea lapped at the harbour wall. She'd stood there for a while, leaning against the railing, deeply breathing in the fresh briny air until her nose had turned cold and her eyes started to water, then she walked briskly up the hill to get a coffee.

She was pleased to see that it was still relatively quiet, as it was only just gone eleven o'clock. She went to the bar and ordered a spiced cinnamon latte, then took it over to a cosy corner near the log burner. She put her coffee down on the small round table, then sat on the soft leather couch and looked around.

The pub was warm and quaint with the log burner glowing and its low ceiling with dark wood beams. The slate tiles on the floor were worn and uneven in places and the tables and chairs were made of reclaimed wood, some of which Grace suspected might be from boats. The semi-circular bar was in the middle of the pub and around the other side was the restaurant, although the menus on the surrounding tables suggested that patrons could eat in this area too. Her stomach gave a rumble; the smells drifting from the kitchen were mouth-watering. But she couldn't eat here: her parents were expecting her home for one-thirty. Besides, it wasn't much fun eating out alone, which was why she rarely did it back home in Cardiff, even though there was an abundance of places to choose from.

Grace couldn't believe it was the first weekend of December and their second in Conwenna. The past few days had flown by while she'd helped her parents to settle into their new home, and squeezed in as much writing as she could when she wasn't moving furniture around to see if it looked better another way, or clearing out the garage to get rid of the previous owner's weird collections – although none of them had been as strange as the prosthetic legs.

The pub owners had already put the Christmas decorations up, but then Grace knew how quickly December passed, so those aiming to drum up festive business had to make the most of the season. And it was nice to enjoy the festive cheer that the large Christmas tree in the corner and the other decorations around the cosy pub offered. The tree, which stood in a large red clay planter, reached the ceiling and was decorated with gold and silver tinsel. Matching baubles adorned its plush branches and in between those, red and green orbs twinkled. At the top was a glittery silver star.

On the slate grate in front of the log burner stood four gold glitter reindeer, each one with a red tinsel collar, and the wooden surround that served as a mantelpiece was draped with bright green holly with fat red berries. Each table in the pub had a golden tealight holder with snowflake cutouts on them, and Grace suspected that when lit they would be very pretty indeed. The overall mood in the Conwenna Arms was festive, and Grace felt a frisson of satisfaction that she was able to enjoy some time there.

She took a sip of her coffee, which was creamy and delicious with its festive spices, then pulled her lightweight laptop and spiral bound notebook from her bag, along with a set of coloured biros. If she was lucky, she'd get a good hour of writing in before the lunchtime rush began. After all, she'd excused herself from her parents' house because they were currently cooking dinner and she'd wanted to get in a good word count before eating; she knew that Sunday dinner always made her drowsy so she wouldn't get much done at all that afternoon.

Grace also knew she was lucky to be able to take her work with her; it made her portable and she could work anywhere as long as she had some peace. Sometimes, she liked to work in the calm quiet of her flat, sometimes she chose a café or a pub to soak up the ambience and to people watch, and sometimes she'd write outdoors. It depended upon her mood, the weather and her deadline. And if she was in need of some inspiration that she couldn't get from sitting home alone.

She pulled the laptop onto her knees, then switched it on and opened her work in progress. She was enjoying writing this one: a twisty psychological thriller. Grace's literary agent in London had drummed up excitement around her debut four years earlier, and she'd just signed her second three-book contract with a big publisher. Her writing career was going extremely well and she hoped it would continue to do so. The thrill of seeing her books on the shelves in shops and supermarkets would never get old.

As she waited for the laptop to finish its page count, she took another sip of her coffee, then selected a pen from her stash and jotted some key words onto a clean page of the notebook that she'd placed on the table. She always did this before she started writing; it was a routine that helped her to focus and to get back into the writing groove if her mind wandered or she hit a plot snag.

Then she started to type and was catapulted into the fictional world she'd created.

'What do these words mean?'

Grace was dragged from her story. She met the light brown eyes of a small boy. His white blond hair was cut shorter at the sides and spiked messily, as was currently fashionable. He looked like he was five going on fifteen, cute but trendy.

She shook her head to free herself from the tense scene she'd just composed.

'Uh…'

She stared at the words in her notebook where: cold, broken, escape, echo and seawater. They taunted her, inviting her to get the full scene typed before the idea slipped from her mind to be lost forever in the void of the unwritten. Grace hated to be interrupted when she was into the flow, but it was a hazard of writing in public.

She saved the document, then closed her laptop.

'They are part of a story I'm writing.'

'A story?'

'Yes, you see I'm an author.'

He nodded.

'Do you know what an author is?'

'An author writes the books and an illustrator draws the pictures.'

'Wow, you're clever. How old are you?'

'Five.'

'Five?' Grace was impressed.

'I know because Eve and Jack came into our school.'

'Who are Eve and Jack?'

'They write books and they came to tell us about the greyhounds.'

'The greyhounds?'

'Up at the farm.'

'At Foxglove Farm?'

'Yes. In the santuery.'

'Santuery?'

'Yes, where they save them.'

'Oh… sanctuary.'

'That's what I said. Can I write on your paper?'

'Uh… okay. Let me just turn that piece over. But don't you think we should introduce ourselves properly first?'

'Okay.'

'I'm Grace Phillips. What's your name?'

'Tom Davenport.' The way he said his surname made Grace's heart squeeze. He was so cute and had the tiniest hint of a babyish lisp. And the name also made her wonder if he was linked to the rude vet she'd met at the café.

'Where are your parents, Tom?'

'My daddy and Maxine and Bampy are over there at the bar. With Amy.'

'Do they know you're here?'

'Yes.'

He sat next to Grace and she held out her pens, 'What colour would you like?'

'Blue, please.'

'Here you are.'

Grace handed him the pen, then the notepad, and watched as he sat down beside her, put the pad on the table and started to write. His tongue poked out of the corner of his mouth and he held the pen tightly in his tiny hand.

'See.' He pointed proudly at the notepad. 'T-O-M. That's my name.'

'Very clever. Can you spell Davenport too?'

'Tom!' A sharp voice came from across the pub.

The little boy looked up. 'Uh oh. That's my Daddy.'

'I thought he knew where you were.'

'He did, but he tells me not to talk to people I don't know.'

'That's very sensible.'

'I'm so sorry.' The tall man met her eyes and realization dawned on his face. 'Grace, right?'

'Oli?'

'Yes. Tom, I told you not to bother people. This lady was trying to, uh…' He frowned. 'What were you doing?'

'Writing. I'm an author.' She offered a brief smile, in spite of her misgivings about this man and their first meeting.

'An author?'

'Yes. And Tom here asked if he could use my notepad.'

'Tom, you say thank you to the nice lady then leave her in peace.'

Tom stood up then held out his hand to Grace. She took it and he shook hers firmly, his small hand warm and soft.

'Thank you Grace for being my friend today.'

'You are very welcome, Tom. Would you like your piece of paper?'

He shook his head. 'You can keep it so you remember how to spell my name.'

'Thank you. That's very kind of you.' She bit her lip to prevent herself from smiling.

'Now go on over to Maxine and tell her what you want for dinner.'

Tom nodded then jogged back around the bar.

'Thanks for that. He has a habit of talking to strangers even though I've warned him not to. One minute he's by my side, the next he's gone. It's just hard sometimes doing this alone...' He bit his lip and his cheeks coloured. 'Sorry. Too much information, there. What I meant to say was... I need eyes in the back of my head.'

Grace felt her lips turn upwards. Was this the same man she'd seen just days before in the café? The same man who was cold, grumpy and distracted? Right now he seemed a bit awkward and bumbling, as if he was uncomfortable in his own skin. Exactly how she often felt.

'Don't worry about it. Tom wasn't bothering me at all. In fact, he's helped me to work out a plot point that I was struggling with.'

'He has?' Relief washed over Oli's face.

'Yes. So I should be thanking you.'

He looked around. 'Are you here with anyone? Nate perhaps?'

'No. It's just me. Why would I be with Nate?'

'I thought you two were…'

'Oh no!' She shook her head. 'Gosh that came out wrong. Not that there would be anything wrong in being with Nate, you know, because he's perfectly lovely and everything, but I just… uh…' she sighed. 'Sorry, I'm babbling. What I meant was that Nate is a really nice person, but we're not involved. I barely know him.'

Oli's smile lit up his face. 'He is a really nice person.'

'I've got to know him because of my visits to the café. In all honesty, I've probably been spending more time there than I should. It's a way to escape some of the unpacking and rearranging that's going on at the cottage.' She shook her head. 'My mother still isn't happy with where the sofa is and my back won't take much more shifting it around. Also, I can write in peace at the café. Today, I just thought I'd check out the pub instead.'

Oli nodded. 'If you get a chance to go, there's a really nice café in Truro called Espresso Yourself. I take the children there quite regularly.'

'I'll try to remember that one. I think Mum did mention doing a bit of Christmas shopping there next Saturday. Are you here for lunch?'

'I've come with my father and his partner. Most Sundays I go to Dad's but they like to eat out at least once a month. Saves him from doing the dishes.'

'Sounds very sensible.'

He rubbed his head then the back of his neck.

'I don't suppose you'd uh… like to… uh, no. Probably not.'

'Like to what?'

'Well, it seems daft you sitting there alone when you could join us for dinner. Tom would no doubt be delighted and I'm sure Amy, my daughter, would be impressed that you're an author.'

'That is such a lovely offer, but my mother has probably made enough for an army and I promised I'd be back...' she checked her watch, 'by one-thirty. In half an hour, in fact. Gosh, time has flown this morning.'

'Oh, okay. No problem. Silly of me to ask, of course you'd have somewhere to be.'

'It wasn't silly. It was very kind, actually. Perhaps another time?'

He smiled. 'That would be nice. Hold on...' he held up a finger then turned and went to the bar. Grace watched as the landlord handed him something.

Oli returned to her table and held out a bottle of red wine.

'By way of apology.'

'Whatever for?'

'For Tom and for me... the first time we met, I think I might have been a bit rude. I can be like that when I've something on my mind and in retrospect, I think I was quite unfriendly.'

'You don't have to give me wine.'

'So I *was* rude! I am so sorry. Please take this.'

Grace accepted the bottle of what she recognized as a very nice Cabernet.

'Well, thank you.'

'My pleasure. I guess I'll see you around?'

'You certainly will.'

He smiled then walked away, leaving Grace with a big grin on her face and a fluttery sensation in her belly. The local vet had just risen in her estimation. Not only did he have a gorgeous little boy, but he was actually quite friendly and even a bit shy. She'd obviously been wrong to judge him so harshly when they first met.

If only she could have joined them for dinner. But then... he had two children.

Her heart sank. So he was likely to be happily married and certainly off limits.

She closed her laptop and put it in her bag along with her notebook and pens.

But that was all fine, as Grace wasn't looking for a man, especially one with a little boy in tow, however cute that little boy might be.

Chapter 4

Oli slammed his pen down on top of the notepad and rubbed his eyes. He was trying to write a list of things he'd need for Amy's eleventh birthday party, but he was struggling to focus. Linda used to do all this; she'd get really excited about special occasions including birthdays, anniversaries, weddings, Christmas and so on. She had made so much effort for him and for the children, until that final Christmas when she was too ill to do anything at all.

Linda had been a strong woman: refusing to ask for help from her own parents who lived in Scotland, even when she knew the end was coming. In fact, she'd insisted that Oli not tell them how ill she was, because she didn't want them rushing to her side where she felt they'd be more hindrance than help. She'd never been particularly close to them, and even though she'd grown up in Conwenna Cove, and returned there after studying textile design at university in Falmouth, her parents had moved away not long after Linda and Oli married. Neither of her parents had been particularly enamoured with parenthood – Linda had always suspected she was an accident – and they apparently felt the same about being grandparents. Amy and Tom received birthday and Christmas cards from them, but that was as far as their relationship went. Having never had them around, Amy and Tom didn't miss them or even seem to think about them that often.

Oli's father, on the other hand, had been amazingly supportive and he didn't know how he'd have managed without him. His mother lived in Helston, having left when Oli was fifteen after falling in love with her boss at the haulage firm where she worked as a PA. She was there if Oli needed her, but he tried not to bother her too often because she always seemed so busy. And anyway, Oli always tried to be strong around his parents because he didn't want his own grief – or, his loneliness – affecting their lives. It wasn't good for them, or for the children who were incredibly intuitive and would pick up on it all.

And so his life went on… day after day, he got up, got the children ready then put one foot in front of the other. But, unfortunately, party planning wasn't his forte and he knew he was working himself up trying to organize this one.

He cocked his head at a noise from upstairs. Probably just one of the children going to the toilet, but he should check. He pushed the kitchen chair back and got up, then went out into the hallway and listened. Sure enough, there was the sound of the toilet flushing then someone padding across the landing.

'Tom?' he called softly.

A white face surrounded by messy blond hair appeared on the landing.

'Did you wash your hands?'

'Oh… No. I had to have a Sunday dinner poo. It was the cabbage, Daddy, it made me stinky.'

'I thought you might have. Go and wash your hands and use soap like I showed you.'

Oli shook his head, knowing that his sleepy little boy would probably fail to do a good job of washing his hands, so he climbed the stairs and supervised Tom's ablutions. When he was done, he guided him back to his bedroom and tucked him in.

'Daddy?'

'Yes.'

'I had a dream.'

'You did?'

Tom nodded, his eyelids already fluttering as tiredness claimed him.

'What did you dream?'

'About the nice lady with the coloured pens. She was so pretty. She had red hair like dragon fire and lots of brown spots on her face like Maxine.'

'Those were freckles.'

'What are freckles?'

'I'll explain tomorrow. Right now you need to get some sleep.'

'Daddy, I really liked her.'

Oli stroked his son's hair before planting a gentle kiss on his forehead.

'I did too,' he whispered as he left the bedroom, making sure that the door was left ajar.

He descended the stairs, thinking about what he'd just admitted. It was silly really; he was a thirty-five year old widower with two young children. He'd felt not even a flicker of interest in women since Linda had died. And now... the beautiful Grace Phillips had appeared in Conwenna and he couldn't get her out of his head. But he knew that she was probably already involved, even if not with Nate, and that she'd have no interest in Oli himself.

39

Why would she? He was hardly an attractive proposition with his emotional baggage and domestic situation. Besides, he couldn't allow another woman into his children's lives, as much as he knew they sometimes wished they had a mother. What if something went wrong and they lost another mother figure? Oli knew he couldn't put Amy and Tom through that, neither could he cope with it himself. He just wasn't strong enough.

He returned to his list and added birthday cake and candles. He'd go to the Conwenna Café tomorrow and speak to Nate about arranging a birthday cake. Of course, he knew that he could ask his father to sort it all out while he was in work, but it just didn't seem fair to lay his responsibilities at Paul's door. He was a wonderfully loving father and grandfather, but Oli was a grown man and he hated the idea of anyone thinking he wasn't coping alone.

He was doing okay. He just had to keep telling himself that. He had to display a strong front because at least if he did that, he could almost believe in it too.

–

Mondays had never been Grace's favourite day of the week, but here in Conwenna it didn't seem so bad. She'd woken in her parents' cottage and appreciated the peace and quiet of a morning in a small seaside village. There was no traffic noise, no drunken student antics happening below her window and no heart-wrenching sirens in the early hours.

When she'd opened her curtains to see the incredible view from her bedroom window, she'd actually been breathless. Over the weekend, her father had worked to clear the brambles from the upstairs windows and to cut the hedge out front, and now there was a clear view out to sea, from the cottage's elevated position. In the early morning sunlight, the sea sparkled as if millions of diamonds were floating on its surface, and just seeing that view had filled her with hopeful anticipation about the day and week ahead.

Initially, Grace had only intended to stay in Conwenna for a week or two, until her parents were settled, but over Sunday lunch yesterday, and following the very nice bottle of wine that Oli Davenport had given her, Grace's mother had persuaded her to stay until the new year. What did Grace have to go back for, she'd asked? A small empty flat and drinks with old school friends if she was lucky – Grace didn't really have any close friends in Cardiff. Growing up, she had focused on her family life and her education, and she had no regrets about that at all. When people her own age were experimenting with drink and sex in their teens, Grace was at home studying or keeping Sam occupied. Her brother had been such a bright young man, such good company and they'd been so close. He would have loved it here and she wished he could see the view. She would have sacrificed the front bedroom for him, just to see him smile.

She rubbed her chest above her heart. Her grief was not as raw or as sharp as it had once been, but her heart still ached whenever she thought of her brother and how much she missed him. The only thing that really helped ease the ache was her writing. When her mind was creating new characters and putting them into difficult situations, she could escape the sorrow for a while. She'd always written growing up and enjoyed creating stories, but after losing Sam, immersing herself in fiction was her escape – her creative therapy. She was grateful every day to the counsellor who had suggested that she try something creative to deal with her grief. Before Sam died, she'd gone to Cardiff University and studied English Literature, which she had adored. Following graduation, she'd spent a few years temping in offices and found it quite boring. Then, in her grief, her love of writing was rekindled. It had started as journaling, but she'd soon found herself writing whole novels and her father had suggested that she send some of them off to literary agents. To her surprise, one of her books had been snapped up by an agent and that had been that. A generous advance meant she hadn't needed to temp any more, much to her relief.

Her mother and father read every word she wrote and were her personal critique partners. She believed that they felt some relief in seeing her create her novels, because it was as if she was leaving something behind in the world, so that even after she'd gone, there would be proof that she existed. Because she'd sworn never to have children of her own; it was far too risky. There was nothing left of Sam, except for photographs, memories and the urn of ashes that her parents had kept on the mantelpiece in their living room in Cardiff, and that was now on the wooden shelf above the fireplace in the cottage. They'd, so far, been unable to let go of the ashes and they'd become like part of the furniture: always there, reassuring in their presence. Grace believed that they'd need to let go of Sam at some point, but when she wasn't yet certain.

Sam had been too young to have a family of his own, his life had barely started, and even if he'd met someone, he never would have risked having a child. It was just something that he and Grace knew they could never do. In fact, they'd made a pact when she was eleven, and he was twelve, that they'd never have children in case those children had to suffer as he had. And Grace still carried the memory of making that promise around with her; it was as vivid as if it had happened yesterday.

But that was life. Everyone had to make sacrifices and Grace wasn't about to allow hers to darken her doorstep. She intended to live for as long as she was able, preferably without hurting anyone else along the way.

And right now, Conwenna Cove seemed like a great place to do just that.

She dressed then went down to the warm kitchen where things were taking shape. She'd helped her mother to unpack their kitchen utensils, pots and pans, and her father had put them where he wanted them; after all, he used them more than his wife or daughter. They'd also hung the dried lavender and herbs – that they'd brought from their Cardiff garden – from the beams on the low ceiling, and just outside the kitchen window, a pretty wind chime tinkled. Sam had loved wind chimes and told his parents that whenever they heard one, they should think of him. Therefore, Louise and Simon had wind chimes wherever they went, and their tinkling had become synonymous with the comfort of home and of the love they'd all shared.

The large oak kitchen table was also from their former house and it easily seated eight people. Not that they entertained that often, but her father liked the idea of being able to invite guests. Under the window that over-looked the back garden and the evergreen trees that bordered it – providing privacy from the rental cottages that sat further along the main road that led through Conwenna – sat an apron-fronted sink with an antique copper mixer tap. The wooden units in the kitchen were painted a very pale blue and had a genuine distressed effect that Grace really liked. In fact, now that the cottage was clean and warm, she could see its character and she found herself actually wishing that she had a cosy little cottage too. She could certainly afford one with the money she was bringing in – and with her lack of commitments – plus she'd been saving for years, but she'd never thought about buying a property like this.

Until now.

She shook her head. The bright morning sunshine and the pretty cottage were playing havoc with her sensibilities. Grace rented a perfectly nice flat in the centre of Cardiff. She could go to the shops or the pubs whenever she chose, and was close to the train station for when she needed to get up to London. Moving to a village like Conwenna Cove would make all of that more difficult: she wouldn't be able to hop on a train whenever she chose. Not that she did just hop onto trains, ever, but at least the option was there.

As she ran through these thoughts, her father appeared in his navy towelling dressing gown with his grey hair sticking up and a relaxed smile on his face. They'd been in the pretty Cornish village a little over a week, and in that time Simon had lost the haunted look that she thought he'd had most of her life. His face seemed to have filled out a bit and the brown of his eyes was somehow warmer. It lifted her heart to see him looking so much better, as if life was giving him a second chance at happiness.

'Morning, Dad.'

'Morning, Grace.'

'Tea?'

'Yes please, and make one for your mother too. She's having a lie-in.'

'She's having a lie-in?'

Grace swallowed her surprise. Louise was usually a whirling dervish, spinning constantly from the moment she woke until she passed out exhausted on the sofa at night and had to be woken by her husband and guided up to bed. And now she was having a lie-in?

'I know, can you believe it? I woke up to find her still softly snoring.'

'The sea air must be having a good effect on her then.'

Her father nodded. 'On me too. I slept better last night than I have done in years.'

'Me too, funnily enough. I thought I'd miss the city noise but apparently not.'

Grace made three mugs of tea.

'You know, Grace, I do think that being here is having a positive effect on us all. We suspected that it might. The locals would say that it's the magic of Conwenna Cove.'

Grace snorted; she couldn't help herself.

'Who've you been talking to, Dad?'

'Yes, my girl, you can mock the idea, but—'

'It's ridiculous. Superstitious nonsense.'

'You might be right. But all I do know is that it's not just the hard work getting this place shipshape that's improved our appetites and helped us to sleep better. Being here is just...' his voice caught then and he blinked hard and stared down at his corduroy slippers. Grace went over to him and stroked his arm. She'd never seen her father get emotional, not even at Sam's funeral. Simon had been a rock for her and her mother, holding them together when their world crumbled around them. But here Simon was, on the verge of tears, his pain bubbling to the surface.

He cleared his throat and his Adam's apple bobbed furiously, 'Must be getting soft in my old age, Grace.'

'You're not old,' she said, as she shook her head.

'Getting there, though. You know, I'd love to see you settled and happy. If you found someone… a good man, then your mother would finally find some sort of peace.'

'Come on, now.' Grace forced a laugh. 'Bit heavy for the morning cuppa, isn't it? You don't need me married off, you know. I'm perfectly fine as I am.'

'You don't have to be on your own forever. And when we're gone, I'd like to think you'll have someone to look out for you. It can be a lonely life.'

'I'll be fine, Dad, and you and Mum will be here for a long time yet.'

He smiled, then leaned forwards and kissed her cheek, being careful not to spill the tea.

'Right, off to grab another hour. See you later.'

'You do that.'

Grace took her tea to the kitchen table and sat down.

It wasn't like her father to be so open about things; it was usually her mother telling her to find a man and settle down. As if that was the magic cure for everything they'd all been through. For Grace, that idea didn't seem realistic, and her parents knew why, as well as she did.

But perhaps she could consider making a change in her circumstances. And a cosy cottage of her own, with a picturesque sea view, seemed more appealing by the minute.

Chapter 5

Grace entered the Conwenna Café and closed the door behind her. She stood still for a moment, catching her breath after having it stolen by the biting sea wind that was sweeping through Conwenna. Her teeth had literally been chattering on her walk from Rosehip Cottage and she'd been glad of the hat, scarf and gloves that her mother had pressed on her before she'd left.

She pulled the hat and gloves off then unwound the scarf, before looking around for somewhere to sit. The air was filled with the mouth-watering scents of festive baking – reminding her again that it was December – and the haunting sound of a church choir drifted from the speakers around the café. In the corner, a large Christmas tree glowed with hundreds of tiny white lights and the front of the counter had been decorated with a colourful string of miniature lanterns.

The table nearest the tree had been taken by a striking looking couple. The woman was very pretty and petite with large green eyes and short blonde hair. Her companion was tall and broad with brown hair and eyes so dark they seemed black. They were currently cooing over the baby that the woman was cradling in her arms and their love for the child was written all over their faces. As Grace watched, an older woman approached the table carrying a tray of mugs and cakes, which she set down on the table. They looked like a perfect little family and Grace wondered if they lived locally.

Grace continued her scan for a table and her cheeks filled with heat as she met the blue-green eyes of Oliver Davenport. Were they destined to keep bumping into each other as if they were the leading roles in a Hollywood blockbuster? Then again, it was a very small village and it was highly likely that she'd bump into him more than once, and she was probably only noticing him because they'd been introduced. There were other faces she'd seen around that were becoming familiar, but she had yet to put a name to them. She held her breath, unsure whether to smile or wave, but as his lips turned upwards and he beckoned her with a wave of his hand, she released the breath and returned his smile.

'Hello, Grace. How're you?'

'Cold.' She removed her coat. 'Actually, I'm freezing.'

'You want to sit down?'

She glanced at the table where he had an empty coffee cup, a plate with a few crumbs on it and a notepad with a pen sitting on top.

'Wouldn't I be disturbing you?'

'Not at all. To be honest, I'd be glad of the distraction.'

'Okay, then. Thanks.'

She hung her coat on the back of the chair and sat down.

'Do you always go out for lunch?'

'No.' He shook his head. 'Only when I need some thinking time... or some cakes.' He laughed. 'I needed to try to get my head around this...' He gestured at the notepad.

'You're writing?'

'Not exactly… more planning.'

'Anything interesting?'

'A birthday party.'

'Who for?'

'My daughter.'

'Oh… that's right, I remember you mentioning her.'

'Yes, Amy. She'll be eleven on Friday. I've left all this a bit late, but things have been busy and then it was the weekend and then…' he sighed. 'I've no excuse really, other than to say that I'm still getting used to doing all this stuff, and I was probably subconsciously delaying because I knew I'd struggle.'

Grace nodded, although she wasn't quite sure what he meant and didn't want to pry. Not when he was being so nice again. She realized who he reminded her of this morning with his short dark hair and eyes the colour of the Caribbean ocean: the actor Tom Hardy. His wife was a lucky woman.

'Hey there, Grace.' Nate had arrived at the table. 'How're you settling in?'

'Really well, thanks. My parents are delighted with the cottage and it's getting more homely by the day. They're not fully unpacked but they're getting there and the view from the front bedroom is gorgeous.'

'Great to hear that. So do you think you'll be likely to stay too?'

Grace glanced at Oli and found his eyes fixed on her face. She dragged her gaze away from him then made eye contact with Nate.

'I… uh… I doubt it. I have a flat back in Cardiff and a… my life is there.'

'Of course it is.' Nate grinned. 'I just thought that, you know… the Conwenna magic might have got under your skin by now.'

'It is really beautiful here. I can see why people would want to settle here, but I—'

'Well you only need to look at Eve over there to see how Conwenna can get under your skin.' Nate gestured at the couple with the baby. 'Isn't that right, Eve?'

The blonde woman looked up. 'Sorry?'

'I was just telling Grace that Conwenna Cove is a fabulous place to live.'

'Oh absolutely! I came here last year in the summer and never left.' She smiled at the man sitting next to her. 'Although Jack here, and our rescue greyhound Gabe, had something to do with it too.'

'And now look at us.' The handsome dark haired man took the baby from Eve. 'We even have this little fella.'

'Are you staying around here then?' the older woman sitting with them asked. 'I'm Mary Millar. I've lived here for years and couldn't imagine living anywhere else.'

'Nice to meet you,' Grace replied. 'My parents bought Rosehip Cottage.'

'The Phillipses, right?' Mary asked.

'That's right.'

'Well, I hope they'll be very happy there.'

'Thank you.'

'And there you have it,' Nate said. 'Happy Conwenna residents. Come on, Grace, tell me you're not tempted.'

'Leave the woman alone, Nate. She's being too polite. I'm sure Grace has a busy social life in Wales, and has no intention of moving to a tiny Cornish village where the pubs still close at eleven and where the windows rattle when the winter gales bring in a storm.'

'Don't listen to him, Grace. Even when we have a storm here, it's still a wonderful place to be. Oli set up his own veterinary practice here so it can't be that bad.'

'It's a convenient location for the practice. I can get to all the local farms in good time. So don't you let Nate put any pressure on you, Grace. Conwenna is beautiful, but it's too quiet an existence for some.'

Grace smiled her thanks at him, although she wasn't sure how to feel about the fact that he was convinced that she wouldn't want to stay. After all, she'd already considered it, but she barely knew these two men and telling them her thoughts before she knew for certain what she wanted to do, didn't seem quite right.

'Well, all I can say is that you haven't seen it in the summer time yet, Grace. So even if you do return to Cardiff, promise that you'll come back here in July or August and enjoy a Conwenna summer.'

'Okay. I promise.'

'What can I get you, Grace?'

'A latte please, and whatever Oli wants.'

'Shall I make that a gingerbread latte? Christmas special?'

'That sounds amazing, thank you.'

'And a mince pie?'

'Oh, go on then.'

Oli checked his mobile. 'I have time for one more, so I'll have one of those gingerbread lattes too, please. But I'd better finish this list.'

'Oh, sorry, do you want me to leave you in peace?'

Grace pushed her chair back to get up.

'No, no. Please stay. Perhaps you can help me?'

His question, accompanied by a dazzling smile, reassured her.

'So your daughter will be eleven, right?'

'I can't believe it. Seems like she was only a baby yesterday. Her mother would be so proud of her.' He bit his lip.

'Would be?'

He looked down at the notebook.

'She uh… she passed away two years ago.'

'I'm so sorry.'

'Me too.'

'That must have been so hard for you. I mean… gosh there are no words to describe how awful it must have been… must still be.' Grace cringed inwardly at her lack of appropriate words.

'It has been difficult. But the children need normality and stability and I try, with the help of my father, to give them that.'

'Of course. So did your wife always do all of this then?'

'All of what?' He frowned and a thin line appeared between his brows, instantly ageing him. Grace noticed that he had similar lines around his mouth, and her heart ached at the realization that they were evidence of his pain and grief, of what he'd been through over the past two years. No one escaped unscathed.

'The party planning.'

'Oh… yes. She loved all of it. She was always planning the next special occasion.'

'What about your father? Could he help with this?'

'I don't like to ask for help all the time. He's already fabulous with the school run and in so many other ways. Besides, I'm perfectly capable of planning a party.'

'Of course you are. I didn't mean that.'

'Sorry.' He held up a hand. 'I get a bit defensive sometimes.'

'That's perfectly natural, I'm sure.'

He smiled. 'You haven't even had a coffee and already you're counselling me.'

'I guess it could be seen that way.'

'So you're an author, but you've also trained as a counsellor?'

'I am an author, but I'm not a counsellor. Although I had some counselling in my past.'

'Did you find it helpful?'

'In some ways, yes.' Grace looked around her. 'Although it's a bit strange talking to a complete stranger about your deepest feelings. It took some getting used to.'

'I had counselling too.' He nodded slowly. 'So I know what it's like.'

There were a few other people in the café, as well as Eve, Jack, Mary and baby Iain, but they were all involved in their food and their own conversations. She rarely spoke about Sam, but knowing that Oli had lost his wife meant that he knew how it felt to lose someone you were close to. So she felt that she could share at least some things anyway.

'My older brother died nine years ago. He had cystic fibrosis. Some people with it live into their late thirties and forties, but Sam's lungs were badly scarred... and he got infection after infection... In the end, he just grew too weak and it was like he gave up. He told me he was tired of fighting all the time, tired of the pain and the effort it took just to live.' She took a shaky breath. 'Sorry, I don't talk about it much.'

'I can understand why.'

He reached across the table and took her hands. She looked down and realized that she'd been tearing a napkin into tiny pieces. His hands were big and strong, his fingers long with short clean nails. Her skin tingled where he held her and she was strangely comforted by his touch; she very rarely had physical contact with anyone other than her parents.

'I just miss him. A lot. I mean… most of the time, I just get on with it. And nine years is a long time. But sometimes, it all comes flooding back doesn't it?'

'I know exactly what you mean.'

Oli gently released her hands as Nate arrived at the table carrying two coffees and a plate with two large mince pies, their golden pastry dusted with soft white icing sugar.

'Here you are, Grace,' he said. 'My uncle's mince pies are delicious. There's one there for you too, Oli.'

'Oh, thanks. That baguette was very filling, but I'm sure I can manage one of these. I also wanted to ask you about a birthday cake.'

'For Amy?'

'Yes. You think your uncle Kevin will be able to make one for Friday?'

'I'm sure he will. I'll check with him and let you know before you leave.'

'Fantastic.'

Nate walked away.

'You'll enjoy that mince pie. They really are the best I've ever tasted.'

'You haven't tried my father's baking yet.'

'Yet?'

Grace smiled into her mug. Why had she said *yet*?

'Oh... I was just thinking that he could... uh... bake some for the party.'

Oli stared at her and she grew hot under the intensity of his gaze.

'I didn't mean that I'm inviting myself, or my father or... uh... or anything like that. Just that if you'd like some cupcakes, I'm sure he'll be happy to make some for you.'

'Doesn't he have enough to do with sorting out his cottage?'

'He likes baking. It relaxes him, and I'm sure he'd be delighted to do it. He doesn't get to try out his recipes on anyone other than me and my mother these days.'

'These days?'

'Oh, when I was in school he used to bake for the school fêtes and PTA evenings and so on. Any excuse to feed people.'

'Well, if you're sure, then that would be wonderful. My mother has already insisted on bringing sandwiches and pasties – that she'll order from her local deli, no doubt – and with a cake from Kevin and cupcakes from your father, I think that'll be enough for the children to eat. What do you think?'

'Jelly and ice cream?'

He laughed. 'I'm not sure that they expect that these days. It's all fancy cakes and nibbles and knowing some of Amy's friends, they'll probably want olives.'

'Olives? Really? I must be out of touch.'

He nodded. 'At the last party she went to they had bruschetta with fresh ricotta and spinach and prunes wrapped in prosciutto.'

'Now you're having me on.'

'Not at all. These kids have grown up on a diet of reality TV. They watch teenagers on MTV having these elaborate parties and they want a slice of it too. I do try to ensure that Amy is not spoilt and I draw the line at a limo to the village hall, but I have to make some concessions or I'll be labelled *the worst daddy ever*!' He gave a dramatic flick of his hand as if he was throwing long hair over his shoulder, and wiggled his eyebrows. 'Come to the party and meet some of the kids. Then you'll see.'

'Are you sure?'

'I'd appreciate the support. And Tom will be pleased if you're there.'

Grace thought about the little boy with the brown eyes and blond hair. A little boy who didn't have a mummy, who'd lost his mummy when he was around three years old. Then there was this handsome man sat opposite her, a man who'd just held her hands when she'd become upset, a man who knew what it was to lose a loved one. A man who could understand.

'I'd love to come. Now let's have a think about some cupcakes that Amy would like and I'll get Dad baking.'

'Brilliant!'

Oli's grateful smile was enough to melt her heart.

–

The next few days passed in a blur of activity for Oli as he treated domestic pets at the surgery, made visits to two local farms to see to larger animals and went to the greyhound sanctuary at Foxglove Farm to check over a new arrival.

'Ruby seems to be in pretty good health, Jack.' Oli stroked the small tan female greyhound and she wagged her tail.

'She is. Lovely girl too.'

'Was she raced?'

'Apparently not. She just wasn't interested in chasing the hare.'

Oli watched Jack's smile broaden. The ex-marine was such a large man yet he was extremely gentle, and he adored the dogs at the rescue sanctuary. He also seemed a lot happier since he'd fallen in love with Eve, in the summer of the previous year, and had a baby boy a couple of months ago. Jack just looked like his life was complete.

'So she was a bit what... lazy?'

'To be honest, I think she's just too bright. She's only been here two days and is already making headway with the wooden puzzles and can get all the treats out quickly. But she does love to roach too.'

Oli pictured the pretty girl lying in the roaching position, on her back with her legs in the air, as sighthounds tended to do when relaxed, and it made him smile.

He crouched down in front of Ruby. 'You'll make someone a lovely companion, won't you?' Ruby licked his chin.

'Be nice if we can find her a home before Christmas, but with two weeks to go it's unlikely. She needs to be properly assessed first anyway.'

'I'm sure she'll find a loving home. I'd offer myself, but it seems like I might have to take in a cat soon, unless we can find an alternative home for her.'

'The one Edward found?'

'That's right. She's a cute little thing and doing a good job of mothering so far.'

'I wouldn't be surprised if Mary wants to home a kitten too.'

'That's what Edward said. So I just need to find homes for the others. Besides, I know that if I start adopting animals, I'll struggle to stop. Amy and Tom ask all the time.'

'Kind of like opening floodgates?'

'Yes, I guess so. I'd end up overrun.' Oli shook his head at the thought.

'You fancy going for a drink later? Eve said I should head for a pint with Nate, now Iain has started to sleep better at night. Thought we'd head over to The Conwenna Arms after dinner. Just for a drink or two.'

'That would have been great, babysitting problems aside, but we have Amy's eleventh birthday party at the village hall. So it's going to be a busy one.'

'No problem. You all sorted for it?'

'Yeah. Should be okay. I've been lucky to have Mum and Dad on board, as well as Grace Phillips.'

'Grace who?' Jack frowned.

'Her parents are the ones who've just moved into Rosehip Cottage and she's staying in the village for a while.'

'Oh yeah... the pretty woman from the café.' Jack's mouth twitched. 'Sounded like Nate, and you no doubt, were trying to persuade her to stay around.'

'No, nothing like that. She just seems like a really nice person.'

'And it helps that she's very attractive?'

'She is. Well, I think so anyway. Not that it matters.'

'I know you've had a difficult few years, Oli, and I'm not dismissing that, but if you find someone you like then you should allow yourself to consider being happy. I never thought I'd find someone to love again, then Eve arrived that summer and I couldn't help myself. And now... I can't imagine life without her.'

Oli nodded. 'I know, and I'm happy for you, Jack. But it's different for me. One, it's still too soon, and two, I have Amy and Tom to consider. If I ever bring someone into my life, she'd have to be good enough for them too. And anyway, how many women would want to take on a widower with two kids?'

'Oh I don't know, I think you're quite a catch. At least Eve tells me you are, you know, from a female perspective.' Jack winked.

'You're so kind.'

'Look, let's have that pint soon. Preferably this side of Christmas.'

'Sure thing.'

Half an hour later, Oli drove down through the country lanes to the surgery. The drive was so pretty in spring and summer but now, in winter, the hedgerows were bare, their naked dark brown branches revealing the fields that lay beyond them. There were still patches of greenery on the ground around them but some of the grass was yellow and dry, and some – where the wintery sun hadn't reached – still bore a crisp white frost. It reminded Oli of how he tried to protect himself by maintaining a cold outer layer, but he also knew that a touch of warmth and his own frosty layer could easily thaw. Which was why he tried to stay so strong. He was worried that he'd melt if he ever got close to anyone again and he just couldn't afford to do that.

He thought about what Jack had said and he knew that Jack wasn't being insensitive. He'd been through hell during his time in the marines and lost comrades, then his first wife when she'd gone off with another man. Jack had been scarred by his experiences and so had Oli. Wasn't everyone damaged in some way? After all, Grace had told him about her brother dying so young from complications linked to his cystic fibrosis. She had scars too. But that just made Oli feel more drawn to her, in spite of his belief that he shouldn't get close to her, because she understood loss and the pain it brought.

He wondered if she understood the loneliness too. Because he did get lonely; there were nights when he'd wake up expecting to find a warm body next to him in bed, but the other side would be cold and empty. And it hurt so damned much that the ache was physical. He'd tried to tell himself that it was the way life would be for him now and he thought he was getting along all right. That was until he met Grace Phillips a week ago and something inside him stirred, a part of him that was tired of being alone. But he didn't know if it was possible, if his feelings would be reciprocated or if it was something he should even be considering. He probably should just let the idea go completely but...

He parked his Land Rover behind the surgery, stopped the engine, then sat there for a moment to compose himself before heading inside. Today was about Amy and making her happy, about trying to show her a good time without her feeling that awful sense that something was missing, that there was a big black hole where her mum should be.

And that was exactly why Oli didn't have the time, or the energy, to spend on falling in love and caring about another human being. His heart was already stretched as far as it would go.

Chapter 6

Grace pressed a hand to her stomach to try to still the butterflies. This wasn't funny; in fact, it was downright ridiculous. Why was she so nervous? She was only going to a child's birthday party, hardly a big date to get herself in a state about, but the thought of seeing Oli again so soon had left her dizzy.

She checked her appearance in the mirror one more time, wondering yet again if she was wearing an appropriate outfit for the occasion. But in her indigo skinny jeans, knee-high grey leather boots, a soft long-sleeved grey tunic and silver scarf, she felt comfortable. Herself. So other people could like it or lump it. She'd left her curly red hair down and applied just a dash of mango lip gloss, not being one for lots of heavy makeup. Some women could trowel it on and they appeared beautiful and flawless as china dolls, but whenever Grace tried to put foundation on, she looked caked and false. So she had stopped bothering years ago. Besides, who would she be doing it for? Her skin felt so much better without layers of cream and powder and she'd finally grown attached to her freckles.

Downstairs, it was obvious that her father had been very busy.

'Thanks again, Dad.'

'What for?'

'Well, all of this. I'm so grateful.'

Grace gestured at the cupcakes on the table, set out in rectangular cake boxes that Simon had brought with him when they'd moved. He'd often baked for local charities and the schools she'd attended, so he had plenty of experience of catering for large numbers. Grace's mouth watered as she cast her eyes over the varieties of cakes on offer: white chocolate topped with a rich fondant and snowy desiccated coconut; carrot cake with cream cheese frosting,; zesty lemon and poppyseed; double chocolate with toffee sprinkles; and vanilla with a raspberry fondant icing.

'Dad... these are amazing.'

'Well, let's hope that birthday girl thinks so too.'

Grace kissed her father's cheek. He was so kind and generous; he'd do anything for anyone and she knew how lucky she was to have him as a father. She was going to miss him a lot when she returned to Cardiff. *If* she returned to Cardiff.

'Will I do?' Louise entered the kitchen. Some of her red hair was pinned to the side with a small diamante clip. She was wearing straight-leg blue jeans, brown leather ankle boots and a crocheted brown sweater over a brown vest top.

'You look incredible, Mum. You could easily pass for thirty.'

'Well, it's a good job you take after me then, darling.' She winked.

'You do look fabulous, Louise.' Simon planted a quick kiss on his wife's cheek. 'Right, we need to get these out to the car,' he said as he checked the kitchen clock. 'Don't want to be late!'

'Definitely not.' Grace took a deep breath, then picked up a box of cakes. Luckily, her father had an estate car, so there was plenty of room in the back and boot for the cakes.

As they made the short journey to the village hall, she took in the beautiful views. The light was fading, but the expanse of sea was dark and calm. The sun glowed just above the line of the horizon, turning the nearest clouds orange and those further away a dusky tiered lilac. They passed the small harbour then turned left and drove through the main street where shops were closing for the day. Colourful Christmas lights twinkled in the shop windows and where they dangled from lamp posts and trees. The window of the Conwenna Café was steamy around the edges, but inside Grace could see Nate cleaning tables and the Christmas tree in the corner dressed with white lights that raced and flashed alternately. They passed Catch of the Day with its giant illuminated fish sign outside, where hungry locals were already queuing for their dinner, and the delicious savoury aroma of freshly cooked fish and chips doused in salt and vinegar made its way into the car.

At the top of the hill, they reached the village hall and Simon pulled into the car park, parked and cut the engine.

Lights glowed in the windows and the back door of the hall was open. Grace's stomach shifted again. She really was nervous about seeing Oli. For some reason, it mattered to her that he thought she looked nice and that he liked her. It was silly of her to allow herself to care, but there was something there between them and she couldn't deny it. Maybe it was just shared experience, and it would probably only lead to friendship, but even so, she was looking forward to spending the evening with him.

She wondered if he felt the same.

–

Oli was juggling too many balls and he knew he was bound to drop one of them sooner or later. He just hoped he could make this a good party for Amy. His father was bringing the children along at five o'clock, so he'd finished work early and come up to the village hall to get things ready.

He'd set up the trestle tables at one side of the main hall and the DJ was on the stage preparing the disco. His mother had arrived at four-thirty to help him prepare. When Oli had told her about the party, he'd been apprehensive about what she'd say, because her relationship with his father was strained at best, but she'd told him she'd love to come and wanted to be there for her granddaughter. Oli's main concern was how she'd react to Maxine. She knew that Paul was seeing the veterinary nurse, but they hadn't all been in the same room yet. Oli just hoped they'd all be civil to one another for the sake of the children, because the last thing he needed to be worrying about was how his parents would behave.

'Oli?'

He turned to find Grace walking towards him carrying a large box in her arms. She could barely see over the top of it, so he hurried towards her to take it.

'Grace! Great to see you.'

'These are from my dad.' She nodded to the man behind her. 'Oli meet Simon. And this is my mum, Louise.'

'Great to meet you both and thanks so much for this.'

'My pleasure,' Simon said. 'Where do you want the cakes?'

'On the end table, please.'

Fifteen minutes later, the buffet table was set up and it looked amazing with the offerings from the deli that his mother had brought, the cupcakes from Simon and the birthday cake that Nate had delivered. Oli's mother was deep in conversation with Simon and Louise, and Grace was speaking to the DJ.

Oli was pretty happy with how things were going so far, although he was hoping he'd get to have an extended conversation with Grace at some point. He'd found his eyes repeatedly drawn to her since she'd arrived. She was dressed casually yet appeared effortlessly beautiful. Her grey top made her hair seem even brighter than usual, and he liked how she didn't seem to be wearing any makeup. She was obviously lucky that she didn't feel the need to pile it on, and he was glad because he liked the cute spattering of freckles over her nose and cheeks. It would be criminal to cover up such pretty skin.

He was about to go to speak to her, when the front door opened and in walked the birthday girl with her brother, Oli's father and Maxine.

Oli took a deep breath then released it slowly, and plastered on a smile. It was going to be a busy evening and he hoped it would all go well.

–

Silence fell over the hall as the candles on the birthday cake were lit, then everyone sang *Happy Birthday* to Amy. Grace's heart fluttered, as the girl's face flushed with pleasure and she gazed around the room at her party guests. When the singing finished, she blew all the candles out in one go and received a round of applause.

'Can I have a go now?' Tom asked.

'Not today, Tom, it's my birthday. Don't be such a baby.' Amy shook her head.

'I'm not a baby.'

'Well, stop acting like one then.'

Amy flounced off to a group of friends and Tom stood next to his father, scowling.

Grace couldn't help herself; she had to go over to him.

'Hi, Tom.'

He frowned and pouted.

'You're not a baby.'

'Amy always says it when she wants to be mean to me.'

'I don't think she meant to be mean.'

'Well, she was.'

'How about if we go into the kitchen?'

'What? Why, Grace?'

'I have an idea.'

He nodded, and Oli paused in his cutting of the cake and raised his eyebrows.

'There's always a possible compromise.'

'There is?'

'Bring some matches.'

'Of course.' Oli waved at his father. 'Would you finish cutting this, Dad? I won't be long.'

Grace led the way through the hall to the small kitchen. She'd picked up one of her father's cupcakes on the way and a spare candle, which she pressed into the fondant icing.

'Now you can blow this candle out in private.'

Tom grinned. 'Really?'

'Yes. But you must remember to make a wish.'

Tom nodded, his face serious.

Oli handed Grace the matches and she lit the candle then lowered it so Tom could reach.

He gazed up at her and she looked at Oli, not sure what Tom was waiting for.

'Tom?' Oli nudged his son. 'What's wrong?'

'You have to sing before I blow it out.'

'Oh!' Grace swallowed her laughter. 'Right... uh... *happy birthday to you...*'

When she'd finished singing, Tom took a deep breath then blew as hard as he could. The candle sputtered then went out, and Tom screwed his eyes shut and whispered behind his hand.

Grace raised her eyes to find Oli smiling at her.

Then she looked back at Tom and he was still whispering.

The heat of Oli's gaze burned into her and she tried not to meet his eyes again. She was sure that if she did, her cheeks would flame and she'd go all red and blotchy, so she kept focused on Tom, as if she was completely unaware that a good-looking man was gazing her way. Finally, Tom lowered his hand and nodded.

'All done.'

'That was a long wish.' Oli tousled his son's hair.

'It was an important one, Daddy.'

'Obviously.'

'Do you want to eat the cake now?' Grace asked.

'Yes please.'

She removed the candle and Tom took the cake from her outstretched hand.

'Hey, Tom, I think they're playing that song you like.'

Tom tilted his head. 'Yes! Can I go dance?'

'Carry on, but no eating on the dance floor.'

Tom ran out of the kitchen, leaving Oli and Grace alone.

'That was a very kind thing for you to do.'

'I couldn't bear to see him upset.'

Oli nodded. 'He does need to learn that every time Amy has a birthday, it's not his too... well, he already knows that... but what I meant was that he can't always blow out the candles as well.'

'He's still very young.'

'I know. I also know that I tend to be guilty of trying to overcompensate.'

'Look, my parents always let me blow out candles on Sam's birthday. Even when he turned twenty-two. It was a family tradition and one we kept going. It wouldn't have been a birthday without several renditions of *Happy Birthday* and relighting of the candles.'

'Well, we're at a party, so... How are you on the dance floor?' He waggled his eyebrows.

'Oh... I'm not exactly ready to enter any dance competitions.'

'Me neither, so come on, let's go and have a dance. I don't want Amy taking herself too seriously. It's all too easy to let that happen and she's eleven not seventeen. So a bit of dad dancing might do her good.'

He held out his hand and Grace took it, then he led her out into the hall where coloured lights roamed the wooden floor and the walls, the beat of the music was hard and strong, and thirty children were dancing around having a fabulous time.

Oli guided Grace through the children to the middle of the floor then pulled her into a ballroom hold. As chaos ensued around them, Grace was only conscious of the beat of the music in her chest, Oli's hands where they held her and the swaying of her body so close to his.

The parents who'd stayed to keep an eye on their children and stood around chatting, faded away. Her own parents near the buffet table, handing out cake, faded away. The children, racing around the dance floor, faded away. And there was just Oli, holding her close. His eyes, as they gazed into hers, were clear and bright blue-green, like tropical waters that would be perfect if she dived into them. She allowed herself to take in his handsome face, to trace the contours of his strong jaw and the tiny lines around his full lips, as if she were running her fingers over them. She could feel the heat of his body, so close but not quite touching hers. And his scent, a woody cologne with a spicy undertone, made something inside her start to unfold like the petals of a rose opening to the sun.

She was breathless.

Enchanted.

Confused.

And emotion rose in her chest, threatening to choke her. She couldn't do this. It was too intense, too much and so unexpected. She wasn't brave enough to feel this way or to give herself to someone else. It was terrifying, overwhelming and dangerous.

She slipped out of his arms as the song ended and gave him a quick smile before hurrying off the dance floor. At the drinks table, she grabbed a plastic cup of lemonade and downed it quickly, keen to wash the lump in her throat back down before the emotional gates opened and all the things she'd been trying to hold back came gushing out like a flash flood. She'd been so good at getting on with life for so long, at staying shut down and not feeling, but here was a man who seemed to have the key to unlock the door to her emotions and she didn't know how to feel about it. She was bewildered at what was happening.

Yet… as she turned to check where Oli was and saw him approaching her, a look of concern on his handsome features, she knew that she couldn't stop this. Whatever it was. Because as difficult as it was, the creeping in of sensation was exhilarating, and she feared that if she shut it down right now, then she might never experience anything like it ever again.

Chapter 7

In the car on the way back to her parents' house, Grace couldn't get Oli's face out of her mind. It was as if it had been emblazoned there for the rest of the night, like some kind of sign that she needed to re-evaluate her life.

But how? What was it that she should do? Right now the whole situation was far more confusing and complicated than she wanted to contemplate.

When her father parked outside Rosehip Cottage, she got out and went inside, then made her excuses about wanting to do some writing.

Her parents had been wonderful at the party, socializing with everyone and getting on particularly well with Paul and Maxine. Then there was cute little Tom and his intelligent and mature sister, Amy. It was almost as if fate had thrown their families together and suggested they see how they all got on.

But Grace didn't believe in fate, only feelings, and her own were now a boiling pot. She went upstairs and into her bedroom then flopped onto the bed, wondering what to do with the rest of the evening. She could write, of course, but she felt too restless to sit in one place. Perhaps a walk would help? Yes, she needed to get out into the fresh air to clear her head.

She pulled on a thick jumper and wrapped a scarf around her neck then picked up her hat from the dresser. Back in Cardiff, she often strolled through the city in the evening, watching as people went about their lives, some leaving work late and some off out to socialize with friends and colleagues. Then she'd return to her small flat alone, and turn on her laptop immersing herself in her latest manuscript. Writing was a good way to lose herself for a few hours, but right now she knew she needed some air before she tried to tackle a particular plot point, or she'd end up staring into space thinking about Oli and how she really shouldn't be thinking about him at all.

Once she'd slipped her feet into wellies, she told her parents she needed a walk to find some inspiration for a scene, then she strolled out of the garden and along the road, appreciating the quiet of the village. Everything was so calm and peaceful, even though it was seven-thirty on a Friday evening. Conwenna was so different to Cardiff and although she loved the bustling city, she did sometimes crave peace and quiet. As she walked, she could smell the salty tang of the sea and hear the waves as they rolled against the shore of the cove. It was comforting and made her feel closer to nature, more a part of something than out on her own, which was how she usually felt.

The end of the road led off in three directions. One was towards the veterinary surgery and attached cottage, which she now knew to be Oli's, the other was down the steep path to the cove and the third was back across the cliffs and towards the harbour. If she went that way, then she'd likely end up bumping into people and she didn't fancy having to make conversation. She certainly wasn't about to go to Oli's cottage, and he might not even be home yet, so she decided that a walk along the beach might be nice. She'd strolled down with her dad earlier in the week, and loved the crashing waves and wind that had left them red faced with streaming noses but feeling refreshed and energised.

The narrow path down to the sand was steep and she took it gingerly, aware that a fall would be unpleasant at the best of times. When she reached the bottom, she stepped onto the sand. The beach was illuminated by the full moon. She walked towards the dark expanse of the water. The tide was on its way out and the sand beneath her boots was wet; it sucked at her soles, making walking harder. But the view was worth it. She gazed out at the water where the moonlight fell across the surface, undulating with the currents, creating a wavy silver ribbon that led to the skyline like a pathway to peace. She stood still, savouring the scene, enjoying the sense of tranquillity that crept into her heart.

And she knew in that moment that Sam would have loved it here. Everything about the pretty fishing village would have made him smile. So why hadn't her parents ever brought them here for a holiday?

She thought she knew the answer to that.

Their own fears and doubts would have held them back. On one hand, they might have thought the sea air would be good for him, on the other they'd have worried that it would have been too cold; they'd have hoped a change of scenery might have helped him, but they'd have worried that the journey would have been too much for him. And then, of course, there was the biggest factor in keeping them tied to their Welsh home. They worried constantly that Sam might need specialist medical attention for his infections that had increased in frequency and severity as Sam had aged, and taking him away somewhere would have meant being further away from his doctors and the hospital. So fear had kept them tied to one place. Not just Sam, but Grace and their parents too.

They'd spent twenty-two years living in fear and in the end the result had been the same. Sam was gone. They couldn't save him. But he'd lived and was loved.

The dull ache in Grace's heart picked up again, for her parents and for her brother and for all that they been through and all that they had lost. Life could be so cruel. Yet it could also be so wonderful, because Sam had been her brother and she'd adored him.

'Are you all right, Grace?'

The question startled Grace and she turned to find Maxine stood just a few feet away, her face bright in the moonlight.

'Oh… yes. Thank you.'

Grace sniffed and realized that her cheeks were wet. She pulled off a glove and rubbed at her skin.

'The cold air making your eyes water?'

Grace nodded.

'Happens to me all the time.'

Maxine's face was so kind and her voice so soothing that Grace suddenly realized she might break down completely. She bit her lip hard and took a few steadying breaths.

Maxine startled her by whistling long and loud, which was soon followed by the pounding of feet heading towards them from out of the darkness. She tensed, wondering what on earth was headed their way, then burst into laughter as she saw two greyhounds circling across the sand. She could just make out their long tongues dangling from their mouths and their powerful leg muscles propelling them at high speed. Just when she thought that one would collide with her, it darted sideways then turned back in the direction it had just come from, before turning again and jogging towards Maxine, its companion doing the same.

'You have two greyhounds?'

Maxine nodded. 'The best thing I ever did was adopt these two. Brother and sister they are… Most beautiful siblings I've ever come across.'

She hooked leads to their harnesses, then gently rubbed their chins before kissing them both on the top of their narrow heads.

'There you go, you two, I promised I'd let you have a run tonight, didn't I?'

The dogs panted in reply, both seeming to smile as they fixed their eyes on their mistress.

'I'm a good listener if you'd like to talk about anything, Grace.'

She smiled at the older woman.

'Thank you. I'm okay though. I was just thinking about someone I lost a long time ago.'

'I'm sorry for your loss, but Conwenna will do that to you. Help you work out your feelings, so to speak.'

'I'm beginning to realize that.'

'Sometimes you need to let it all go, lovely. Allow yourself to feel the pain in all its glorious technicolour then release it.'

'I'll try. But it's difficult.'

Maxine nodded.

'On another note, did you enjoy the party?'

'Yes, very much. Oli's children are lovely and it was nice to meet more of the locals.'

They started to walk automatically, taking a slow pace across the sand towards the cliffs and rock pools. Grace inhaled the cold air, filling her lungs with it as if it could cleanse her from the inside out.

'Have you always lived here?' Grace asked.

'I grew up here, but moved away in my twenties. I was convinced I wanted to travel the world and escape my loving but rather domineering parents. So I did for a while, I lived in France, Belgium, Italy… I had some elicit love affairs.' She laughed. 'They were wonderfully exciting at the time, but all came to nothing. Then I moved back to Cornwall and rented a small cottage in Porthleven. Close enough to visit Mum and Dad but not on their doorstep. It was a beautiful village but, after a few years, the landlord wanted to sell and I didn't have the funds to buy the place. Then my parents died within months of each other, and left me their cottage in Conwenna and the job at the surgery came up. I'd had some training assisting a vet nurse during my travels, so I applied for the job. I didn't expect to get it, but Oli said I could study for my level three diploma in veterinary nursing apprenticeship-style while working at the practice. With his help and support, I qualified. He's a lovely man, he'd do anything for anyone.'

'He would?'

'And he's had such an awful time of it.'

'With losing his wife?'

'Yes. For a while there I thought we'd lose him too, but then he picked himself up and soldiered on.'

'What was his wife like?'

'Linda was… bohemian. She was a very pretty girl with fine blonde hair and gentle brown eyes. She ran her own online bespoke clothing business and could make a dress out of a tea towel. Very talented, she was.'

'Impressive.'

'Yes. They complimented each other as a couple and always seemed to be laughing.'

'The perfect marriage.'

'I guess so.'

The breeze picked up and Grace swayed, almost losing her boot as the sand sucked it down while the wind pushed her to the side. She wobbled then regained her balance.

'You guess so?'

'What I mean is that they went through a terrible time. I don't want to share too much because it's Oli's business, but I see that he likes you and I want him to be happy.'

'He likes me?'

Maxine stopped walking and turned to Grace. The moonlight lit up her cheeks and forehead and made dark hollows of her eyes.

'It was obvious when I saw you together this evening. The way he looked at you was just… well I haven't seen him look at anyone like that in the two years since Linda died.'

'Oh.'

'Look, I might seem out of turn saying this but… please be gentle with him. Linda was diagnosed with breast cancer towards the end of her pregnancy with Tom. She was given the option to terminate the pregnancy and have treatment, or to have treatment and risk the baby, or to wait until after she delivered. She insisted on waiting. They induced her a few weeks before her due date so they could start treatment right away. She had chemo and radiotherapy and the cancer went into remission for three years, but after that… it returned with a vengeance.'

'That's so sad.'

'And it's why I worry about Oli. He's been like a closed book ever since. The only things that get close to him are the children and the animals he treats. When he's cuddling Amy or Tom, or treating a dog, I see a flicker of the man he was before Linda got sick. But it doesn't last long. I think it's why he sometimes comes across as cold and aloof, it's kind of a protective layer he assumes. But today, I saw that flicker when he danced with you.'

'I really don't think it was anything other than his friendly nature emerging.'

Grace's stomach rolled uncomfortably. She liked Oli, but he'd been through so much. Could Maxine be telling her the truth or just what she wanted to hear? Or, of course, what Maxine wanted to believe because she obviously cared about the single father.

'I know Oli quite well. Not only have I worked with him for five years, but I'm also involved with his father. I see him on a daily basis and therefore see the ups and downs. Take my word for it, you have permeated his protective veneer. So if you have no interest in him, then please back off right now so he doesn't fall for you. However, if you genuinely like him, then make him happy.' Maxine reached out and squeezed Grace's shoulder. 'I know that Paul would be as delighted as me to see Oli with a new life ahead of him and those children with a mother. They're so young, you know?'

Grace swallowed hard. Yes, she was attracted to Oli and she knew that could probably develop into something more – but the children? Adorable, sweet, and Tom had definitely squeezed his way into her heart already, but to become a mother figure to them? That would be a huge responsibility. It sounded like Linda was beautiful, talented and gentle. And she was dead. Forever perfect in everyone's memories. So to attempt to take her place would be madness and something Grace would never do. Yet was there a way to fit into Oli's life and into his children's lives that would suit them all?

She sighed.

'Look, Maxine... please don't take this the wrong way but I think you've read far more into the situation. I like Oli, and his children, but I barely know them. With what they've all been through, it sounds like they just need some time and space. I mean... you know them better than me, but you don't know me or what I want from life.'

'Sorry, love, it's a lot to consider. And perhaps I am being an interfering old so and so.' Maxine took her arm. 'Take your time. Be sure before you decide yay or nay. Life is short. Love is wonderful and it's the only thing worth fighting for.'

They made their way towards the steep path, then Maxine gestured for Grace to go first. As she walked, she tried to empty her mind. It was the best way for her to process information. She would spend a few hours writing when she got back to Rosehip, then hopefully have a decent night's sleep.

Tomorrow would be another day at Conwenna Cove and she would see where it took her; right now, she had no idea where that would be.

Chapter 8

'Daddy can we put the Christmas decorations up now, please?'

Tom looked up from his bowl of porridge and smiled, exposing his small white milk teeth. He had a speck of porridge on his chin, so Oli used a tissue to wipe it off.

'I guess so.'

'Yay!' Tom wiggled on his chair.

The previous year, Oli had suggested that they wait until Amy's birthday had passed before they decorated. It was, in part, a way of not stealing her thunder, because he'd hung birthday banners around the cottage and stuck balloons outside the house, but it was also because he just found the whole process so damned hard. However, now it was Saturday morning, the day after Amy's party, and Oli really had no excuse to delay any further.

'Are they in the attic?' Amy asked.

Oli nodded and his stomach lurched. It was another reason why he was reluctant, because he'd have to go up there where Linda's things sat in their boxes: silent reminders that he was about to spend another Christmas with his children – alone. After she'd died not long before Christmas, he'd left everything as it was until the new year. Then suddenly, he'd woken up one morning in February, burning with rage at the unfairness of it all and after taking

81

the children to school, gone into the surgery and grabbed a load of old boxes, then marched into the cottage and packed everything of hers up. He'd stuffed clothes and shoes, jewellery, brushes, perfumes and body lotions, her sewing machine, her notebooks and even the books she'd been reading – that had sat on the bedside table for months – into boxes then taped them shut. He'd carried them up the ladder to the small attic and pushed them to the back, behind everything else, ending up sweaty and dusty from his efforts. He'd known, even in his deepest grief, that he had to keep Linda's things for the children, but he couldn't bear to look at them for a moment longer.

Now he would have to venture near them to get the two plastic containers of Christmas trimmings.

'Can I come up in the attic and help you?' Tom asked.

Oli shook his head. 'Better not. There's all sorts up there. Big fat spiders, ancient cobwebs, woodlice and lots of dust. I'll go up and hand the boxes down, then you and Amy can unpack things.'

'Okay, Daddy.'

Amy nodded. 'That's a good plan, Daddy.' Her face had paled and he knew it was the talk of spiders. She had had a phobia of them ever since someone at school had told her that now she was in the ground her mummy would be eaten by spiders. It had given Amy nightmares for weeks and taken a visit to the school from Oli to get the issue dealt with. Amy hadn't been troubled by such bullying again, but Oli knew that children could be blunt and cruel; he hoped his children wouldn't have to deal with more as it made their grief all the more difficult to handle, especially as he was still trying to navigate his way through his own.

As Amy lowered her eyes and stared into her bowl, Oli realized that there was something different about her appearance. Her eyelashes looked longer and darker. As if she was wearing...

'Amy?'

'Yes, Daddy?'

As she met his eyes again, he saw that she did, in fact, have longer lashes this morning.

'Are you wearing mascara?'

She rolled her eyes and he stifled a laugh.

'Yes, Daddy. Brogan bought it for my birthday.'

'Your eleven-year-old friend bought you make-up for your eleventh birthday?'

'Well, yeah...' She bridled as if he'd just said the most ridiculous thing he could think of.

'Oh. I see. Don't you think you're a bit... young for all that? I mean, it wasn't so long ago that you were playing with Barbie and Sylvanians.'

'Daddy, you're so behind the times.' She flicked her blonde hair.

'And you've made your hair all wavy. I knew there was something else different about you.'

'It's fashionable, Daddy. I did it with my new straighteners from Lauren.'

'So it would seem.'

'I am eleven now, Daddy and that's almost a teenager.'

'Almost.'

Oli drained his mug then carried the breakfast things over to the sink. He turned on the tap and waited for the water to get hot, using the time to get his head around his daughter's comment. She was right, of course, she was growing up and quickly. But was it too quickly?

As he had so many times before, he wished he had someone to talk to about it, someone who understood how it felt to look at his daughter and see the serious, precocious pre-teen who had taken the place of his sweet, happy little girl.

But there was no one to discuss it with.

Because Oli was all alone.

–

'Shall we get a hot chocolate first?' Louise asked her daughter as they strolled through the town.

They'd driven into Truro to spend Saturday morning soaking up some of the pre-Christmas build up, and because Louise wanted to buy some festive decorations for her new home.

Grace yawned. 'I don't know about hot chocolate, think I need coffee.'

'Well, if you will write until the early hours, what do you expect?'

Grace knew that her mother understood her writing processes and that once she was on a roll she had to keep going, no matter what the time. She became so involved in her plots, so engrossed in her characters, that they took precedence over everything else. If she'd had a husband and family to worry about, then she suspected it would have been different but for Grace, her writing was her life.

'I know, I know. But I had to get the ending just right.'

'So that's another book finished then?'

'Well, the first draft yes, but I'll need to revise it and edit it before sending it to my agent.'

'Of course. And you want me to read it before you send it?'

'As always, Mum, you know it can't go anywhere until you've done a critique for me.'

Grace was really grateful for her mother's no-nonsense feedback; she knew her mum would want her books to be as good as they could be before anyone else saw them. On a few occasions, they'd debated about the best way for a plot to go, or for the most exciting way to end a scene, but they always ended up laughing and agreeing, and Grace appreciated her mother's honesty. It was just one of many things that made them so close; she didn't know what she'd do without her mother.

Which was another reason why she should consider moving to Cornwall. The thought of being so far away from her parents, even though she could drive it in a few hours, was getting more worrisome by the day. Instead of looking forward to returning to her quiet flat and locking herself away to write, Grace found that she was starting to dread the day she had to leave.

'Oli mentioned a place called Espresso Yourself. He said it's really nice.'

'Did he now?' Louise smiled. 'Well, let's see if we can find it.'

The small café was nestled between a bookshop and a shoe shop. The interior was warm and cosy, the window steamy as the warm air met the cold of the glass. The aromas of freshly ground coffee and baking met Grace's nostrils and her mouth watered instantly.

'There's a table.' Grace pointed at the far corner, so they headed over to it.

'I'll get the drinks in. So do you want a cappuccino?'

'Yes, please.'

'Anything to eat?'

'I shouldn't really.'

Louise smiled. 'Are you sure?'

'Oh, go on then. Surprise me.'

As her mother went over to the counter, Grace removed her warm duck-feather gilet and the thick black fleece she wore underneath. She knew her mother would have told her to do as much, just so she'd 'feel the benefit of them' when they went back out into the cold air. Grace had grown up hearing those words and it was instinctive now to act on them. *A mother's wisdom*. Amy and Tom popped into her mind. Those poor children didn't have what Grace was still enjoying in her thirties. They didn't have a mum to advise them, to comfort them or to take shopping trips with. It was so incredibly sad and her heart went out to them.

She gazed around the café. There were random words painted on the dark orange walls in swirly black ink: coffee, cake, tea-break, biscuit, muffin, shortbread... *Certainly some not so subtle subliminal messaging going on there*, she thought, as her stomach growled. She'd only had breakfast an hour ago, so shouldn't really be hungry, but she found she suddenly was.

The tables were low and round, and the seating consisted of large, squishy fake leather armchairs that swallowed you when you sat down. It was sort of comforting, although Grace suspected that a few coffees had probably been spilt as patrons sat down, not realizing how much bodily control they'd lose once within the grasp of the chairs. In fact, they were like chair-beanbag hybrids.

As it wasn't yet ten o'clock, the café was still relatively quiet, with a few spare tables, but Grace suspected that as there were only three Saturdays left before Christmas, that the café would fill up fairly soon. Better to get her caffeine fix now before the queues got too long.

Louise soon returned to the table with a tray. She placed it on the table then went to sit down.

'Careful!' Grace warned.

'What? Why?' Her mother looked around her, then at her chair. 'There's nothing on the seat is there?'

'No, but once you sit down, it's hard to get back up.'

Louise giggled. 'We should get your father one of these then. Do him good to sit still every now and then. Boy does that man like to keep active.'

'I'm surprised he didn't want to come today.'

Simon loved a good shopping trip, but today he had declined.

'He said he wanted to finish sanding the bedroom floor.' Louise rolled her eyes. 'I told him it could wait, but he said he wanted it done before Christmas.'

'But it's the spare room, no one will be sleeping in it.'

Grace started as the reality of her words sank in. Had Sam survived, it would have been his room. But any place they lived in that had a third bedroom would always have a spare room.

Louise lowered herself carefully into her seat.

'It's okay, Grace. It is the spare room. We have to accept that. To be honest, I think it's actually easier to say that here, because in our old house the room was always going to be Sam's room... even after all this time. But now, we're in a cottage he never lived in, and although I thought that would make me sad, it's actually a bit easier. I'll never

ever forget him, obviously. I mean… he was my baby boy. But he's gone and we had to make a decision about what to do at this stage in our lives. Your father always loved Cornwall, so this seemed like the best place to choose.'

'You love it too though, don't you?'

'Oh, yes. But after years of watching your dad living a kind of half-life, I wanted him to have what he really wanted. He's such a good man and he deserves to have what he wants. Don't tell him this, but I'd have been happy moving anywhere, even to a small apartment in the south of France. But your dad had his heart set on Conwenna Cove and now that we've moved, well, I'm certain we made the right choice.'

Grace nodded then leaned forwards and picked up her cappuccino.

'I got you a cherry Bakewell tart. Is that okay?'

'Fabulous. Just what I need before we hit the shops.'

Grace sipped her drink, savouring the frothy surface of the coffee and the bitterness underneath tempered by the creamy milk. She hadn't know that Conwenna was mainly her father's choice, had always thought her parents agreed on just about everything. But then that was probably why they got on so well. A relationship was about give and take and being prepared to make compromises. Kind of like a good cappuccino, where the milk and coffee went so well together. Would she go well with Oli, Amy and Tom? They were very different, had lived different lives, although they had both been through a devastating loss. Would that bond them? Was there more beneath the surface that would bring them together?

She shook herself. She was getting way ahead of herself and it wasn't like her. Grace was not a hopeless romantic:

she was a pragmatist. She got things done and didn't waste time swooning around over handsome men. Yet with Oli, she was convinced there was something more there. Something they had only just scratched the surface of and she wanted to find out more, to see if they could be more than just people who shared the loss of a loved one.

'Have your tart, Grace, and stop daydreaming.'

'Yes, Mum.'

'Anyone would think you'd recently bumped into a handsome vet, wouldn't they?'

Her mother winked.

Heat rushed into Grace's cheeks. What had her mother seen? First Maxine and now her own mum. She stretched forwards and grabbed her Bakewell tart, then took a bite. At least with a mouth full of cherry and almond deliciousness, she could avoid responding to the topic her mother had just hinted at.

Ten minutes later, Grace heaved herself out of the chair and pulled on her fleece and her gilet. She slipped her bag across her body then turned back to her mother.

'Mum? What is it?'

Louise was bright red, her eyes bulging and her hands white as she gripped the sides of the chair.

'I can't get up.'

'Of course you can.'

'I can't. I'm really stuck.'

'Hang on, I'll help you.'

Grace went around the table and took her mother's hands.

'After three.'

'One… two… three!' Grace pulled, but just as her mother was almost on her feet, she lost her balance and Grace ended up being dragged back down on top of her.

'Grace!' Louise squealed.

'Hold on, Mum.'

Grace tried to move, but she couldn't budge her knee without putting it somewhere that would hurt her mother. So she tried to use her hands to push herself upwards on the arms of the chair, but she just couldn't hoist herself high enough.

'It looks like I was giving you some sort of bizarre lap dance that went wrong.'

Grace started to giggle and beneath her, she felt her mother laughing too.

'This is ridiculous.'

'Grace, get up. I'm too warm now. It's my age!'

'I can't, Mum, I'm stuck.'

'Morning ladies, need a hand?'

Grace raised her head to find herself looking at Oli. Either side of him were Amy and Tom, their mouths open and their eyes wide as they took in the spectacle before them.

'What are you doing?' Tom asked. 'Are you playing Twister?'

Grace started giggling again.

'Hold on.' Oli went around behind her. 'I'll have to put my hands on your waist, Grace. Is that okay?'

'Of course.'

'I'll pull you backwards so you don't accidentally knee your mother in the stomach or something. Just don't change your position.'

Grace was still giggling. 'I can't move. I'm weak.'

'Right, I've got hold of you. Ready...'

Oli tightened his grip on Grace but his fingers tickled as they dug into her sides, so when he pulled, she wriggled, still weak with laughter but finally upright again.

'Easy, Grace,' he whispered into her ear, his warm breath caressing the sensitive skin there. 'So you're ticklish are you? Useful information.'

A tiny shiver ran down her spine and the hairs on her arms stood on end.

What did he mean? How could that be useful? Tickling was such an intimate thing. She stood there trying to compose herself as he moved around her and went to her mother.

'There. Now let me help you up too, Louise.'

He took Louise's hands and with one firm tug, pulled her out of the chair.

There was a round of applause in the café and Grace realized that they'd become the morning's entertainment. In her weakness, she hadn't noticed what was going on around her.

'Well that was fun,' Oli said, his eyes twinkling as he held Grace's gaze.

'Fun?' she asked. 'Embarrassing more like.'

'Oh, I don't know. Coming to the rescue of two beautiful redheads is certainly my idea of fun.'

'Get on with you, Oli!' Louise laughed. 'I'm old enough to be your mother.'

'And our granny.'

They all looked at Tom who gazed at them, his face the picture of innocence.

'I guess I am, Tom.' Louise smiled at him. 'Now there's a thought.'

'We're going to put our Christmas decorations up today!' Tom clapped his hands. 'Want to come and help?'

'Oh... uh...'

Grace looked at Oli to try to gauge his reaction to his son's question, but he was removing his coat and a strange expression had taken over his face, as if he'd been transported far away to a different time and place.

'Perhaps, Tom. It depends on how long my mum keeps me walking around the shops.' Grace pulled a face at the little boy and he nodded his understanding.

'Daddy, can we have milkshakes now, please?' Amy tugged at Oli's hand.

Oli glanced up again as if he'd suddenly been dragged back into the moment.

'Yes, Amy. Of course.'

'They're on me.' Grace pulled her purse out of her bag. 'It's the least we can do.'

Chapter 9

'What about this one?'

'Yes, that's lovely too, Mum.'

'Why don't you try something on?'

'Not yet. I'll find something closer to Christmas.'

'It'll be here before you know it.'

Her mother disappeared back into the changing room.

Grace was sitting on a small blue sofa outside the changing rooms of a department store, as Louise tried on several outfits she thought might be nice for Christmas. It was a tradition of theirs to find a new outfit for Christmas Day as well as one for Boxing Day and New Year's Eve. It had been one of Louise's many coping strategies after Sam had died. She said that they had to celebrate occasions in style, to make an effort to live life because that was what Sam would have wanted them to do.

And really, when Grace thought about it, life was mapped out by the occasions they celebrated. The days in between passed by, but the Friday night movie and popcorn, the Saturday night curry and wine, the Sunday dinner, the birthdays, weddings and festive periods, were what it all came down to. Without those markers of time, life would have just been a series of days. So Louise was right to insist upon keeping their little traditions going.

Christmas music drifted out from the speakers and tinsel shone everywhere she looked. The mannequins were decked out in Christmas jumpers, and Santa hats and Christmas trees positioned around the store featured the range of lights that the retail chain had for sale this year.

When they'd left the café earlier, Grace had still been giggling as Tom had been begging Oli to let him sit in the sticky chair. In his innocence, he'd thought Louise and then Grace had been stuck because the chair was covered in some adhesive substance. Oli had been trying not to laugh himself as he explained that Tom could sit in the chair, but might find that Louise had taken all the stickiness with her. This had led to Tom diving into the chair and bouncing up and down to test its stickiness. Grace hadn't wanted to leave them, and it had been strange saying goodbye, because she'd sensed that Oli had more to say but circumstances and present company made it difficult for him. So they'd held each other's gaze for a moment longer than would be expected from mere acquaintances, then Grace had turned and left the café. But at least she knew there was a chance she'd see him again soon. Especially seeing as how Tom had given her an opening by asking her to help them with the Christmas trimmings.

As the opening chords of Wham!'s *Last Christmas* floated out into the store, a memory flashed into her head, as vivid as if it had been yesterday. Grace and Sam, just five and six, sneaking carefully downstairs in the dawn light on Christmas Day, keen to see if Santa had been. They'd held hands, both trembling with excitement, and when they'd entered the living room of their family home, they'd paused, their mouths falling open in awe. Gifts had been piled on both of the sofas, their wrapping paper different – gold for Grace and silver for Sam – as well as under the tree. Grace had wanted to start tearing through the paper immediately to find out what was inside but Sam had cautioned her, wise even at six years old. He'd told her to wait for their parents to get up, because they'd want to see what Santa had brought too. As a compromise, he'd allowed her to sneeze loudly at the bottom of the stairs, and soon Louise and Simon had appeared, hair sticking out, bleary-eyed, but awake. And a wonderfully happy Christmas day had begun. Sam had always known how to do things to ensure that everyone enjoyed themselves. It was as if he had been born with that knowledge, as if he'd known from the outset that his life would be short, so he'd need to live every moment to the full and in the best way he could.

She wondered what he would think about Oli. Then she cringed. She couldn't believe that they'd been rescued by Oli in the café. What a coincidence that he'd come in just as they were stuck on the squishy seat. And she'd been a giggling mess sprawled on top of her mother. What must he have thought of her?

And what about the thing he'd said about tickling? Every time she thought about it and the way his breath had gently caressed her neck as he'd whispered into her ear, she tingled all over. Did Oli want to get to know her better? Her body certainly wanted to get to know him even if her mind was trying to reason with her.

Sometimes she wished she could just switch off her mind like she could a set of flashing fairy lights. It would be nice to stop thinking, just for an hour or two. Writing did that for her by distracting her, but when she wasn't writing, it was as if her brain offered up an open house to all and sundry ponderings and the subsequent disquiet they could cause.

'Grace?'

'Oh, that's gorgeous!'

Louise did a slow turn and the purple sequins on the tunic top sparkled.

'It really suits you.'

'Right, I'll get this one then.'

'You should.'

'And the black silk trousers?'

'Definitely.'

'Your father will have a fit at the price tag.'

'Well, he should have come to keep an eye on your spending then. Anyway, Mum, they can be my treat.'

'Nonsense! What else has your dad got to spend his money on?'

Grace shrugged. She often thought the same thing about her own money. She earned a good wage from her writing and had plenty saved up for a rainy day. Perhaps it was time to start spending some of it, because as she well knew, and as Sam would have reminded her, life was for living and tomorrow is not guaranteed.

–

Grace tucked her arm into her mother's as they walked through the compact streets. The UK's most southerly city reminded her a bit of Cardiff with its variety of shops, its cosmopolitan feel and fascinating architecture. The city was dominated by the cathedral with its gothic towers that reached up into the winter sky, and she kept finding her eyes drawn to them, wondering what they had seen and heard in their time above the city in the heart of Cornwall.

They passed wonderful Christmas window displays that sparked a frisson of childish excitement in Grace. One, in a card shop window, featured a life-size sleigh complete with six reindeer and a jolly Santa Claus who faced outwards towards the street as if looking for all the well-behaved children. Another, in a shoe shop, had a wide range of shoes and boots in every shade of red, propped up in fake snow. Grace rarely wore heels but she had to admit that the red stilettos on show were very appealing, and she was even tempted to go in and try them on. Her favourite display was that of a lighting shop, where lights in a variety of shapes hung from wooden beams suspended from the ceiling. There were intricately detailed hearts that glowed from within, gingerbread men with red and green glowing buttons, miniature Christmas trees adorned with tiny colourful lights and snowmen with glowing smiles and illuminated hats and scarves.

As well as the shops, Truro boasted fancy coffee houses, trendy cocktail bars and inviting ice cream parlours. The aromas that seeped out onto the streets were mouth-watering and even though Grace had eaten breakfast and a Bakewell tart, she could easily have gone into one of the venues and eaten more. The Cornish air and appreciation of good food were certainly rousing her appetite.

Everywhere she looked, she saw happy families: parents and children were smiling and chatting excitedly about the approaching festivities and what gifts they needed to buy. For a moment, Grace was hit by a wave of frustration. She would never have that, never have her own children to enjoy Christmas with. It just wasn't possible. But then her thoughts strayed to her mother and she squeezed her arm tighter. Louise had had that, once, a long time ago. And lost it. She'd never have grandchildren and never know the excitement of seeing Sam or Grace's children as they opened their gifts or enjoyed their Christmas dinner.

'You okay, Mum?'

'Yes, love, why?'

'I was just thinking about the things that we'll never have. Not meaning to bring you down, but sometimes it's hard to ignore it.'

Louise nodded. 'I know. But I try to think instead of what we do have and what we once had. I'm luckier than so many people. I had a wonderful son, and I still have a beautiful daughter and a loving husband. Many never have that. So even though I lost Sam, at least I had him for as long as I did. I'm not saying that I've never considered what I'd sacrifice to have him back, because I'm only human, but I know that's not possible and that life has to go on. Besides, you could still have a husband and a family. If you wanted it.'

'We've talked about this, Mum, and it's not going to happen.'

Louise shook her head. 'Never say never, Grace. If you meet the right man and he wants to have a family with you, then it's something you may well consider then.'

'And go through what you and Dad did?' Grace shuddered. 'I just couldn't bear it.'

'I'd go through it all again just to have Sam for the time I did. Look at what light and laughter he brought with him.'

'He did bring so much love.' Grace swallowed hard. Perhaps she was being unfair on her parents by being so adamant that children were not on her horizon; the risks were so great, that it was more than she could imagine opening herself up to at any point in the future. But she didn't know if she was strong enough to take those chances or to expose her parents to more heartache. It was far safer to stay single and not to want what she could not have. Besides, not everyone had to have a husband and children; sometimes life just took a different course.

'Ah there's that cookery shop I wanted to go into. Come on, let's see if we can find your father the deep muffin tin he's wanted since he saw it on TV.'

'Okay.' Grace nodded, glad of the diversion because cakes were always a good distraction.

–

Oli had taken the children into Truro after getting the boxes down from the attic, because he'd needed to give himself a breather. Not because he was physically tired, but because of the emotional wear and tear it had caused him.

He'd suggested they go for a milkshake and cake, got them both into their warm coats and hats, and into the Land Rover. Then he'd driven away from Conwenna, not really sure where he was going. He'd ended up in Truro, as if guided there by some mystical force; although he now suspected it had something to do with remembering that Grace had mentioned a Christmas shopping trip with her mother. So, when he'd taken the children into Espresso Yourself, and seen Grace and her mother in hysterics, unable to get out of the squishy chair, he'd been delighted.

Helping Grace to get up had been quite an experience. He'd needed to take hold of her waist and to lift her to prevent her from sticking a knee or an elbow into Louise. In his arms, just as she had when they'd danced at Amy's party, Grace had been warm, soft and smelt so good, he'd been tempted to bury his face in her neck right then and there just to inhale her gorgeous scent.

He knew now, for sure, that being around Grace was having a strange effect upon him. He'd been immune to women, disinterested in their charms for what felt like a lifetime, and now one redheaded, blue-eyed beauty had walked into his world and he just couldn't get her out of his mind. It was a little unsettling, but also rather welcome as he knew that he could feel alive, that parts of him that had been numb for so long did still want to work. And they wanted to work with Grace. He'd had to force all wicked thoughts from his mind as he'd drunk a coffee, and listened to Amy and Tom debate the merits of strawberry versus banana milkshake. But try as he might, he couldn't prevent himself from imagining what it would be like to kiss her, to delve his tongue into her mouth and taste her, then…

'Daddy, shouldn't you be straightening the branches?'

He blinked hard and realized that he was standing in front of the old Christmas tree, and staring absently out of the front window of his cottage at the pale winter horizon. After the milkshake, he'd decided it was best to get on with the decorations rather than put them off, so here they were trying to make the tree look respectable.

'Oh!' He met Amy's bright eyes. 'Yes, indeed. I drifted off there.'

She frowned at him and folded her arms.

'What were you thinking about?'

'Uh… about how this tree is quite old and we should probably have picked up a new one.'

'But I like this tree. Mummy chose it.'

'I know she did.'

'So we should keep it.'

'Yes… of course.'

He began straightening the branches, unfolding them from the position they'd been in since last January when he'd packed them away. The musty smell of Christmases gone by assaulted him, and he struggled against the wave of emotion, breathing through his mouth to avoid the memories.

He wondered if the tree lights still worked and realized that he should have checked them too – before they'd left – because he could have picked up some replacements. But it was too late now; if they didn't work, they'd have to manage until next weekend when he'd have a chance to go and buy some more.

'Daddy?'

'Yes?' He braced himself for another tree comment.

'How is the cat doing?'

'The cat?'

'Yes… the one with the kittens.'

He stopped what he was doing and turned to his daughter.

'She's doing well.'

'Oh, good.'

Amy's cheeks turned red.

'Is everything all right, Amy?'

'Yes.'

'Are you sure?'

'Yes, Daddy.'

'Is there anything you want to tell me? Do you know something about the cat and the kittens?'

Amy hung her head. 'No.'

'Amy?'

'I said no, Daddy! I just wanted to know if she was okay because the kittens need her.'

'Okay...' He decided to leave it for now, but he suspected that Amy might know something about the cat that she hadn't shared with him.

Ten minutes later, he stood in front of the tree with a very disappointed Amy and Tom. And there was nothing as harsh as disappointed children at Christmas time.

'Oh, guys, I'm so sorry.'

Amy shook her head, then folded her arms across her chest. 'Why don't they work, Daddy?'

'The bulbs must have blown or the fuse has gone... and I don't think I have any new ones here.'

Tom's lip wobbled. 'I liked those lights, Daddy.'

'I know.'

Oli felt like the worst dad in the history of the world. Why hadn't he thought to check the damned lights? Linda would have done so. Probably before the children even got up that morning. Wouldn't she?

'Look, let's have some lunch then we could go back out.'

'What, more shopping?' Tom groaned.

'Well, if you want lights on the tree today then we'll have to.'

'But I wanted to watch that Christmas film,' Tom whined.

Oli sighed. He could ring his father and ask him to watch the children, but he didn't like to keep asking for favours. Paul had Maxine now and she'd already worked the morning at the surgery, feeding and cleaning out the cat and kittens as well as their other two weekend resident dogs who'd come in for treatment. His father deserved to have some peace and quiet with his girlfriend. So there was no one else he could ask, was there?

Just then, there was knocking at the door.

'Who's that?' Amy asked, her eyes wide. 'Are we expecting anyone?'

Oli bit his lip, again amazed by how mature she sounded.

'I don't think so.'

'You two have a look through that box of decorations to see if there's anything you want to use and I'll go see who it is.'

He headed out into the hallway and ran his hands through his hair. When they'd got home, he'd slung on an old pair of jogging bottoms that hung low on his hips because the elastic was stretched and a faded grey t-shirt that was a bit clingy after he'd accidentally boiled it. But he hadn't been expecting company and hadn't wanted to wear decent clothing to go through dusty old boxes.

And now someone was knocking at the door.

He opened it slowly, trying to hide his bottom half with the door, and peered outside.

'Oli? Hi, sorry to arrive unannounced but I uh...' Grace's eyes roamed over him and he felt his cheeks flush. She was probably wondering why he was hiding behind the door. 'Sorry am I interrupting something?'

'No, no.' He opened the door properly. 'Of course not. I was just sorting through our old Christmas decorations. Which is why I'm dressed like this.' He gestured at himself and Grace looked him up and down again. She must think he looked like a sack of potatoes.

'You look... uh... fine.' She smiled and her eyes sparkled. The tip of her nose was pink and there were two matching spots on her cheeks. As she spoke, her breath emerged like smoke in the icy air.

'Wow, I'm so sorry. I should invite you in. It's getting colder out there.'

'Oh, it's okay!' She waved a hand. 'I just wanted to see if you wanted these.' She held up two carrier bags. 'My parents were going through their old Christmas stuff and they thought you might want some of these decorations and lights for the children. Tom said earlier that you were going to be decorating and...'

'Oh. Right. Of course he did.'

'Oh my goodness, I'm so sorry. Of course you don't want these. That seems awful doesn't it, pushing old trimmings and lights onto you.'

'Actually,' he said, reaching for her arm and pulling her gently inside, 'you're a lifesaver. I was just surprised that you'd turned up like some beautiful guardian angel, when I was having a complete crisis.'

He closed the door and relieved her of the bags then set them down on the hallway floor.

'Crisis?' She frowned.

'Here, take your hat and coat off and come on through.' She did as Oli suggested and he took her coat and hung it on the stand behind the front door. It smelt of Grace, her signature perfume with its vanilla and cherry blossom combination, a scent that made his heart beat faster. She handed him her hat and he put it on top of her coat. 'Yes, see, I put the tree up then got the lights ready, actually spent ages untangling them, then found that they don't bloody work. So I've two very disappointed children in there and I'm currently a contender for Worst Daddy in Cornwall.'

'Is that an actual competition then?' Her lips twitched.

'Yes, didn't you know? Here in Cornwall we like to celebrate all things disappointing.'

'Well, I don't think you need to worry. That's hardly a terrible thing to do, is it?'

'You obviously don't have children.'

He smiled, but his stomach dropped to the wooden floor as he saw her expression change.

'Oh god, I've said the wrong thing haven't I? I'm so, so sorry, Grace. I didn't mean it like that.'

'It's okay. You're not the first to mention it and you certainly won't be the last.'

'Really?' He reached out and placed his hand on her arm. His heart was thudding now, as he really didn't want to upset her. The smile she'd freely offered him when she'd arrived, a smile that had brightened his day, had been replaced by an air of sadness that made him want to gather her in his arms and hold her tight. He wanted to make it all better for her.

He looked at his hand, where it held her arm, their skin separated only by her black sleeve, and instantly pulled away. Whenever he was around Grace, he found himself wanting to touch her and sometimes doing it without being fully aware of it, as if it was the most natural thing in the world.

'Really. It's fine.' She smiled again, but her eyes showed that she wasn't in the same frame of mind as she had been.

Oli resolved to try to bring her real smile back, the one that lit her up from within and made him want to watch her smiling all day long.

'So what's in the bags?'

Just then, there was a loud scream.

'Hold that thought!'

He hurried through to the living room and gasped. Amy and Tom were standing on the sofa, their cheeks red and their faces scrunched up in fury as they tugged something red and white between them. Tom was growling like a small feral animal and Amy was puce-faced and crying.

'What are they fighting over?' Grace asked, as she peered around Oli.

'I have no idea. KIDS! What are you doing? You two don't fight like this. Not ever.'

Amy turned her watery eyes to him. 'It's mine, Daddy, tell him.'

'Amy...' Oli suppressed the urge to tell her that she was much older than Tom, and should therefore be more sensible as she was clearly distressed. 'I can't see what it is.'

And with that there was the sound of old material tearing and his children collapsed onto the sofa, each one holding half of the offending object. Amy burst into fresh tears, and Tom wailed as if he'd just kicked a brick with no shoes on.

Oli went over to Tom and opened his hands gently then lifted the object up. It was a stuffed Santa toy that Linda had made years ago, the Christmas Amy was born if he remembered correctly. The material was ripe with age and smelt of damp, even though it had been wrapped in plastic and the attic was dry enough to store things.

He then took the other half from Amy. The Santa grinned up at him, unaware that it had just been torn apart.

'Oh kids, you mustn't fight. Look what happens.'

He shook his head.

'Let me have it, Daddy, I can sew it back together,' Amy held out her hands. Her bottom lip trembled and she had mascara smudges down her cheeks.

'I don't think you can, sweetheart. I think he's had better days.'

'But Mummy made it...' She buried her face in her hands and sobbed.

Oli turned to Grace and shook his head. 'I'm so sorry. I don't know what's got into them.'

'Christmas can be an emotional time,' she whispered. 'Let me have a look at that and see what I can do.'

He handed her the Santa then went to the sofa and sat down. He opened his arms and Amy snuggled into his chest, her tears instantly soaking his t-shirt.

'Tom, do you want to show me where you have a pair of scissors and some cotton?' Grace asked.

Tom looked up at Oli.

'I think there's some in the kitchen drawer.'

'You have one of those too?'

'Sorry?' He smoothed Amy's hair back from her hot face.

'A drawer. The magic one where everything is stored.'

'Oh... yes. Have to have a drawer.'

'Come with me then, Tom.'

As Grace left the room, Oli rocked his daughter in his arms. For all that she sometimes seemed so mature, she was still just a little girl and one who'd lost her mum.

He thought she held up so well, but at times like these, which didn't happen often, he was reminded that she was still trying to work her way through her own grief. It was inevitable that she'd miss her mum and want to keep things that reminded her of Linda. Perhaps it was time now to get some of Linda's belongings down for his children to sort through. They had a right to remember their mother as vividly as possible, and he had a responsibility to help them with that. It was just so damned tough trying to get it all right for them, and he worried that he'd do the wrong thing or make their pain worse.

He could hear Grace's voice floating in from the kitchen and her gentle tones were soothing to him as well as to Tom, who replied and even laughed.

Well, this certainly wasn't the best way to get to know a woman better but then that was single fatherhood. Oli came as a package deal and the days of taking a woman out and wooing her with fine food and wine, then perhaps a night of passionate lovemaking were long gone. He was a father first and foremost and that would surely scare a lot of women away.

He just hoped that Grace wasn't one of those women.

But he had a feeling that she had more about her than that.

Chapter 10

Grace snipped the cotton then held up the Santa to appraise her efforts.

'What do you think, Tom?'

He peered at the toy then nodded. 'He's all fixed like you did an operation on him.'

'Do you want to take him through to Amy?'

'Yes, please.'

After Tom had left the kitchen, Grace tidied away the sewing things into the drawer where she'd found them. The drawer was stuffed with bits and bobs, from needles and cotton, to Sellotape, drawing pins and a ticket from a fairground ride. As she'd pulled the cotton out, it had been stuck to an old mint that she'd thrown in the bin. There was also a bar of coal tar soap with its strong nostalgic antiseptic smell, a frayed tape measure and a few foreign coins. Nestled in the corner was a small notebook with a chewed pencil, an unopened pack of dog treats and a box of matches. Kitchen drawers could tell stories about their owners and what they'd been through in their lives.

She leaned against the counter and looked around. The rectangular kitchen had a table and chairs at one end next to French doors that appeared to lead onto a patio area, and the kitchen cupboards, Aga and apron-front sink were at the other. The ceiling was low with wide oak beams and had a lot of similar features to her parents' cottage. Grace liked the kitchen; it smelt of wood, thyme and garlic, as if years of the Aga burning and cooking meals had permeated the very walls. It had a homely lived-in appeal and she could imagine Oli and his children sitting down together to eat, talking and laughing and enjoying their time together.

Tom was such a cute boy and he made her smile. Before she'd sewn Santa's legs back on, he'd been dancing them across the worktop, creating a rather disturbing scenario where Santa had lost his torso by getting it stuck in the chimney, so his legs had run away. She'd had to stifle her laughter as she'd taken the legs from him, then she'd pricked her finger twice as she'd sewn, because she'd been shaking as she tried to suppress her laughter again.

'Hey...' Oli entered the kitchen. 'Thanks so much for putting Santa back together.'

'I'm no expert seamstress but he should hold, at least if there's no more fighting over him.'

'The children have been warned.' He leaned against the unit next to her. 'I've lit the fire and put a DVD on for them. Amy's still quite upset so I'm hoping it'll distract her.'

'She's bound to be. Losing her mum so young must be hard.'

'She doesn't deal with it as well as Tom because he was just a baby really when Linda died. But Amy knew her mum, she felt what it was like to be loved by Linda and she feels her loss all the more.'

'And special occasions bring it all back don't they?'

He nodded then turned around and placed his hands flat on the worktop. 'Are you hungry?'

'A bit… I think.' She rubbed her belly. 'Yes, actually I am.'

'Well, how about I make us some food?'

'That would be lovely. Do you need a hand?'

'No, but I'd be grateful if you'd go in there and keep an eye on those two. Just to make sure that Santa doesn't have another *accident*.'

'Of course.'

On the way back to the living room, Grace sent her mother a text to tell her where she was and that she wouldn't be home for dinner. She found Amy and Tom on the sofa, their eyes glued to the TV, the Santa sitting between them. In the corner of the room the old Christmas tree looked sad and forgotten, unadorned except for a set of lights that weren't glowing. Grace went over to the tree and turned the plug on but the lights stayed dark.

'They're the broken ones.' Tom shook his head. 'Daddy said we need new ones.'

'Yes he did, didn't he?'

Grace pulled the plug out of the socket, then carefully unwound the lights from the branches. She put the old lights into a plastic bag, then went back to the hallway and retrieved the bags she'd brought with her and carried them into the living room. While cartoon characters sang about Christmas on the TV, Grace wrapped two sets of lights around the tree. She knew they worked as she'd tested them earlier, so once she'd finished, she plugged them in but didn't turn them on.

'Amy, Tom. Do you want to decorate the tree now?'

'Yes please!' they both responded.

Fifteen minutes later, they had used all of the decorations she'd brought from her parents. The tree was literally groaning with the weight of them, but the children had been so enthusiastic about the tiny snowmen, reindeer, Santa Clauses and the tinsel, that Grace hadn't wanted to curb their excitement by suggesting they hold back. Then they'd added some of their own from the boxes on the floor, and now the tree could have given the one at the Rockefeller Centre in New York a run for its money.

'There's one thing left to do…' Grace pressed the switches on and the tree came to life, sparkling with the racing white lights and glowing like a rainbow with the small coloured set.

'I love it.' Tom came to stand next to her then slipped his small hand into hers.

'Me too.' Amy gazed at the tree, the lights reflecting in her eyes and over her face as she stepped closer. 'Thank you, Grace. I thought it was going to be a rubbish tree. And that would have made Daddy sad.'

'It's my pleasure. No one should be sad, especially at Christmas time.'

Grace bit her lip. She sounded like she'd just stepped out of the TV. But she did know that she wanted these children to be happy, and that if they were happy then Oli would be too.

'Now, that looks incredible.' Oli was standing in the doorway, a big smile on his face.

'You think so?'

He nodded. 'You didn't have to do that.'

'I wanted to help.' Grace shrugged, a bit embarrassed now.

'And you have. I've finished dinner if you're all hungry. Kids, pause the movie.'

In the kitchen, the children went to the table and took what must be their regular seats. Grace looked at the two spare chairs, suddenly feeling incredibly awkward. She didn't want to take Oli's seat but neither did she want to take Linda's. That would just feel wrong.

'It's a new table,' Oli said, as if sensing her discomfort. 'I bought it in the summer. Sit where you want.'

Grace flashed him a look of gratitude then sat next to Tom and opposite Amy.

'That's Daddy's chair.' Amy pointed at her.

'Oh.' Grace stood up. 'Shall I come round there?'

Amy eyed her, a frown settling on her pretty face. 'No it's okay, you can sit there. But you might have to cut Tom's food up.'

'No, she won't!' Tom slammed his fork onto the table. 'Don't be silly, Amy, I'm not a baby.'

'Sometimes you are,' Amy said.

Grace watched Amy carefully, but she seemed to be innocent enough as she cast the judgement on her brother. Sometimes siblings could be mean, but Grace hoped Amy hadn't intended to hurt Tom.

Suddenly, Tom snorted then he nudged Grace. 'Sometimes I am a baby.'

Amy and her brother both giggled at this, and Grace met Oli's eyes as he set a bowl of mashed potatoes and a smaller one of peas on the table. He returned with four plates, then a baking tray with four breaded pieces of fish.

'Can I have tomato sauce, please?' Amy asked.

'You know where it is.' Oli nodded before taking a seat. 'Oh… drinks!' He jumped up and got four glasses from a cupboard then brought over a carton of juice from the fridge.

Grace polished off her food quickly. It was simple yet delicious and she enjoyed listening to the gentle chatter of the children and Oli's additions to their conversation. The three of them were evidently close and had many shared stories and jokes. It made her think of Sam and how they'd shared so much, how they'd had their own in-jokes and how they'd made their parents laugh many times over dinner. She missed the closeness she'd shared with her brother, and hoped that Amy and Tom would remain close as they grew older. A good relationship with a sibling was something to treasure.

She caught Oli's eyes on her a few times and when he realized she'd seen him, he'd quickly looked away. Was he comparing her to Linda, wishing she was here, or was he just enjoying her company?

Grace helped him to take the plates to the dishwasher, then Oli replenished their drinks before bringing four bowls of chocolate ice cream to the table.

'It's from Foxglove Farm.'

'I shouldn't really, but I can't refuse ice cream,' Grace said as she spooned some into her mouth. It was smooth and creamy and the sweet hit she craved after a meal. 'Delicious.'

'I know. I pick some up every week because it's just so good.'

'Another reason to stay in Conwenna Cove.'

Oli's eyes widened. 'You're thinking of staying?'

'Oh… uh… I've considered staying until the New Year. But I'll have to go home then… I have a flat and… things.'

Things? What things? Belongings that could be moved anywhere easily enough?

'Of course you do.'

Was that disappointment that just flashed across his features?

'Are you married, Grace?' Amy asked as she stood up and carried the bowls to the dishwasher.

'No… never been married.'

'Do you have children?'

'No. No children.'

'A boyfriend—'

'Amy!' Oli snapped. 'That's enough.'

'I'm only asking, Daddy. People always ask me if I have a boyfriend.' She placed a hand on Grace's arm and leaned forwards. 'To be honest, Grace, it gets on my nerves. Why would I want a boyfriend? The boys in my class are all so childish.' She shook her head then tutted.

'Right kids, chores time.'

Tom rolled his eyes at Grace and she hid a smile behind her hand by pretending to cough. She watched in amazement as Amy loaded the dishwasher then popped in a capsule and switched it on. Tom cleaned the table with kitchen roll and an antibacterial spray that Grace wanted to tell him to be careful with, but then she realized that Oli was supervising him discreetly.

'What now, Tom?' Oli asked.

'Wash my hands very well.'

'Good lad.'

Grace felt like a complete lazybones for not helping with anything, but every time she'd tried, Oli had raised a hand and shaken his head. When the kitchen was clean and tidy, Oli gestured at the doorway.

'Shall we go and put the rest of the movie on?'

'What time is it?' Grace asked. 'I've completely lost track.'

'Six.'

'Already?'

'The weekends fly past. We even forgot to have lunch because I was about to make some when you arrived. Although those two did have a snack in town so that's probably why they didn't ask for anything else. Do you fancy a glass of wine?'

'That would be nice.'

'You go on through and I'll catch up in a moment.'

Grace went through with the children and Tom pushed her towards the sofa. 'Sit by me, Grace.'

'Okay...' She sat down between the children then wriggled as she realized she was on Santa's rather inadequate lap. 'I've been very good, can I have a new book, please?'

'What?' Amy frowned at her.

'I'm sitting on Santa's lap,' Grace said, raising herself so she could pull the toy out from beneath her.

'Oh!' Amy smiled. 'Funny.'

Grace chewed her bottom lip. Amy was so lovely at times then almost spikey at others. It was confusing, but then Grace had little experience of children and no frame of reference, except for her own time as a child. Perhaps it was linked to Amy's age, or perhaps it was because of what she'd been through. And, of course, she hardly knew Grace so might warm to her as time went on. Although Grace would probably be leaving, so that probably wouldn't happen.

'How's this?' Oli held a glass of wine out to her. 'It's a pinot noir. Light and fruity.'

'Fantastic, thanks.' Grace took a sip of the ruby liquid and sighed as it slid down her throat. 'That's delicious.'

'I like wine, so it has to be good.'

When they were all seated, Grace in between the children and Oli in the chair by the fireplace, Tom put the movie back on and festive music filled the air.

The fire crackled in the grate, the lights twinkled on the tree and soon, Tom was sleeping against Grace's arm, his weight warm and solid – reassuring. Melting her heart. Because it was nice. Nice to be a part of a family, nice to be able to cast glances at Oli that he returned with smiles, nice to see Amy shuffle closer and closer to her until she was able to rest her head on Grace's shoulder, and nice to be a part of this little family.

It might not be her own, but right now she was enjoying their company and she could almost imagine what it might be like if they were hers.

Almost…

Chapter 11

Oli padded down the stairs, listening carefully for noise from above. It was instinctive now; his ears were trained to capture any sound, even a cough, from his children, and he often spent his evenings running up and down the stairs to check on them. He knew he could be described as overprotective, but having lost one person he loved, this had left him anxious about Amy and Tom in case they became ill too. Losing them would be absolutely unbearable. But it happened; he knew that. After all, the woman sitting on his sofa knew that better than most: her parents had lost their son.

He entered the living room and goosebumps rose on his arms. It was a combination of the twinkling tree lights, the fire glowing in the grate, the department store Christmas advert playing on the TV and that fact that the room wasn't empty. He had company and beautiful company at that.

He went to sit on the chair but changed his mind, and instead took a seat on the sofa. Grace had moved over so that there was a whole cushion between them, and it seemed strange to take the chair when there was a space closer to her.

'Are they sleeping?'

'Tom is and Amy will drop off soon. She has to read a chapter of her book first though, whatever time she goes to bed. It's a ritual and who am I to discourage reading? Sometimes, I creep back up ten minutes after bedtime and I'll find her sleeping with the book in front of her nose.'

'Do they always go to bed at the same time?'

He shook his head. 'That wouldn't be fair with Amy being older. I try to stagger their bedtimes, but tonight was different as it's been a very busy day and I think Tom would have kicked off if she'd stayed up because you're here. He does seem very fond of you.'

Grace chewed her lip.

'He's very sweet. They both are.'

'I know Amy can be more difficult to win round, but I think it's all down to what she's been through. She takes a while to get to know people, especially women. Not that there's been women as in dating and that... uh...' He shook his head. 'What I meant was with any women who enter our lives. But I hope that with time, she'll lose that wariness. I just want her to be able to be a child, you know?'

'Childhood doesn't last long these days does it?'

'If it ever did. I think there's something else bothering her though.'

'Like what?'

'Linked to the cat and kittens that came into the surgery recently. I suspect that Amy knows more about them than she's letting on.'

'Have you asked her about them?'

He nodded. 'But she clammed up.'

'Is there someone else she might talk to?'

'Possibly. But it's hard to tell with my daughter.'

'I could always try if you like? Not that I'm being presumptuous or anything. It's just sometimes easier to speak to someone you don't know very well.'

'If the opportunity arises naturally, I'd appreciate that. Thank you.'

Grace drained her glass.

'Would you like another?'

'I shouldn't really. I guess I should be heading home.'

His heart sank.

'Of course.'

'Although… I have nothing to rush off for.' She smiled. 'Go on, let's have another one.'

'You sure?'

'Yes, please. It is delicious.'

Oli filled their glasses then handed one to Grace.

'Would you like to watch a film or something else?'

'I really don't mind. I'm thoroughly relaxed.'

'Put your feet up if you want.'

'Are you sure?'

'Of course. I want you to feel comfortable.'

While Grace tucked her feet up under her then leaned against the arm of the sofa, Oli flicked through the channels. He found an old action film that had just started.

'Is this okay?'

She nodded.

They watched the film in companionable silence – except for the three times Oli had excused himself to go and check on the children who were both sleeping soundly – and Oli enjoyed every minute of it. He knew he'd missed having adult company in the evenings but this just confirmed it. Just having someone sitting close, enjoying the same wine and breathing the same air was more comforting than he'd thought it could be. A few times, he experienced a flicker of guilt that he was with a woman other than Linda. But then he reassured himself with the fact that nothing had happened between him and Grace. And nothing was going to bring Linda back, however hard he might have wished it could in the past, and he knew that she wouldn't have wanted him to spend the rest of his life alone.

As the credits rolled, he stretched and yawned. Grace's mobile beeped in her pocket and Oli watched as she checked the screen.

'Oooh!'

'What is it?'

She met his eyes.

'Mum and Dad have asked if you'd like to join us for lunch tomorrow. If you're not busy that is. Dad cooks a mean roast and his Yorkshire puddings are melt in the mouth!'

'That would be lovely. We usually go to Dad's, but I'll text him and tell him we've got an invite to Rosehip Cottage.'

'Won't he mind?'

'No. He's quite easy going, and it'll mean less washing up.'

'Well, come for lunch then. Mum said about one.'

'Fantastic. Please thank them for me.'

Grace nodded then stood up.

'I really had better go now.'

They went out into the hallway, and she put on her boots and coat and opened the front door. Icy air swirled into the hallway making Oli shudder.

'Temperature's dropped then. It was cold earlier but that's freezing now.'

'Do you have much snow here?'

'Sometimes. Not every year and not always a lot, but we have had white Christmases.'

'I hope we do this year. I'd love to see the village covered with snow.'

'It's not much fun when I have to go out on a call in the middle of the night though.'

'How do you manage… with the children?'

'A quick call to Dad, usually. I tend to share the on-call with other local vets in nearby towns, so I'm not expected to go out every night if something happens.'

'Well, uh… see you tomorrow then?' Grace stepped over the threshold.

Oli followed her. 'I'd walk you home, but I can't leave the children.'

'Of course not. It's not far anyway.'

'No it's not. But even so… it's something I would do if I could.'

She gazed up at him and her pupils dilated in her pretty eyes. In the moonlight, her freckles were dark on her pale skin and her lips were full and inviting. She could have been a fairy from one of the children's storybooks or an angel fallen to earth.

His heart thudded and he reached out and gently stroked her cheek. Her lips parted and a small sigh escaped. Her eyes closed and her eyelids fluttered as he moved his thumb softly over her mouth.

Heat coursed through Oli and he reacted by slipping his hand behind her head and pulling her to him, kissing her. At first, he kissed her gently but soon his passion surfaced and the kiss deepened. He was overwhelmed by desire and need, and something that he hadn't experienced in a long time. It was the simple joy of being alive and connecting with another being.

He broke away from the kiss and tried to catch his breath. Grace was breathless too and she was leaning on him heavily, as if her ability to stand unaided had deserted her.

'Grace… I'm sorry. Was that… wrong?'

She made an effort to stand up straight but still held on to him.

'No. It was so right. I'm positively weak though. I wasn't expecting it and I'm not sure if it's the wine making me a bit lightheaded but… wow!'

'Wow?' He laughed. 'So I haven't lost it then?'

Relief coursed through him. Oli didn't make a habit of kissing women, especially not on his doorstep when his children were sleeping upstairs. But it had seemed inevitable that this would happen with Grace, as if he'd known it from the first moment he'd seen her and wished that she wasn't with Nate.

Grace giggled. 'Whatever it is, you certainly haven't lost it. Now I should go because if you kiss me like that again, I won't be able to tear myself away.'

'I won't be able to let you go. Text me when you're home.'

They gazed into each other's eyes for a moment longer, as something between them grew and flourished like a flower opening its petals to the sun, then Grace pulled on her hat and set off. Oli watched her go, until she reached the main road and disappeared from view.

He stood there for a while, taking deep breaths and gazing out at the sea where the moonlight bathed the water in a silvery glow. His heart was pounding, which was not an unfamiliar sensation for him, but tonight it was not because of anything negative.

Tonight, it was down to desire, excitement and something he was delighted to feel again.

That something was hope.

–

Grace fluttered around the kitchen like a moth round a lightbulb the next day. Last night had been wonderful and completely unexpected, but it changed a lot for her. And, she suspected, for Oli.

She couldn't help wondering if it was down to the Christmas decorations, and the wine and the relaxing evening. But what if Oli had woken up this morning regretting their kiss? And oh that kiss… it had been wonderful. Grace had been lit up from within as she'd walked home, and she'd danced around her parents' cottage, relieved that Simon and Louise had turned in for an early night so she didn't have to explain her high spirits.

Only now, in the cold light of day, did doubts start to creep in. It wasn't that she didn't like Oli, because she certainly did, but there was so much to consider and she knew Oli would feel the same. He was a widower and a father, and he couldn't make decisions about his life without considering the children; they had to come first.

The kitchen was filled with the delicious aroma of roast beef, Yorkshire puddings and a variety of side dishes that her father had whipped up as if they were as easy as scrambled egg. They weren't, of course. Grace knew because she hadn't been able to create several of the dishes before when she'd tried, but her dad was very talented in the kitchen.

'Grace, will you sit down?' Her father pointed at a chair.

'I can't.'

'Why not? What's wrong with you?'

'Anyone would think she was nervous.' Her mother smiled as she set the table.

'Are you nervous?' her father asked.

'No. Why would I be?'

She caught a knowing glance passing between her parents.

'What was that about?' she asked as she forced herself onto a chair, then began folding up napkins.

'Grace, we know you like this man.' Her mother smiled. 'And it's okay.'

'What?'

'You've been singing in the shower, you've been dancing around lately when you think we can't see you, and your face lit up when you danced with Oli at the party. It's been a while since we've seen you like this.' Her mother's comment made her bristle; she was being too obvious.

'He's a nice guy and that's all. He's a father and widowed. I'm not seeing him or anything.'

'We know that, love.' Her dad came to stand behind her and squeezed her shoulders. 'But if you like him then that's okay.'

She slumped in her chair.

'But it's not really is it? I hardly know him and he has a whole load of responsibilities. I'm going back to Cardiff soon so nothing can come of this… flirtation or whatever it is, anyway.'

Her mother nodded. 'Perhaps. And you don't need me to tell you to be careful. His children will be his priority. But sometimes, darling, love blossoms where you least expect it.'

'Mum!' Grace rolled her eyes. 'Who said anything about love? This is about like and nothing more. I like Oli. I like his children. Yesterday I took the old decorations over and we put them up, and he made me dinner and we watched a movie. Well, actually I watched one and a half movies as the children put one on too. But it's not a big deal. It was just lovely to spend some time with him, Amy and Tom.'

'Sounds like the start of something to me.' Her father planted a kiss on the top of her head then returned to stirring the gravy.

Grace folded the rest of the napkins, then straightened the cutlery. When it all met with her satisfaction, she got up and went to the door to check if there was any sign of Oli. She'd sent a text last night after getting home, and her phone had pinged almost immediately with a reply. Oli had just written: *Night X.* She'd stared at the kiss for ages, thinking about the incredible physical kiss they'd shared.

A noise from outside made her start, so she leaned forwards to see more of the road. Tom came into view first, his blond head bouncing as he rode his scooter towards her.

'Grace!' he called as his little leg met the ground repeatedly, propelling him forward.

She waved at him, her heart filling with warmth.

Just as he reached her and pulled a rucksack from his back, and dropped it on the ground next to the doorstep, Oli and Amy emerged from the trees lining the roadside, both wrapped up in their coats. Amy wore a purple beret and matching scarf with leather gloves. Grace was impressed at her style. Oli's head was bare like Tom's and his short brown hair was windswept. His cheeks glowed pink from the cold and the tip of his nose matched them.

And he took her breath away.

'Grace, can I show you my tricks?' Tom asked. 'I can do lots and lots on my scooter.'

'Yes, of course.' She stepped outside in her slippers. 'But be careful.'

As she watched, Tom rode his scooter across the path then did a small hop that reminded Grace of a rabbit.

She clapped enthusiastically. 'Well done, Tom! Very impressive.'

He returned to her side.

'Now you have a go.'

'Oh, I really couldn't, Tom. It's years since I've been on a scooter.'

'Try it. You'll be good'

'Tom, leave Grace alone.' Oli had reached the path in front of the cottage. 'I'm sure she doesn't want to risk life and limb on the scooter. And talking of that, where's your helmet?'

Tom pulled a face.

'You know you need to wear it. What if you fell off and banged your head?'

'I put it in my bag.' Tom kicked at the ground. 'I don't like it. It pinches.'

Grace lowered into a crouch. 'How does it pinch, Tom?'

'My hair and by here.' He pointed at his forehead, and Grace moved his hair to reveal a red line where the helmet had clearly dug in.

'Oh, Tom, let me see the helmet.'

He opened his rucksack and pulled it out, then handed it to her. She peered inside and found what she was looking for. 'There's a strap here to make the helmet looser. See.' She adjusted it. 'Try it now.'

He put it on then smiled. 'That fits!'

Grace nodded.

'Tom, have you been messing about with the strap?' Oli asked, a frown darkening his features.

Tom nodded. 'I didn't know what it was so I tried to pull it out.'

'And in the process tightened it.' Oli met Grace's eyes and shook his head. 'He'd have everyone think I'm neglectful, even if he doesn't do it deliberately.'

'Can I do some more tricks, Daddy?' Tom asked.

'Yes, now that you've got your helmet on.'

Oli stood next to Grace with Amy at his other side, as they watched Tom trying to perform a variety of moves that he'd apparently seen on TV. Oli caught his breath a few times, and she saw his hands fly up as Tom swung the scooter around and between his legs, but then he pushed them into his coat pockets, clearly trying to allow Tom to have some fun.

'You know, every school morning I put his uniform out for him – clean shirt, jumper, trousers, socks and pants. Every morning. A few weeks ago, I was having a good tidy up and I found about ten odd socks under the bed.

All of them clean. I don't know if it was deliberate or if he was bouncing on the bed and they fell off, but he must have been wearing the same socks more than once. I did wonder why he had a sock shortage, but assumed they'd gone to sock heaven or that secret place in the tumble dryer.'

Grace laughed. 'So he was wearing smelly socks to school?'

Oli nodded. 'Imagine what it must have been like when he changed for P.E. I bet there was a terrible stink in the changing room.'

'Oh dear.'

'Parenthood, eh?'

'Something smells lovely right now though.' It was Amy, leaning around her father.

'That's our dinner, Amy. My dad is such a good cook and you are in for a treat.'

Amy smiled. 'Are there roast potatoes?'

'Like you wouldn't believe.'

'They're my favourite.'

'Then you shall have extra!'

Amy's eyes lit up.

'Shall we go inside, I don't know about you but I'm freezing.' Grace rubbed her hands together then gestured for Amy to go in before her.

'I'm not surprised, you have no coat on.' Oli removed a glove then touched her hand. She jolted as their skin met. His was so warm and her own so cold. As she turned to go inside, she caught his eyes on her mouth, and her heart skipped a beat.

If only she could read his thoughts, then she'd have a better idea of what was going on here. Unless, of course,

Oli was as clueless as her. And if that was the case, then they had better work together to try to navigate their way through whatever it was that was happening between them.

Chapter 12

Dinner was enjoyable. Grace sat at the table in her parents' cosy kitchen and she couldn't stop smiling. Her parents were wonderful hosts, attentive to their guests and making a fuss of the children. Tom chattered away to her father about his love of drawing and riding his scooter, and Amy tucked into her food with gusto, leaving the roast potatoes until last so she could enjoy them all in one go.

When Grace had helped to clear the plates away, her father went to the fridge and brought out the honeyed peach and pistachio pavlova he'd made once their dinner invitation had been accepted. The children gasped as he set it on the table and Grace knew why, because the meringues were like shiny white icebergs on top of which sat a thick layer of whipped cream imbued with peach syrup. This was finished off with honeyed peaches that her father had preserved in the summer and kept for occasions such as this. Chopped green pistachios were scattered over the top, creating a tempting combination.

'That looks incredible,' Oli said. 'We really are being spoilt.'

'And so you should be,' Louise said. 'Grace, do you want to serve?'

As Grace started cutting into the pavlova, the knife cracked through the crisp meringues scattering tiny white pieces onto the table and made her think of snow. A buzzing came from beneath the table. Oli pushed back his chair and pulled his mobile from his pocket.

'Sorry, I'd better take this.' He swiped the screen then left the kitchen and went out into the garden.

'Don't worry, Grace, Daddy sometimes has calls like this,' Amy said. 'And then he has to go to work.'

'Do you think it's work then?'

'Probably.' Amy nodded.

'Most likely,' Tom added.

'I hope it's not bad news about the cat and the kittens.' Amy blanched.

'What do you mean?' Grace asked.

'Oh… I… Daddy has a mother cat and her three kittens at the surgery. They're going to need homes. He said Edward and Mary are thinking about homing one of them, but I don't think it's the mummy cat they want.'

'Is that right?' Grace caught her father winking at her mother. 'Kittens needing homes, eh, Louise.'

'I'll think about it.'

'Thank you.'

Louise sighed and shook her head. 'If Oli needs to find them homes, then we'll happily take one.'

'One?' Simon raised his eyebrows.

'Oh, okay, then two. But only if they still need homes.'

'And that's why I love you, Louise,' Simon smiled at his wife.

Grace turned to Amy, but the little girl was chewing her bottom lip. Perhaps she'd hoped to home all the kittens herself, and didn't want other people offering to take them. Grace would speak to Oli about it later, just to ensure that her parents weren't jumping in too quickly here.

'Serve the children's dessert, Grace. We can wait until Oli's done.'

Oli returned to the kitchen within two minutes. His face was white, and the relaxed expression he'd had just moments ago had been replaced with tension that was evident in the stiff way he held his jaw.

'I am so sorry, but I have to go up to the farm.'

'Why, what's wrong?' Grace got up.

'There's um…' He looked at his children. 'It's complicated.'

'Let's go and check that the shed is locked, shall we? I have an awful feeling I didn't shut it properly,' Grace said. 'And I don't want a fox wandering in there and getting stuck.'

'Yes, that's a good idea.'

'Daddy I'm not a baby, you know.' Amy shook her head. 'It's one of the dogs isn't it?'

'Yes… one of the greyhounds isn't very well. A new girl who recently arrived. I have to go to check on her.'

'She doesn't have puppies does she?'

'No, Amy. Try not to worry now.'

'I'll come with you.'

'What?' Oli met Grace's eyes.

'I mean… only if you want me to.'

'Amy and Tom can stay with us,' Louise said. 'I have some cards here that I've been hoping to use for a while, so we can play some games.'

'Cards?' Amy asked.

'Yes, Amy, do you know any card games?'

The girl shook her head.

'Then Simon and I will teach you.'

'Okay!' Amy beamed.

'Are you sure that's okay, Louise? I can always drop them at my father's.'

'It's fine, Oli. Simon and I will enjoy having some company. And they haven't even finished dessert yet.'

'Thank you. That's very kind. I'll come straight back afterwards to collect them.'

Louise waved a hand. 'No rush.'

'Grace, you can come if you're sure you want to,' Oli said quietly. 'According to Neil Burton, the owner of the farm and sanctuary, it's not looking good for the poor greyhound though.'

'I want to.' Grace felt certain that she did. If Oli had to rush up there half way through his Sunday lunch then she wanted to accompany him. She wanted to be there for him, to support him with whatever the afternoon would bring.

'Right grab a warm coat, and whatever else you need, and we'd better go. Kids, be on your best behaviour and I'll see you soon.'

Grace collected her coat, gloves and hat then they left the cottage and marched back to Oli's cottage to pick up his bag and his Land Rover. Once inside, he drove them up through the lanes to Foxglove Farm.

'So what's wrong with this dog then?'

'He didn't give me much information, just said someone had brought her in and she's in a bad way. Probably suffering from exposure, as she was freezing when she was found, and she's got some nasty looking wounds. Possibly from a fox or badger.'

'Poor thing.'

He nodded. 'Some greyhounds and lurchers are used for poaching and baiting.'

'I've read about that.'

'It's awful for the dogs and for the wild animals. Some people are just…'

Grace noticed that a muscle in his jaw was twitching and his knuckles were white where he gripped the steering wheel.

'Are you all right, Oli?'

He glanced at her. 'I just get so mad.'

Grace gently touched his arm. She wanted to say something to offer him comfort, but what words were adequate in this situation? People did terrible things to animals and Oli saw this on an almost daily basis. He dealt with the consequences of other people's actions and that had to be tough, especially when he had to try to treat the animals afterwards, to heal them physically and mentally. But Grace knew that even if physical scars healed, emotional ones took a lot longer, and sometimes they never faded completely.

Oli parked the vehicle and they got out. A man with a big grey beard, wearing a flat cap, scruffy trousers, wellies and a baggy jumper – that strained over his belly and appeared to be unravelling at the hem – met them outside a long outbuilding. Dogs were barking nearby and Grace realized they must be the ones in the sanctuary.

'Oli, thanks for coming so quickly.'

'Of course. This is Grace Phillips. Her parents just bought Rosehip Cottage. Grace this is Neil.'

'Pleased to meet you.' Grace removed her glove and Neil shook her hand firmly. His palm was calloused and his nails broken and stained from years of manual labour.

'Likewise. Hope you'll be very happy here in Conwenna.'

'Oh… I'm not staying here. At least I don't think so. It's my parents who've bought the cottage.'

Neil assessed her quietly. 'See how it goes. You might decide to stay. Worse places to be that's for sure.' He turned to Oli. 'I've put the greyhound in the assessment room because, to be honest, I didn't want to put her in one of the kennels. She's in a bad way.'

'Well, let's take a look then.'

Grace hurried along to keep up with Oli's determined strides as they went around the back of the stables, then towards a door at the end. Her stomach was knotted with tension at the thought of what she was going to see.

Neil opened the door and ushered Grace and Oli in first. The room was like a lounge with two sofas covered in colourful patchworks, a coffee table and an old portable TV. A small window overlooked the yard. There was another window in the back wall, and Grace supposed it led to some sort of office or kitchen area.

And on the floor, was a woman kneeling next to a dog that was covered with a blanket. Grace could only see its head. As they approached, the dog lifted her head and whined softly.

'Elena, how's she doing?' Neil asked.

'She's exhausted.' The older woman met their eyes in turn. Her face was weathered and kind and she smiled at Grace but her eyes were sad.

'This is Grace,' Oli said. 'Grace, meet Elena, Neil's wife.'

'Hello.' They both nodded, understanding that Elena couldn't shake hands right now, as she was gently stroking the dog's head.

Oli shrugged out of his coat and laid it on one of the sofas. He knelt next to the dog then gently removed the blanket, revealing her beautiful brindle coat. The dog blinked but didn't move as Oli spoke to her, telling her what he was going to do before he even touched her. Grace stood back, not wanting to get in the way, but her heart was in her mouth as he conducted a full examination.

When he'd finished, he sat back on his heels.

'She has signs of hypothermia... slow pulse, shallow breathing... but you've done the right thing getting her warmed up. I think she has frost bite on her ears, so that may require further attention. The wounds are consistent with bites from another animal, most likely a badger.' Neil and Elena nodded as he ran through his findings. 'There is a risk of infection, in fact, this one here on her leg is already looking quite nasty, so we need to get her on a course of antibiotics. She's malnourished and skinny, even for a greyhound, and I'd hazard a guess that she's had puppies within the last twelve months.'

'Oh, love her.' Grace bit her lip as anger burned in her gut.

'I'm going to need to take her into the surgery and monitor her there. She'll need blood and urine tests. I'll give her an injection now because as her ears thaw, it's going to be very painful, so I can ease that a bit for her.'

'Will she be okay?' Grace asked.

Oli sighed. 'If we get her treated quickly, she might be. There are no guarantees because until I have the bloods back, I don't know what's going on inside her. She's clearly been outdoors for a while and the shock of what she's been through could be enough to…' he stopped talking and looked at Grace.

'Enough to what?'

'She might not make it,' Elena said as she stood up. 'That's what Oli meant. It's so hard to accept that a lovely greyhound like this one might die because of appalling treatment by human beings, but when a dog has been through what this girl has, it's sometimes kinder to let them go.'

A flash of fury pierced Grace's chest. This beautiful greyhound might die? Because she'd been mistreated by people. How could someone be so callous as to hurt an innocent animal?

'Neil, I'll reverse the Land Rover up and we'll need to get her in the back.'

'I'll sit with her.'

'Thanks, Grace. We'll take it slowly down to the surgery then get her inside. I'll just give Maxine a call and ask her to meet us there.'

Ten minutes later, Grace was sat in the back of Oli's Land Rover as he drove them down to the surgery. She spoke constantly, words of reassurance that she hoped would help keep the greyhound calm. To know that a dog had been through so much made her heart ache and she wished she could take it all away. She meant every word when she told her that she'd never let any harm come to her again. The greyhound gazed up at her, with big amber eyes full of knowledge and pain, blinking slowly, seemingly aware that her fate was in their hands.

'I think we should give you a name,' Grace whispered. 'Don't give up, sweetheart. I know you've been through an awful time. Things will get better for you, I promise. Don't give up hope.'

'What's that?' Oli asked as he pulled into the surgery car park.

'I told her not to give up hope. In fact, as we don't know her name, I think we should call her, Hope.'

Oli got out then came around and opened the boot. He paused and rubbed his hand over his hair. 'Look, Grace, naming her is... it will bond you to her. You know that don't you? It will be harder for you then if she...'

'I know. But she has to have a name, Oli. The poor girl deserves a name and anyway, she won't give up. We've had words and she knows that her life is about to change. We are her last hope and we won't let her down.'

'She certainly won't suffer like that again,' Oli said. 'But her experiences might mean that she's not suitable to live in a normal home. She might not—'

'Oli... she'll be fine. She's going to recover. I know it.'

He gave her a brief smile, but his eyes were dark with sadness.

'Well, we'll do our best. Come on then, Hope. Let's get you inside.'

Maxine met them at the door and helped Oli to get Hope onto the examination table.

Grace watched as they ran through some tests and a more detailed examination. Hope lifted her head a few times, but Oli and Maxine were so kind and calm that the dog let them do what they needed to. Soon, she was taken into another room and settled in a crate, covered in a warm blanket.

'She'll sleep now. It's what she needs more than anything and when she wakes I'll try her with some food.' Maxine wrote something on a clipboard, then hooked it over the edge of the crate.

'Will you stay with her?'

'Yes. She'll need to be observed overnight.'

'You'll stay here?'

'It's not far from home for me and Oli's just next door. He'll take over at some point. Sometimes, Pamela comes in too if we have a lot of animals in.'

Grace scanned the other crates and could make out the dark shape of a cat in one of the higher ones, and three smaller shapes that she assumed were the kittens. She'd have liked a closer look, but didn't think it was the right time.

'Grace?' Oli had gone to call Neil to give him an update on Hope but had now returned. 'I'll get you home, collect the children then drop them at my father's.'

'There's no need for that. If you're going to be back and forth tonight, I could watch them.'

'I couldn't ask you to do that.' He buried his hands in his pockets. 'You have things to do.'

'Remember that I work from home, cafés, pubs… wherever I want. Of course I can come and babysit. Besides, it's not like you're a million miles away. You can get them settled, as I expect that Mum and Dad will also be happy to give them tea too, and I'll just sit at your kitchen table with my laptop. I'll be there if they need anything, but I can give you a shout if need be.'

He roamed her face with his eyes, and a flush crawled up Grace's throat and into her cheeks. She wasn't sure why, but Oli's gaze was so intense, his eyes were so full of her and it made her acutely aware of how much she liked him. And of how much she wanted him to reciprocate that feeling.

'You are amazing,' he said. 'You know that?'

'Ahem.' It was Maxine, grinning at them both. 'I just need your approval on a few things, Oli, then you're good to go.'

'Of course.'

He handed Grace his car keys. 'You go on out and I'll catch up.'

Grace made her way out to the car, opened it and climbed in. Although it was only the afternoon, she was lightheaded with tiredness. It had been an intense day, full of emotion: she'd learnt more about Oli and his children, and seen how badly treated this beautiful greyhound had been. A greyhound she'd felt a connection with; something about the sadness in the dog's eyes, and in her quiet acceptance of what was done to her as she was examined and treated, really penetrated Grace's heart. It made her think of Sam, the way that Hope had kept silent about her pain, about the heartbreak she must have been feeling, and Grace knew how it felt to hold things inside. To nurse her pain as though it were a burden that she alone had to bear.

If only she could offer Hope a home, a place to come to after she had recovered. A place where she would be loved and fed and cared for, a safe haven where she could live and be loved.

And something inside Grace suddenly uncoiled.

Because she knew, in that moment, that if Hope made it through the night, then she would be there for her. It was the way it had to be.

Chapter 13

Grey morning light gave the lounge an eerie appearance when Oli opened his eyes. Something was different. Then he realized what it was: the Christmas decorations gave the room an unfamiliar appearance. His head was tight, his eyes gritty and he ached all over from sleeping in the chair. But then he had only managed to grab about three hours in total, because he'd been back and forth to the surgery next door to check on Hope.

In spite of his exhaustion, he smiled. Grace had fallen for the greyhound instantly. She had a compassionate heart. In some ways, he knew that should worry him because Hope wasn't out of the woods yet, but at the same time, knowing that Grace was such a good person lifted his spirits. Even if she was in Conwenna Cove for a short time, just being around her gave him a lift; she made him hope that life could be good again.

A gentle sigh made him turn his head. Of course, Grace was on the sofa. He'd told her to take his bed, reassured her that he'd changed the bedding just yesterday, but when he'd come home in the early hours, he'd found her sleeping on the sofa. She'd been out cold and he hadn't liked to disturb her, so he'd covered her with a blanket, made himself a cup of tea, then passed out as soon as he'd drunk it.

He watched her for a moment, her eyelids fluttering, her red–gold hair tumbling over her shoulder. Her face was so serene, so beautiful and so…

He sat up.

He rubbed his eyes.

He took a deep breath.

What was he going to do? In spite of his vow to focus entirely on Amy and Tom, he was falling for Grace. She was kind and funny and his children liked her. Oli liked her and he enjoyed her company. But he also had to be sure that he wasn't confusing his loneliness and the relief she offered him from that with other emotions. What if it was her friendship that he craved most? He shook his head. He knew that wasn't true. Just looking at her confirmed that for him. If he could, he would sweep her up in his arms and carry her up to his bed, wind his fingers in her hair, kiss her sweet mouth then make love to her all morning.

A creaking floorboard upstairs cut into his thoughts. There'd be no finding out if Grace desired him as much as he did her, because his two children were upstairs and it seemed like Tom was already rising. At least his children stopped him rushing anything with Grace. Sex would surely just muddy the waters even more, although it would be so good to be held again and to love again.

But Grace was going back to Cardiff. Oli couldn't exactly have a long distance relationship with her, could he? Not with two children. So he'd have to enjoy her company over Christmas then wave goodbye. He wouldn't allow himself to think about how hard that would be right now; it made his chest hurt.

Footsteps on the stairs made him jump up. He should get to Tom before he came in and startled Grace. He went out into the hallway and found his son on the bottom stair.

'Hi Daddy.'

'Hey Tom.' He put a finger over his lips.

'Why have we got to be quiet?'

'Grace is sleeping.'

'Grace had a sleepover?' Tom's eyes widened. 'I want to see her.'

Oli shook his head. 'Not yet. Let her wake up first.'

'Can't I just have a peep?'

Tom tilted his head on one side and gazed up at his father with his big brown eyes.

'Go on then, but keep quiet.'

He stepped back and let Tom peer into the lounge.

'She's so pretty, Daddy.' Tom turned round and tiptoed towards the kitchen. 'I wish she was staying here for ever.'

Oli bit his lip to stop himself replying.

Because in his head, he blurted the words, *So do I.*

—

Grace washed her hands then splashed some cold water over her face. In Oli's bathroom mirror, she looked pale and her hair was wild from sleeping on the sofa. She didn't have a clip or a band to tie it back, so she raked her fingers through it, then shrugged, it would have to do. As she turned around, she eyed the bath longingly. She was cold and a bubble bath would be delicious right now, especially in that freestanding Victorian roll-top tub. The whole bathroom was lovely with a double walk-in shower and pale beige wall tiles. She wondered if Oli had chosen the décor or if it had been his wife.

His wife.

The lovely Linda. Grace's heart ached for the woman who had lived here, who had died before her children had grown. It must have been devastating to know that she wouldn't see Amy grow into a woman, or Tom as he became a man. She would miss out on so much; just as Grace would do. Because Grace would never have children.

But to have had them, then be aware that you wouldn't be there for them would be unbearable. Poor Linda. Grace wished that she could go back in time and offer the other woman comfort.

She shook herself, then left the bathroom and padded down the stairs. The sound of laughter coming from the kitchen made her smile. Tom and Oli were evidently having a good time.

'Yes, Daddy, like that!' Tom squealed as a pancake flew up in the air.

'Morning!' Grace called as she entered the kitchen.

'Ah…' Oli turned to greet her and the pancake in the air came down and missed the frying pan, landing instead on his foot. He stared at it, Grace stared at it and Tom said, 'Uh oh! That one's no good now, Daddy, and you'll need to wash your slipper.'

'Sorry, Oli, it's my fault. I startled you.'

'It's fine.' He smiled, then leant over and peeled the pancake from his foot and dropped it in the bin. 'No worries at all. Plenty more batter here. Would you like tea or coffee?'

'I'll make it. You carry on with that.'

'Okay then! Ready, Tom?' He poured batter into the frying pan with a flourish, causing Tom to giggle again. 'Ready, steady... go!'

Grace dropped a teabag into a mug that was already set out in front of the kettle. 'You want tea too?'

'No, thanks. Have had two already,' Oli said.

Grace switched the kettle on then gazed around the kitchen. The window above the apron-fronted sink had small panes and ruby curtains held in place with yellow tiebacks. French doors next to the table led out onto the patio.

The kettle clicked off so she poured water onto the teabag then waited for it to brew.

'Grace, do you want syrup on your pancakes?'

'Yes please, Tom.'

When her tea was ready, she carried it to the table and sat down next to Tom, in the seat she'd taken last time she'd eaten with them. Tom was already eating his pancakes.

'Isn't Amy having any?' she asked.

'Still sleeping. She's a lazybones.' Tom shook his head.

'It has only just gone seven, Tom.'

Oli placed a plate laden with pancakes on the table. 'Help yourself, Grace. Plenty here. Tom thinks everyone should be up by six a.m.'

'I see.' Grace nudged Tom. 'I'm usually up early, too.'

'And Daddy is. He doesn't sleep very well, do you, Daddy?'

Grace met Oli's eyes. 'I, uh... haven't slept well for years, really.'

She nodded. After what he'd been through, it wasn't surprising.

'What are your plans today, Tom? Are you off to school?' she teased.

'Nope. We've finished for Christmas!' He grinned. 'Two weeks off to have fun and watch cartoons and ride my scooter.'

'That sounds like a brilliant plan.'

'Want to stay?' Tom asked. 'We can take turns on my scooter and you can pick the cartoons.'

'Not today, Tom.' Oli pointed his fork at his son. 'You're off to Grandad's, remember? I've got to work. Not all of us get two weeks off.'

'Oh yeah… I forgot. Grandad's taking us to the park.'

'Well, it depends on how the weather is, Tom.'

'I know.' Tom pulled a face. 'But I think it will be sunny.'

'You have to admire his optimism, right?' Oli raised his eyebrows at Grace.

'I like the positivity; it's refreshing. Oh to be five again…' Grace hid her smile behind a forkful of pancake.

'Sometimes I think it would be nice to start all over again, to be a child with a clean slate. But then I think about how lucky I am to have great kids and a job I love and to live in Conwenna Cove. And I also appreciate how much I'm enjoying the present company.' He held her gaze. 'That is also very refreshing.'

Grace swallowed hard to push the pancake down, past her surprise. What did Oli mean? Did he like her that much?

As she ate the rest of her breakfast, sneaking glances at Oli's handsome face, she tried to keep her emotions in check. She liked him so much and couldn't help wondering if there was a way to see more of him. After all, she had already decided to be here for Hope, so perhaps she could be here for Oli too.

–

Grace entered her parents' kitchen through the back door. They'd known that she was staying at Oli's to babysit while he saw to the greyhound, but she still felt a bit awkward returning after staying out all night: a bit like she imagined a teenager would. Of course, she wouldn't know because she hadn't had much of a social life, preferring to stay in with Sam.

Simon and Louise were at the kitchen table reading newspapers. Her parents still liked to read actual papers rather than online versions; they claimed it was their age, but Grace knew that they just enjoyed the routine of going to pick up the papers early in the morning then settling down with coffee and breakfast together.

'Morning, Mum and Dad.'

'Hi lovely, how did it go?'

Grace took a seat at the table, and shrugged out of her coat then slipped off her boots.

'Well, the babysitting was fun.'

'Those children are adorable. And they think a lot of you already.'

Grace flushed slightly. Despite having told her mother many times that she didn't plan to marry or have children, she knew she worried about her and wanted to see her settled; even though Grace had protested thousands of times that she didn't need to be with someone in order to be happy.

'I know.'

'How's the dog?'

148

'Hope?'

Her mother nodded.

'Well, I didn't get a chance to talk to Oli about her for long because the children were around, but he said she got through the night and they kept her comfortable. Oh, Mum, she's just gorgeous. In fact… I want to adopt her.'

'Adopt her?' Simon peered out from behind his paper. 'You?'

'Why not, Dad?'

'Well… your mother is just coming round to the idea of us homing a kitten or two. And now you want a dog?'

Grace nodded. 'I know it sounds ridiculous, as I only have a flat, but I can't bear the thought of her being unhappy after all she's been through.'

'And you do work from home,' Louise added.

'True, so I'd be there for her.'

'But won't she need rehabilitation and aftercare?' Her father folded his paper and placed it on the table.

'Possibly. But she's just the sweetest thing and even though she was in great discomfort, she was still so gentle.' Grace's vision blurred. Thinking about Hope's beautiful amber eyes and the sadness she'd seen there made her heart break. No creature should have to go through that. Ever.

'Well, love, there are also other options.' Her mother took her hand. 'You could always move here.'

Grace lowered her eyes. 'Do you think it would be a good idea?'

'Grace, are you considering it?' Louise squeezed her hand.

'I might be.'

'Oh, my darling, it would be wonderful if you did. You will always have a home with us, you know that, don't you? You and your dog... or your twenty dogs.'

'Steady on there, Louise. Twenty dogs?' Simon coughed.

'You know what I mean.'

'Thanks, Mum, and yes I do know that. However, I think if I do decide to come here permanently, I will need to get my own place.'

Somewhere I can spend time alone with Oli...

Where had that thought come from?

'I understand that, love. But in the first instance, you can stay here. Until you find somewhere you like.'

'Thank you. Right, I'm going to jump in the shower then go to see Hope. I want to check on her progress.'

'Of course, love.'

'And remember, I'm considering moving here but I might not actually move, so don't get too excited.'

'I won't.' Her mother winked. 'Or about the possibility that there could be romance blossoming...'

'Mum!'

Grace shook her head then stomped up the stairs, pretending to be far more indignant than she really was.

Chapter 14

The surgery was busy when Grace walked in, rubbing her hands together to try to improve the circulation and warm up. She stood in the line in front of the reception desk, trying not to stare at the people around her.

The smell of animals and wet coats hung heavily in the air. Outside, a cold drizzle was falling from the leaden sky and it clung to Grace's coat and hat, making her shiver even though she was now indoors.

'Toby, stop that!'

Grace turned to find a small white terrier sniffing around her feet.

'Oh, it's okay, honestly,' she smiled at the elderly woman in front of her.

'You won't be saying that if he... Oh, Toby! Now that's naughty!'

Grace looked down to see the dog cocking his leg and a stream of yellow urine covered her boot. She instinctively shook her leg, which caused the urine to splash over the man queuing behind her.

'Watch what you're doing,' he growled.

'Sorry.' She grimaced.

'Here...' The woman handed her some tissues. 'I'm so sorry. He only wees over people he likes.'

'Great. That makes me feel much better.'

'I hope they're not your best ones.'

'No, they're an old pair and so far they've been water-proof, so fingers crossed.'

Grace dabbed the tissues over her foot, hoping that the black leather boots really would stay waterproof. She didn't fancy having a urine-soaked sock.

When she got to the desk, she smiled at the recep-tionist.

'Hi, I'm Grace.'

'And I'm Pamela. What animal are you bringing in?' The woman hovered her fingers above a keyboard and peered over her glasses at Grace.

'Oh, I'm not bringing one in.'

'So you're here to collect one then?'

'Uh, no. Actually I'm here to see Hope.'

'But she's not yours?'

'No.'

'Hang on a minute...' Pamela chewed a pencil she'd pulled from behind her ear. 'You're the woman Maxine told me about. Oooh! I shouldn't have said that out loud.'

'What? I mean, excuse me?'

'Nothing!' Pamela winked. 'Right, dear, if you just go on through that door, then through the next one, you'll find Hope. But you know where it is anyway, don't you? The greyhound is, thankfully, a bit perkier this morning.'

'Thank you.'

When Grace entered the recovery room, the combined smell of antiseptic and disinfectant hit her like a wall. It was overpowering and laced with the strong doggy smell from reception. She paused for a moment to allow her nose to adjust.

'Hello, Grace. How are you?'

She met Maxine's kind eyes.

'Hi Maxine, I'm not bad at all thank you. And you?'

'A bit tired but can't grumble. I take it you're here to see Hope?'

'That's right.' Grace approached the crate where Hope lay on her side. 'How is she?'

'Well, we've stabilized her now and she's responding well to the antibiotics. She also managed to eat a small breakfast, so the fact that she has an appetite is very positive.'

'That's great news. Do you think she'll be all right now?' Grace knelt by the crate and gazed at the dog. Hope was sleeping soundly, her pink tongue lolling from the side of her mouth.

'I should think so, as long as those wounds heal and she puts on weight. As for mentally though… it depends. She's been through a lot.'

'I wonder what happened to her pups.'

'Probably sold on for racing or being groomed to use as hunting dogs.'

'It's so awful isn't it?'

'Many things we see are, Grace. But there are also lots of wonderful things too. Like the fact that our resident cat is doing so well with her little ones.'

Grace followed Maxine's finger to a crate set higher up. She got to her feet and peered into it. 'Oh, aren't they adorable. Oli told us all about them over lunch yesterday, and Mum and Dad seemed keen to meet them when they're ready for homing.'

'And what about you? You seem to have taken a shine to this little girl?'

Maxine had returned to Hope's crate.

'I would love to give her a home. I mean, I know I'd have to be checked out and all that to ensure suitability. But my main problem is that I live so far away... and in a flat.'

'Well, that's not always a problem as long as the dog will be exercised, but if she was going to be alone for long periods of time then it might be an issue.'

'She wouldn't be because I work from home. In fact, I can work anywhere because I write.'

'That must be nice.'

'Actually,' Grace watched Maxine carefully for her reaction, 'I'm thinking of possibly relocating.'

'To Conwenna?'

'Yes. It's only an idea at the moment, but my parents would like it and I'll miss them terribly if I don't and...' She bit her lip. 'Well... it's just something I've been mulling over.'

Maxine's smile widened. 'Can't say I blame you.'

'My parents love it here and now I've been here for a while, I can see why. If they're here, then it's quite a distance from Cardiff and we've always been so close. I'll really miss them. So, maybe, I'll move.'

'Nothing to keep you in Wales then?'

Grace shook her head. 'Nothing at all to be honest.'

'Yet Conwenna Cove holds many attractions.'

'It does.'

'Just remember what we spoke about at the beach, Grace. Oli's a good guy and those children are so precious. Be sure before you make any big decisions. I couldn't bear to see him hurt.'

'There's nothing to worry about there. As I said before—'

'Grace, that man has a spring in his step for the first time in years. And I'm fairly certain it's because of you. So if you have feelings for him, go for it.'

'Go for what?' Oli's deep voice interrupted them.

Grace froze and Maxine gasped.

'Oh… uh… Maxine was just telling me to try the local…'

'Ice cream.'

'Yes. Ice cream.'

'Sounded like quite a serious conversation to me. Rather serious indeed if it was about ice cream.'

'Well, it is very cold to be eating ice cream, I suppose.' Maxine handed him a chart, then went to the door. 'Just popping to the loo.'

When they were left alone, Oli moved closer. 'She's doing okay, Grace. I think she'll make a full recovery. It's early days obviously but she ate this morning, and she's been to the toilet, so they're good signs.'

'Will she be able to trust people again?'

'That's the one thing we can't predict. But every time I've examined her, she's been… grateful. It's the only way I can describe it. She even licked my hand this morning. You'd think she'd be terrified of me, as I suspect her owners were male, but although she's a bit anxious at times, she seems to sense that I won't hurt her.'

He was right next to her now and Grace's heart was pounding at his proximity. She tilted her head and met his blue-green gaze.

'Of course you wouldn't hurt her.'

'It's not in my nature to hurt anyone or anything.'

He leaned closer.

'Or mine.'

He lowered his head and covered her mouth with his. His lips were soft and warm and his breath tickled her skin.

'So what do you think about Grace moving to Conwenna Cove then?'

Oli and Grace jumped apart as Maxine entered the room.

'What?' Oli stared at Grace. 'You're moving here?'

He ran a hand through his hair then rubbed his face.

'I'm considering it.'

'Oh… that's…' Oli opened and closed his mouth a few times.

What was wrong? Grace hadn't wanted him to find out like that but he seemed shocked. Didn't he like the idea of her moving here permanently? Had he just wanted some fun then to wave goodbye?

'Grace… that's great.'

'Thanks.' She knelt back down by Hope's crate and stroked her paw where it lay against the thin bars.

'Right, uh… I have patients to see. We'll speak later?'

Grace nodded, but didn't raise her eyes.

Oli's reaction had cut her to the core. Had it shown that he didn't want her around long term? Well, that was fine. She hadn't made any concrete plans anyway, so she'd just revert to her original plan and go home after she'd seen in the New Year.

But if it was fine, why was her stomach now a boiling pot of acid? And why were there hot tears burning her eyes?

–

Oli checked the house from top to bottom again: Lights off. Plugs off. Windows closed. Children ready.

'I'm excited, Daddy,' Amy said, peering out from under her woolly hat.

'And me!' Tom hoped from one foot to the other.

'Tom have you been to the toilet?'

'Uh…'

'I told you to go, didn't I? Otherwise you'll want to go as soon as we get to the cove. I know you.' Oli shook his head. 'Go on and be quick!'

Tom nodded then pulled off his gloves and hurried to the downstairs toilet that led off the kitchen.

'Do you need to go?' Oli asked his daughter.

'No, Daddy.' She rolled her eyes. 'I already went.'

'Great. Right I checked everything, so we're good to go.'

He patted his coat pockets.

'Nope. I don't have my mobile.'

'It's in the kitchen on the table.'

'Thanks, Amy. What would I do without you?'

He rushed through to the kitchen and located his mobile then automatically checked it as he picked it up. No messages and no missed calls. The cheerful veneer he'd assumed all day wavered. It was now Thursday, and he hadn't seen or heard from Grace since Monday when she'd come to the surgery to see Hope. She'd been in again on Tuesday and Wednesday, but only when he wasn't around.

Oli had sent Grace three text messages asking if she was all right and in the third one, he'd invited her to Carols at the Cove this evening, but she hadn't replied. He knew it could be because she was having problems with her mobile; the signal for some networks wasn't always strong in Conwenna, or it could be that she'd not had time to reply. However, he doubted that it was either of those. In fact, he suspected that he'd upset her on Monday when Maxine had blurted out that Grace was thinking of moving to Conwenna Cove permanently.

It was a good thing, a very good thing, especially if she did go ahead and adopt Hope. But for some reason, he'd been shocked when Maxine had told him and Grace had seen his reaction. Then he'd mumbled some excuse about having patients to see and hurried away. He'd acted like a gawky teenager afraid to talk about feelings and now he was cursing himself for it. His reaction had been inexcusable, yet he knew why it had happened. He'd analysed his own emotions enough over the past few years to know that he'd been struck by fear, the crippling paralysis of terror that overtook him when he worried about losing someone. Which was ironic really, because if Grace moved to Conwenna they actually had a chance of making a go of things between them, whereas, if she returned to Cardiff then a long distance relationship wouldn't be ideal. Wouldn't work at all logistically.

In fact, it had made him afraid, because suddenly, what had been an enjoyable flirtation – although his feelings for Grace were undeniably growing stronger – could now become serious. And he didn't know if he was ready for that, or if his children were ready for it.

So he hadn't gone to Grace's parents' cottage to try to find out if there was a problem with her phone signal, or to discover if she hated him now. He had shrunk back into himself and taken care of his children and done his job. It was what he'd done for two years, and he didn't know if he had the energy to try to convince Grace that he wanted to be with her because he couldn't be fully certain that he actually did. It was all so risky and he'd been hurt enough for one lifetime.

He'd even considered not going down to the cove this evening for the traditional carols but Amy and Tom had been keen to go, telling him that all their friends would be there and that they'd be the odd ones out if they didn't go. And he knew that Linda would have insisted they attend; she had loved Carols at the Cove, telling him that it was the proper start to the festivities, the way to know that Christmas had really arrived.

'Ready, Daddy.' Tom emerged from the toilet and held up his hands so Oli could put his gloves back on.

'Come on then, let's go.'

They went out into the front garden and Oli locked the door, then he took Tom's hand and they walked out past the surgery, where the lights were on in the back room, casting a glow through the side window, then out onto the main road and across to the steep path that led down to the beach. The sky was clear, the moon a semicircle above the sea, casting its ethereal glow over the black water below. The air was sharp, the ground frosty, crunching beneath their boots.

'Amy, hold my hand.'

'I don't want to, I'm too old for that.'

'No you're not. Besides, the ground is slippery, so you need to be careful.'

She shook her head and almost immediately skidded on a patch of ice. She flailed her arms around, and Oli reached out and grabbed her hand just in time to stop her falling on her bottom.

'Thanks, Daddy.'

'See, I told you to hold on.'

She met his eyes and nodded.

As they made their way down the path, they could see the beach below. The tide was out, and the sand seemed endless as it stretched out to meet the sea and to the rocks at either end of the beach. It was an open space, a secret cove, where anything seemed possible. A few dark shapes moved around and lanterns bobbed as the scene was prepared for the evening's celebrations.

When Oli reached the bottom of the path, he helped the children down, then hopped onto the sand himself. He could see about thirty people milling around, their faces now illuminated by the moon and by the lanterns hanging from the canes planted in a semicircle in the sand. The local choir was there too, a combination of people from Conwenna Cove and nearby towns and villages.

'Daddy, there's Billy. Can I go and play with him?' Tom asked.

Oli followed Tom's pointing finger.

'Yes, but stay close and do not go anywhere near the water.'

'Yes, Daddy.'

'Amy, are any of your friends here?'

She scanned the beach. 'Yes, Tabitha and Frankie are sitting by the rocks.'

'Well, go and see them if you want but remember the rules.'

'I know, Daddy. No climbing and no swimming.'

'Definitely not.' She grinned then walked away.

Oli went up to the trestle table that had been set up by Nate. A large stainless steel urn sat on the table and Oli knew that it would contain the café's popular mulled wine, and that under the lid, segments of orange and lemon, as well as cinnamon sticks, would be floating in the warm spiced red wine.

'Evening, Nate.'

'Hi, Oli.'

'Nice night for it.'

'Perfect, right?'

Nate's beany was artfully positioned on the back of his head, in that fashionable slouchy way, and his blond hair stuck out from the front. His teeth glowed white in the moonlight and, as usual, he was smiling broadly, as if life was an easy journey that never fazed him at all.

'Many locals coming?' Oli asked, trying to seem nonchalant, but he felt like he'd just as well have a neon sign above his head saying, Grace, Come This Way!

'I expect so. Kicks off in about ten minutes, so they'd better hurry up.'

Oli nodded.

'You want a mulled wine?'

'I really do.'

Nate handed him a plastic cup wrapped in a serviette and Oli's mouth watered at the delicious aroma of cinnamon, cloves and berries.

'I'll pay for drinks for the children if that's okay, then they can come pick them up when they're thirsty.'

Oli handed Nate some money, then stood back to let other customers near the table.

He looked around to check on his children and was pleased to see that they were both nearby, so he wandered back to the rocks at one side of the path and perched on the edge of one to give himself a good vantage point to watch Amy and Tom.

It really was a perfect evening and he should be feeling happy, festive and optimistic.

But he wasn't.

Inside, something was gnawing at him, making him uneasy.

He tried to brush it away, but he knew himself well enough to understand that only one thing would make this any better.

And that was Grace.

–

Grace walked slowly down the path to the cove. Her stomach was churning and she kept grinding her teeth. She wished she could attribute the tension in her jaw to the cold, but she was wrapped up in so many layers that it couldn't be down to that. It was, instead, because she was nervous. In case she saw Oli at the beach. Her parents had made their way down earlier but she'd delayed, not wanting to be hanging around waiting to see if Oli arrived.

Yet another thought was far worse than that: the one where she didn't see him at the beach.

She was a melting pot of contradiction: longing to see him, yet fearing the pain of being close to him but not being able to hold or kiss him. Knowing that he didn't like her as much as she'd come to believe. That would be so awful.

When she reached the steep descent, she paused and listened. A beautiful, haunting sound was drifting up from the beach below, and it made goosebumps stand out on her arms while the tiny hairs rose on the back of her neck. She stood still for a moment and took in the beautiful scene spread out before her.

People had gathered in a semicircle facing off to the left. Each one of them held a small candle that twinkled like a tiny star fallen to earth. The moon was high now and its glow bathed the scene in a silvery hue, and highlighted the soft white flakes of snow that had started to fall. The melancholy strains of *Oh Holy Night* drifted around her, curling upwards like smoke and enveloping her, until she felt her heart would burst. It had been Sam's favourite carol and she had the strangest feeling that he was right there beside her, smiling at the sheer perfection of the moment.

'I love you, Sam.'

She waited until the song had finished then took a few deep breaths. Losing loved ones was so difficult and at times like this, when emotion was running high anyway, the sense of loss was heightened. But she also experienced something else, something deep and comforting; even though Sam was gone, he would always be in her heart. He would exist through her and her parents for as long as they lived, and she had many memories to treasure.

And Grace owed it to Sam to live a full life. His had been cut short and if she wasted hers then she was letting him down too.

She should follow her heart, because at the end of the day, what else was there but love?

Suddenly she lurched forwards, as if someone had pushed her in the small of her back. She gasped and looked around but there was no one there. Her rational mind told her that she was imagining things, that it was a gust of wind, but her heart told her it was Sam giving her the encouragement she needed to get down to the beach. Even if he was working through her own subconscious.

'That was silly,' she said. 'I could have fallen down the path.'

She glanced around again, but she was completely alone. And she realized that she didn't want to be alone any more. Not now that she'd experienced what it was like to have a connection to another human being.

She hurried down to the beach, as carefully as she could do, and made her way to the table where Nate was standing.

'Hi Nate,' she spoke quietly to avoid disturbing the singing.

'Hello, Grace. You want a drink?' he replied softly.

'Yes, please.'

'Here you go.' He handed her a cup of mulled wine then gave her a candle.

'Thank you.'

She smiled, then turned and walked around the outside of the semicircle of people, which she estimated to be around a hundred in total, and stood at the back of the crowd to try to get a good look at who was there. She spotted Eve and Jack with a fancy looking pushchair, and she could only just make out Iain's eyes and nose because he was tucked up so snugly under blankets and a hat. A handsome black greyhound in a warm green fleece was standing next to the pushchair like a guard dog and Grace realized that it must be their rescue dog, Gabe. Mary was also with them and a man who she guessed to be Mary's husband, Edward, because he was gazing at the older woman adoringly.

'Hello, Grace!' Tom appeared next to her.

'Hello, Tom, how're you?'

'Playing with my friends. Can I have your candle?'

'I don't think that would be a good idea, do you? Unless you're going to stay with me.'

'Oh…' His eyes darted around and landed on another boy of about his age who was waving at him. 'Never mind, I'm playing tag.'

With that, he ran off.

So that meant Oli was here too, probably with Amy. And possibly his father and Maxine.

Her legs started to tremble so she locked her knees. She wished she could blame the cold, but she knew it was because Oli was here, in this crowd, possibly trying to avoid her.

'Grace.'

She turned and a small sigh escaped as she met Oli's concerned gaze.

'Oli.'

'I didn't know if you'd be here.'

'I didn't know if I would either.' She gave a wry laugh.

'Didn't you get my text? Oh, never mind. Well, I'm glad you are here.'

'You are?'

'Of course.' He looked around him for a moment, obviously aware that they were very close to other people. 'Look, I really want to speak to you, but… not here.'

'Okay.'

'Could we… just enjoy the evening then have a good talk later, or tomorrow?'

'I'd like that.'

'But I do need to let you know that…' He took a deep breath. 'I'm sorry if I didn't seem happy that you might stay in Conwenna. My initial reaction was because I was just so surprised. I know it might have seemed different but I really am delighted. I would love it if you stayed.'

Grace swallowed the remaining sadness that had been lurking since Monday, and let the sensation of happiness replace it, then she nodded. 'Thank you.'

'I should have said something the other day. I'm just an awkward idiot at times. Anyway… we're off to the Christmas market in Truro tomorrow. Would you like to come?'

'Uh… I think my parents were hoping to go somewhere for some last minute shopping.'

'We could all go together?'

'You, me, the children and my parents?'

'Yes.'

'I'll ask them and let you know.'

'Brilliant. Now let's get your candle lit.'

He held hers steady while he touched his to it and when the tiny flame glowed, he stood back. She shivered.

'Cold?'

'A bit.'

'Come here.'

He wrapped his free arm around her shoulders and pulled her close to his side as the crowd started to sing *In the Bleak Midwinter*, Simon's all-time favourite carol.

And as Grace joined in, sharing in Oli's delicious warmth, and watching as Tom and his friend raced around, while a little way off, Amy perched on a rock with two girls her own age, the evening really did seem perfect.

She raised her head and gazed into the night sky, smiling as the soft white snowflakes drifted down, coating her eyelashes and melting on her cheeks. Now she knew Oli was happy she was seriously considering staying at the cove. And that thought warmed her right through.

Chapter 15

'I'm so glad Oli asked us to join him and the children today,' Louise said as she brushed her hair in front of the hallway mirror. 'It will be magical at the Christmas market with the children.'

Grace nodded.

She still felt pretty magical after Carols at the Cove: the combination of Oli's company, the delicious and rather potent mulled wine, the carols and the dusting of snow that had fallen; these had all combined to create a very festive evening. After the carols had finished, she'd taken Oli to her parents and asked how they felt about a combined shopping trip. They'd been delighted. It meant taking two cars, which Grace was a bit disappointed about, but at least they'd get to spend time together once they reached their destination.

An hour later, after more faffing from her mother about what shoes to wear, Simon had followed Oli's Land Rover and they were now circling the open-air car park trying to find spaces.

When they finally parked, which took a while because it was busy, even though it was still early, Oli suggested a plan for the day that included browsing the market, visiting the high street shops and lunch.

They made their way to the centre of Truro first, to the Lemon Quay Piazza, where the Victorian Christmas Market was housed in a huge, heated marquee.

'Shall we wander round together or split up and meet up later for lunch?' Oli asked.

Grace looked at her parents. She didn't want to part from Oli and the children, but she didn't want her parents to feel abandoned either.

'Well, I haven't got a thing for Grace yet,' Louise said, nudging her husband.

'Oh… no, not a thing. So perhaps it's best if she goes with you, and we'll meet up here around one and find somewhere to eat?'

'Does that suit you, Grace?' Oli asked.

'Yes, lovely.'

Grace peered at her mother, who was gazing around her innocently, as if she hadn't just manufactured the situation.

'See you later, then.'

Grace watched her parents walk away, then turned back to Oli.

'Where first?'

'Shall we just wander around and see where we end up?'

'Okay.'

Amy and Tom took the lead, rushing enthusiastically to each stall then waiting for Grace and Oli to catch up. The stallholders were dressed in Victorian costumes and Tom was fascinated by them, especially by the top hats that some of the men sported.

The marquee was split into two zones: a food hall with meat, cheese, preserves, chocolate, alcohol, and with a large café and seating area; and the Arts, Crafts and Gifts Hall, which stocked clothes, jewellery, books, artwork, pottery and more. Grace was soon dizzy from staring at so many lovely products.

'Daddy, can I have a top hat for Christmas?' Tom asked.

'Really?' Oli raised his eyebrows.

'Yes, then I will be smart and taller.'

Oli smiled at Grace. 'You certainly would seem taller but I'm not sure about it making you smarter.'

'Yay! I'm having a top hat, Amy! Did you hear that?'

Amy rolled her eyes at Grace and Oli.

'Do you want a top hat too Amy?'

'No, Daddy, don't be silly. But I would like a new scarf.' She pointed at the next stall.

'Gosh they're pretty,' Grace said as she looked at the rack of scarves with Amy. 'Which one's your favourite?'

Amy ran her hand over the silky material in a rainbow of colours, then she paused at a navy blue one printed with tiny silver stars.

'I like this one.' She held it for a moment then gently released it.

'Do you have enough money for it, Amy?' Oli asked.

She opened her small handbag and took out her purse. 'I have twenty pounds.'

'How much is the scarf?' Grace asked.

Amy turned the label over and frowned.

'It doesn't matter. I don't need it.'

Grace watched the girl's face cloud over. 'Is it too expensive?'

'No, it's fine. I don't want it.'

Amy walked away from the stall.

'I'll go and speak to her,' Oli said.

'Oli… could I have a word with Amy instead? I just have a feeling about this.'

He nodded, then allowed Tom to lead him to look at some carved wooden masks.

'Amy?' Grace placed a hand on the girl's shoulder. 'Can I buy the scarf for you?'

'No… it's not that.' Amy chewed her bottom lip.

'What is it then, sweetheart?'

'Well, I do like it and it's really pretty, but I need to keep my money to get Tom and Daddy presents. They don't have any from Mummy any more, and I wanted to get them something really special. Sometimes, Daddy's so sad, even though he tries not to show it, and I wanted to make him happy this Christmas.'

'Well Amy, I think that's lovely, and I have an idea.'

'You do?'

Amy gazed at her with her soft brown eyes. Sometimes she seemed so mature and at others she was just a little girl, torn between the child and the woman she would become. Grace wanted to hug her and tell her everything would be all right, but she knew that would probably startle Amy and that it also wouldn't be true. She couldn't make everything all right; no one could bring Linda back, but Grace could help out today and ease Amy's worries a bit, possibly even make her smile.

'I wanted to get you and Tom a Christmas present today, anyway. I was planning on finding out what you like then buying it when you were looking at something else.'

Amy stared at her, a smile forming on her lips.

'I'm going to buy that scarf then wrap it up for you for Christmas. Is that okay?'

'You don't have to do that.'

'I know I don't have to, but I want to.'

'But I don't have anything for you…'

'I don't expect anything.'

'But I can't not get you a present if you're getting me one.'

'Yes you can—'

'Amy, don't worry!' It was Oli. 'I've got a solution for that anyway. Come here.'

Tom held Grace's hand while Oli led Amy a few paces away then whispered in her ear. She grinned as she listened. 'Good plan, Daddy.'

'So we're all sorted?' Grace asked when they returned to her.

'Yes.' Amy nodded. 'And thank you, Grace.'

Grace purchased the scarf then tucked it into her bag. 'Tom?'

'Yes, Grace.'

'I need to get you something too. Care to give me some ideas?'

The next half an hour proved highly amusing as Tom led Grace around by the hand, showing her all sorts of things he would like: from a large golden Santa ornament; to a basket of assorted fudge including lemon meringue, rum and raisin and banoffee pie; to a carved stag's head complete with marble eyes; a full wooden train set painted red and green; and finally a snow globe with a skull inside that could be lit up at the flick of a switch.

At each stall, Oli shook his head at Grace, and she fought to suppress her giggles. When Tom held up the snow globe and shook it, then sighed with admiration,

Oli leaned closer to Grace and whispered, 'That would give him nightmares for weeks. Cool as it might be.'

'Okay Tom, thank you for giving me some inspiration.' Grace smiled. 'Perhaps I should nip back round then and see what I can find to meet your requirements.'

'What are requirements?' Tom asked, his eyes wide.

'It means what you want and need,' Amy said quickly; keen to show her own knowledge. 'Shall I come with you?'

Grace opened her mouth to reply, but Oli jumped in.

'Perhaps Grace doesn't want you to know what she's buying for Tom.'

'He knows what she's bought me.'

'And so do you.'

'Yes but...' Amy sniffed loudly and folded her arms.

'That's okay. Come with me, Amy, and you can help me decide. Meet you at the entrance in fifteen minutes?' Grace asked Oli.

'See you then.'

Grace strolled around the stalls again, hoping for inspiration to strike. She stopped at a stall selling toys.

'I think he'd like that.' Amy pointed at a box the size of an A3 piece of paper. Grace picked up the box that had a picture of a fort on the front and read it. It would need to be assembled from scratch, and it came complete with small medieval figures to go inside and a book about the history of castles.

'You don't think this would be too difficult for him?'

Amy shook her head. 'He loves building things and besides, Daddy will help him.'

'What about the book?'

'We can all read it to him and help him to learn to read better.'

'It does look lovely. Okay, I'll get this.' Grace paid for the castle and the stallholder tucked it into a shiny plastic bag with a Victorian scene printed on it.

'Do you know what you want to get for Tom?'

'Yes. I'll get him some animals to go in his castle.' Amy pointed at several boxes of assorted animals including horses, pigs, sheep and chickens.

'That's a good idea.'

Amy nodded, her cheeks flushing at the praise.

'What about for your Dad?'

'I'm not sure yet.'

Amy paid for two boxes of animals then slipped her carrier bag over her arm.

'Grace?'

'Yes?'

'Can I ask you something?'

'Of course.'

Grace met the girl's serious gaze.

'Do um… do mother cats get put to sleep when their kittens have been homed?'

Grace frowned. 'Not to my knowledge. Why do you ask?'

Amy stared at her shoes. 'Someone I know said that to me.'

'Really? Who?'

'It doesn't matter.'

'Are you sure?'

Amy nodded then sighed. 'It was a girl I know from school. One of my friends. She told me that if a cat and kittens are found then all the kittens will find homes, but the mother will be k… put to sleep because she's older and no one will want her.'

'Oh, Amy, I'm sure that's not true. Why don't you speak to your dad about it? I'm certain he could reassure you?'

Amy's cheeks coloured. 'I can't because then he'll know.'

'Know what?'

'What I did.'

Grace watched Amy carefully, not sure whether to ask her to elaborate. Amy had told her this much, and she was worried that if she pushed her further then Amy might clam up altogether.'

'If you want to tell me about it, you can talk to me.'

Amy nodded. 'But you might have to tell Daddy, right? The teachers in school always say that. We can tell them things but they can't ever promise to keep a secret in case it's something bad.'

'But I'm sure you haven't done anything bad, have you?'

Amy shook her head. 'No, but I did something I shouldn't have done and Daddy will be cross.'

'You know, Amy, you could try talking to him about it. I'm sure he'll be understanding. Even if he's a bit cross at first.'

'I know.'

As they left the toy stall, Grace felt a tugging at her sleeve. She turned to find Amy gesturing at her to pull her free hand out of her pocket. Grace did and Amy slipped her hand into Grace's. Not wanting to make Amy feel uncomfortable, Grace acted as if it was an everyday occurrence, but she had to fight to stop herself pulling Amy into a bear hug. Amy had not warmed to her as quickly as Tom had, and Grace hadn't wanted to push Amy to befriend her, as she knew that the whole situation was tricky. But now, Amy had taken the lead and shown Grace that she was accepting her, even if it was just as a family friend. Or as her friend.

They paused by a stall selling jams, chutneys and liqueurs. 'Some of those look delicious, don't they?' Grace pointed at the chutneys.

'Daddy loves cheese. He'd like one of those chutneys.'

'Why don't you get him one then?'

'I don't know which one he'd like most though.'

They eyed the range on offer then Grace read the sign behind the counter.

'You can get three for the price of two, Amy. So why not get him a selection?'

'Good idea. Can I have a chilli one, a ginger one and a plum one, please?' she asked the man in a top hat.

'Of course you can, missy.' He wrapped the jars in tissue paper, sellotaped it and tucked them into a bag, which he handed to Amy before she paid him.

'You've done well,' Grace said. 'Is there anything else you'd like to get?'

'I don't think so, but if you're looking for an idea for Daddy then he does like wine.'

Grace smiled. 'Let's find him one he'll enjoy.'

They headed for a stall selling a variety of wines and ales.

'How about… strawberry wine?'

Amy shook her head. 'That'll be too sweet for him.'

'Blackberry?'

Amy wrinkled her nose.

'Mead?'

'What's mead?'

'It's a drink made with honey and spices. It's sweet, but good with cheese.'

'Yes, get him that.'

Purchase made, they left the stall and Grace checked her mobile. 'Goodness, we were longer than expected. We'd better go and meet your dad.'

'Wait!' Amy held up a hand.

'What is it?'

Amy's cheeks coloured and she stared down at her feet. 'I just... wanted to say thank you.'

'What for?'

'I... I wanted to say thank you for taking me shopping like this. It was very nice. And thanks for listening to me.'

'Oh, Amy. I'll gladly take you shopping any time you like, and I'm always glad to listen and advise you if I can.'

'But you won't be here. Daddy said you're going back to Cardiff.'

Grace's heart thudded as she looked at Amy's downcast eyes, at the way her hair flicked up at the ends and at her long fair lashes.

'Did he?'

Amy nodded.

'I might not.'

'What?' Amy met her eyes. 'Really?'

'I'm not one hundred per cent certain yet... but I am thinking of staying in Conwenna. My parents are here and... Hope is here and... well, you, Tom and your Daddy are here and now you're all my friends.'

'I'm your friend?'

'Of course.'

Amy's lips curved upwards and her eyes shone.

'I'd like you to stay.'

'You would?'

'You make my Daddy happy and he hasn't been happy for a long time. I think he gets lonely.'

Grace couldn't help herself then, she pulled Amy into the hug she'd imagined giving her. At first, the girl stiffened, but then she relaxed and wrapped her own arms around Grace. They stood there for a while, holding on, clinging to the comfort of human contact.

All around them people bustled along, purchasing Christmas gifts for friends and loved ones, and browsing the wonderful wares that the stalls had to offer. Carols from the Salvation Army band at the entrance filled the air and the scents of food, spices, mulled wine and coffee tantalized their nostrils. Outside, snow started to fall, big fat flakes that soon created a white carpet on pavements, vehicles and the roofs of buildings.

Grace was filled with happiness, because a motherless little girl who clearly needed to be loved had accepted her as a friend, a little girl who was taking on too much responsibility for someone so young. A little girl who loved her father desperately and hated to see him sad. A little girl who could benefit from having a friend who understood the pain of loss.

Grace hoped that she would be able to help Amy, Tom and Oli. Even if it was as their friend. Although she hoped she could be so much more.

Chapter 16

Oli and Tom were waiting near the entrance when Grace and Amy reached it.

'We thought you'd got lost,' Tom said, as he shook his head.

'We were buying your presents!' Amy told him. She waved a bag at him.

'What is it?' His eyes lit up.

'A secret and you can't know until Christmas Day.'

'Awwww...' He pouted, but his excitement was obviously too powerful for him to be disappointed for long.

'Shall we go and find a table and wait for your parents?' Oli asked.

'Good idea. I'm hungry now, but being surrounded by gorgeous food always has that effect upon me.'

They made their way through the crowd to the café and scanned the seating area. Grace spotted a family leaving a large table, so Amy and Tom rushed over as soon as the family had left.

When they were seated, they tucked their bags under the table.

'Grace!' Louise waved as she approached. 'Thank goodness we found you. It's so busy in here and outside.'

'Thought I was going to pass out from hunger,' Simon said as he wiggled his eyebrows at Tom, then took a seat. 'What're we having young man?'

'Garlic bread.'

'Garlic bread? What with?' Simon frowned.

'Garlic bread.'

'You're just having garlic bread?'

Tom nodded.

'No, you're not, Tom. You need to have something else as well.'

'He's mad about garlic bread,' Amy explained. 'He'd have it for breakfast, lunch and dinner if he could.'

As they perused the menus, Grace looked up and found Oli watching her. He lowered his gaze immediately, but when she'd caught his eye, she'd seen something there. Something deep, as if he was lost in thought. She wished they could have five minutes alone just to talk properly. She was glad of his friendship and of his children's acceptance, but she also couldn't deny her intense attraction to him, the desire right now to sit next to him and hold his hand. Was that wrong? Was she confusing desire with something more?

Grace had always held back emotionally from men, but Conwenna Cove had loosened something inside her and she was experiencing an emotional rollercoaster around Oli that she had never ridden before. He was a good man, a good father, he loved animals, and he was polite and warm towards her parents. She suspected that he would have got on with Sam too.

Oli was everything she could want.

But could she offer him everything he wanted and needed in return?

'I'll have a Cornish hot pot,' she said, trying to break the spell she was under.

'That sounds nice, Grace. I will too.' Her mum patted her hand.

'Amy and Tom? What do you want?' Oli asked.

'Cheese and ham toastie, please,' Amy replied.

'Garlic—'

'Tom, you are not just having garlic bread. How many times?' Oli shook his head. 'I'll get you some but you're having some pasta with it.'

'Okay, Daddy.' Tom pouted.

'Shall we go and order the food, Oli?' Simon asked.

Oli nodded then went up to the counter with Grace's father. When they returned, Simon was carrying a tray of drinks.

'We took the liberty of ordering mulled wine for the adults and hot chocolates for the children,' Simon said.

'Just a small one for Simon and me as we're driving, but you ladies get a large one each.'

Grace accepted her drink and sipped it. The spiced wine was warm and delicious, and combined with the music, the atmosphere and the company, she knew in that moment that there was nowhere else she'd rather be. If she allowed herself, she could almost believe that Oli was her man and that Amy and Tom were her children. How wonderful would that be?

A tiny shiver ran down her spine. If they were her children she'd be worrying about them constantly, fretting that they'd inherited the gene that had left Sam so unwell, that had robbed him of his life so early and so unfairly. She wouldn't want to bring a child into the world to lose it as she had Sam.

Yet even as these thoughts rushed through her mind, she also knew that it was wrong to think that way. The counsellor had encouraged her to be aware of her own thought processes and how to reason with them. It was selfish, perhaps, to think like that if she did have a child like Sam; he or she could live a perfectly happy life well into his or her forties and maybe even longer. But if she was thinking about herself, and her parents, about preservation and carrying on through her life, she knew she couldn't bear to go through what her parents had. And that was why she had sworn never to get pregnant and never to bring a child into the world, because she knew that she would truly break and never be able to put herself back together if she lost that child.

'Don't be sad, Grace.' Tom had got up, and was standing right next to her gazing into her face.

'Oh… I'm okay.'

'It's Christmas. Be happy.' Tom took her hand. 'You've got us to have fun with now.'

'Thank you, Tom. I'd say that makes me the luckiest woman in the world.'

'You are,' he said, causing her to smile in spite of the direction of her thoughts.

'What are you two grinning about?' Oli asked.

'Nothing…' Grace shrugged nonchalantly. 'Just enjoying the day.'

Oli nodded at her, his eyes full of something, as if he had a thousand things he wanted to say to her but he didn't know where to start.

'Me too, Grace. Me too.'

–

After lunch, they wandered around the rest of the city, taking in the sights and soaking up the atmosphere. Tom held firmly on to Grace's hand, making her feel like she was very important to him. That was the wonderful thing about children and animals, they had the ability to live fiercely in the moment, to put the past and future from their minds and enjoy just existing. Tom was helping Grace to do the same.

Outside one department store was a sign that made Tom gasp.

'Daddy! Santa's in there!'

'And it looks like there's a queue to see him.' Oli pointed at the line snaking out of the shop doorway.

'I don't mind queuing, Daddy. It's very important that I speak to him.'

Oli looked around him. 'Uh… there might be another Santa here somewhere.'

'Daddy…' Tom shook his head. 'There's only one Santa. I'm only five and even I know that.'

'I'll take him in. I don't mind queuing.' Grace looked at Tom and he rewarded her with a beaming smile.

'Thank you, Grace!'

'You don't have to do that,' Oli said.

'Daddy, I don't want to see Santa!' Amy scowled. 'Imagine if I see anyone I know.'

'Tell you what,' Louise cut in, 'why don't Simon and I take Amy around some more shops then meet you back here in an hour?'

Relief crossed Amy's face. 'Can we go in that new clothes shop? And the make up one?'

'Of course we can.' Louise smiled. 'See you three in an hour then.'

Grace, Oli and Tom took a place in the queue.

"Have you seen Santa before, Grace?'

'Oh yes. On several occasions, actually.'

'Is he nice?'

'Always.'

'Daddy let me see him last year, but I don't remember much as I was only four. I did have a photo with him.'

'He did.' Oli nodded.

'He's magic, Grace, and he has elves and reindeer and a Mrs Santa and a house in the North Pole and a big fat belly and...' He took a deep breath as if it was all just too exciting.

'So I believe.' Grace stroked his hair back from his face.

'Are you excited now?'

'Very.'

'What will you ask him for?'

'Oh, I don't know... I don't think grownups can ask for anything. It's only children.'

'That's right, Tom,' Oli added. 'He only takes children's requests.'

'Then tell me what you want and I'll ask him for you.'

'No, Tom, it's all right. You ask for whatever it is that you want. Just think carefully about it before you go in.'

They queued for over half an hour before a female elf in a stripy red and green outfit, tights and a hat topped with a small golden bell, took their money then showed them into the grotto. Oli had to duck to go through the entrance, which made the elf giggle. Inside, it was darker and Grace blinked as her eyes adjusted. They walked along a short corridor then into a round room where Santa sat on what appeared to be a throne draped in red blankets. He laughed and held his belly as they approached him.

'And who do we have here?' he asked from behind his thick white beard.

'I'm Tom.'

'Well, come here, Tom, and tell me what you'd like for Christmas.'

Tom looked at Grace and she nodded, so he went forward.

'Think he hit the mince pies early this year,' Oli whispered at Grace and she coughed to cover her laugh.

'Have you been a good boy, Tom?' Santa asked as Tom stood next to his throne.

'Uh… I think so. Have I, Daddy?'

'Yes, he has. He's always very good.'

'Well then, young man, tell me what's on your Christmas list. I'm listening carefully.'

Tom paused for a moment then leaned closer and whispered in Santa's ear. He paused then glanced back at Grace and Oli. Then he whispered some more.

Santa nodded. 'That's quite an ask, young man. But you are entitled to request whatever you want.'

'It is what I want more than anything, Santa.'

'What about toys? Are there any of those that you'd like too?'

Tom chewed his lip.

'I don't mind. But I do want everyone to be happy.'

'Ho! Ho! Ho! Then I shall do my best to make that happen.'

'Thank you, Santa.' Tom shook his hand then rushed over to Grace and Oli.

'Don't go just yet, Tom. There's something here for you.' Santa held up a rectangular package wrapped in paper covered with tiny penguins.

'Wow! Thank you.'

Tom accepted the gift, then Oli led the way out of the grotto.

Back on the ground floor of the department store, they all blinked in the bright strip lighting.

'Happy now, Tom?' Oli asked, as he ruffled his son's hair.

'Yes, Daddy, because now we can have the best Christmas ever.'

A shadow flickered over Oli's face, but he quickly collected himself. Grace understood; he was probably thinking about Linda and the Christmases they'd shared in the past. Of course he was. It must be so difficult for him, especially during the festive season. Tom might not remember Christmases gone by but Oli and Amy would.

'We certainly will have a lovely Christmas, Tom.'

Grace was jostled by an elderly woman carrying too many bags. The woman looked stressed and exhausted and mumbled *sorry* as she hurried away.

'It's getting busy,' Oli said. 'Might be a good time to head on home.'

'Well, you hold Grace's one hand, Daddy, and I'll hold the other and we can stay together safely. It's easy to get lost in a crowd. That's what my teacher always says.' Tom placed Grace's hand in Oli's.

'Yes, Tom, of course.' Oli squeezed Grace's hand and she met his eyes.

'Yes, Tom.'

Oli squeezed her hand again, so she squeezed him back.

'Don't get lost, Grace,' he whispered. 'I'm getting used to having you around.'

'I'll try not to.'

And joined together, they made their way out into the December afternoon, and all the while, Grace was acutely conscious of where Oli's skin met hers, and wondering what Tom had asked Santa for, because it might just be the same thing she wanted for Christmas too.

Chapter 17

Before they got into their cars, Louise nudged Simon, 'Go on then.'

'We were thinking, seeing as how it's a Friday and so close to Christmas, whether you'd like to extend the day and come and have dinner with us?'

'Oh… that would be fantastic.' Oli unwound his scarf. 'To be honest, I wasn't sure what I was going to make for us, and we've all had such a great day that it does seem a shame to cut it short. Are you sure?'

'Absolutely,' Louise said. 'We have a fridge and freezer full of food and drink. It's Simon, you see, he has to stock up at normal times and at Christmas… sheesh! Grace and I feel obliged to eat whatever he cooks, and it would be so nice to have some help eating it all this year.'

'We'd be delighted to join you.' Oli looked at Amy and Tom. 'Wouldn't we, kids?'

Amy nodded. 'Can I do a makeover on you?' she asked Louise.

'I would love that, Amy.'

'What about me?' Grace asked.

'Really?' Amy's face lit up.

'Well, yes, of course.'

'Can I do your hair too?'

'I'd love you to do my hair.'

Amy's cheeks flushed with pleasure.

'I'll need to pop into the surgery to check on Hope and the other animals we have in, but we'll head over to yours after that.'

'Wonderful.' Louise smiled.

'I'd like to see Hope too.' Grace glanced at her parents. 'If that's okay with everyone.'

'Of course. Why don't you come in our car?'

'Yay!' Tom jumped up and down. 'Come in our car, Grace and you can tell me stories in the back.'

'Tom! Grace might not feel like telling stories.' Oli shook his head.

'It's fine, honestly. I know lots of stories, Tom.'

Grace got into the back with the little boy and helped him to fasten his seatbelt over his booster seat. Amy was up front next to her father.

Oli turned the radio on and Christmas music filled the vehicle.

'Sorry about the dog hairs on the back seat, Grace,' Oli said as he met her eyes in the rear-view mirror. 'Hazard of the job.'

'It's fine. Don't worry.'

'Tell me a story then, Grace.' Tom patted her hand.

'Okay. Have you heard the one about the little boy who found a balloon with a note inside it?'

He shook his head, his brown eyes wide.

'Right then...'

The journey back to Conwenna passed quickly as Grace told Tom three stories and he lapped each one up, asking plenty of questions, some of which she had to think quickly to answer. He was such a bright child and so funny with the way he reacted to the stories and to the world around him. His mind was open, innocent and eager to be filled and Grace realized how wonderful it would be to help with that. To be a part of shaping the man he would become by filling his mind with knowledge and understanding, and by feeding his enthusiasm for learning.

It made her think about her writing and how she loved to research for her books. Lifelong learning was something that she'd always clung to, she believed that no one could ever take the thirst for knowledge away from a person and she enjoyed weaving what she learnt into her stories.

When they pulled up in the surgery, Tom's eyes were heavy and she knew if they'd been in the car for much longer that he'd probably have fallen asleep.

'Hey Tom, we're home.'

She undid his seatbelt, then Oli came around and helped him out of the Land Rover, while Grace got out and stood next to Amy.

'We'll go into the surgery first, then pop into the house to freshen up.'

In the reception they were greeted by the smiling Pamela.

'Everything okay?' Oli asked.

'Yes, all good. That locum vet isn't bad, you know.'

'He comes highly commended.' Oli nodded. 'He's helping out over Christmas here and with the sanctuary, and he works in a few of the local towns. He's also worked here before – for a few weeks when I was… uh… unable to put in my normal hours – but I'm considering offering him something a bit more permanent, so that I can have more free time for the children and for…' He stopped himself and his cheeks flushed. 'For you know, whatever else might happen.'

'I see.' Grace laughed. 'Well, it's always important to have some free time.'

'Let's go and see how Hope's getting on, shall we?'

They went through the surgery; Grace was struck again by the familiar scents. They made the surgery smell clean yet slightly intimidating, because for some animals, this place would quite literally be where they hovered between life and death. Oli had so much responsibility on his shoulders and it must be hard for him not having a companion to lean on, someone to rub those broad shoulders in the evening and to reassure him that he was doing everything he could for the animals he treated. Didn't everyone deserve someone like that to help them through each day? Grace had never dwelt on such thoughts before, but Oli brought them to the surface of her mind and tantalized her with images of how life could be if she fell in love and actually allowed herself to care for him. Life could be so good, if only they wanted the same things and if only Oli reciprocated her feelings.

Hope was lying down, but she lifted her head when they entered the room and gave a strange sort of drawn out squeak as she opened and closed her jaw, a bit like a greeting.

'Oh my goodness! What's wrong with her?'

'Nothing.' Oli smiled. 'That's what greyhounds sometimes do to welcome you. It's a kind of hello.'

'Oh. Hello, Hope.' Grace knelt by the crate and pressed her hands to the bars. The greyhound licked her fingers, her long, warm tongue tickling her skin.

'Show me the kittens!' Tom said to his sister.

Amy struggled to lift Tom up to see into the raised crate.

'Awwww… can we have one, Daddy?' Tom asked.

Grace looked over at the children and thought about what Amy had said earlier about the cat. Her concerns for the mother's welfare had been genuine and Grace hoped that Amy would speak to Oli about her fears. She decided to raise the subject now, hoping that a gentle prompt wouldn't hurt.

'What will happen to the cat and her kittens, Oli?'

'Well, I'm hoping that your parents will definitely want one of the kittens when they see them, even better if they want two, and Edward and Mary want one. That just leaves the mother.'

'And what will happen to her if you can't find her a home?' Grace asked, her gaze flickering from Oli to Amy and back again.

'I'm sure we'll find her a home.'

'Daddy?' Amy lowered Tom gently to his feet, then moved closer to Oli.

'Yes, angel?'

'Could we give her a home?'

He smiled down at his daughter. 'Amy, you know what I've always said about this.'

'Yes, but… I'm worried about her.'

'You don't need to be, Amy.'

'But I am. I feel… responsible for her.'

Oli glanced at Grace then placed a hand on Amy's shoulder. 'What's going on?'

Amy chewed her bottom lip then turned to Grace.

'It's okay, Amy.' Grace nodded, offering the reassurance the girl obviously craved.

Amy released a long sigh.

'Okay, Daddy, but you have to promise not to be mad.'

'Uh oh…' Tom came and stood next to Grace. 'Amy's done something naughty.'

'I haven't!' Amy snapped then rolled her eyes. 'Well, I have but I don't think it's terribly naughty. Daddy… I put the cat and the kittens in the park under the slide.'

'What?' Oli frowned at her.

'It was me.'

'But where did you find them?'

Amy took a deep breath. 'I rode my bike up to Rosehip Cottage. Before Grace moved in there with Simon and Louise. And I heard meowing from the shed.'

'Ahhhh…' Grace nodded. 'Mum said it smelt as if cats had been living in there.'

'You found the cat and the kittens in the shed?' Oli asked.

'No. At first it was just the kittens and I was worried that they were lost, so I decided to bring them to you. But then I was worried in case you'd be angry because you told me not to go to the cottage on my own.'

'Then why did you?'

'For a dare.'

'Amy!' Oli shook his head and two spots of colour appeared high in his cheeks. 'Why did I tell you not to go there?'

'You said that the house had been empty for a long time, and therefore I shouldn't go near it in case the building was dangerous or something else.'

Oli met Grace's eyes. 'I was just worried. I didn't really think there would be anything wrong with the building but you never know if some older kids might have been there drinking or some out-of-towners or something. Besides, it's trespassing.'

Grace nodded. Oli had been worried that there could be someone squatting or something similar. She supposed such things could happen, even in a village as small as Conwenna. She also knew that Oli worried about his children enough for two people; he was doing the job of two parents after all.

'Well, do you see why I told you not to go there, Amy?'

'Yes, Daddy. But there wasn't anyone there and then I heard the kittens and I was worried about them.'

'What did you do?'

'I tucked them into my rucksack and was about to leave when I saw the mother watching me from the garden. So I called her and she came to me, so I tucked her into my coat. I was going to bring them to the surgery and risk you being mad with me, but on the way I kept thinking about how sad you've been and how disappointed you'd be and I couldn't bear it.'

Grace lowered her gaze to Hope. She felt as if she was intruding now on a very private father-daughter moment. Amy was confessing to her father and revealing her deepest feelings. Grace pushed herself up and was about to leave the recovery room when Amy rushed over to her and took her hand.

'Daddy, I told Grace a little bit about this today and she said I should talk to you.'

Oli met Grace's eyes. 'Did you?'

She nodded. 'Amy was worrying that the mother would be put to sleep when the kittens were homed.'

'I would never let that happen, Amy.'

'I know.' Amy's lip wobbled, and Grace squeezed her hand. 'Grace told me she wouldn't be, and then I thought I would try to tell you the truth. Please don't be angry at me, Daddy. I just did what I thought was right and I never wanted to lie to you, but I didn't want you to be angry or disappointed with me either.'

'Come here, sweetheart.' Oli opened his arms and Amy rushed into them. 'I'm not angry or disappointed – I'm just glad you told me. Of course, we have no idea where she came from in the first place, but perhaps she found herself pregnant and wandered into town searching for somewhere to give birth.'

Tom was still standing next to Hope's crate and he gave a small laugh. 'See, Amy! Daddy's not cross because you told the truth. You should always tell the truth even if it's difficult. My teacher says that.'

'I guess we'd better give her a home then.' Oli smiled at his daughter.

'Really?'

'Well, yes. I can't have you worrying about her, can I?'

'Thank you, Daddy.' Amy buried her face in his chest and he smiled at Grace and mouthed, 'Thank you.'

'Now that's all sorted, I just need to have a word with the locum and with Maxine. Won't be long.'

Grace returned to Tom, crouched down and stroked Hope's silky chin; the greyhound emitted a long grunt. Her tail flapped up and down and thumped against the blanket she was lying on.

'Oh you like that, do you?'

Hope's tail wagged again in response.

Amy and Tom knelt by Grace.

'Are you going to adopt her?' Amy asked.

'Maybe. I'm hoping so.'

'That's why she's called Hope.'

'Yes, I guess it is.'

'She's hoping you'll give her a home and you're hoping you can give her a home.'

'Yes.'

Grace marvelled at how wise Amy could be.

'And I'm hoping we can give you a home.'

Tom's eyes widened as he realized what he'd said.

'Uh oh...'

'Tom!' Amy nudged him. 'You can't say things like that.'

Grace met Tom's eyes and he blinked at her. 'I can if I want to. And I do want Grace to live with us. She makes Daddy happy and she gets you to tell the truth.'

Amy nodded, as if he'd said the most natural thing in the world, and Grace struggled to find the right words to reply.

When Oli walked back in a few minutes later, the three of them were snuggled up next to Hope's crate and the dog had drifted off to sleep.

'See, Grace, she just needs a warm home and a family. She's obviously comforted by your presence and by your voice.'

'I *hope* so,' Grace said, causing Amy and Tom to giggle.

Oli frowned 'What is it?'

'They've been trying to use the word hope in as many sentences as possible.'

'I see.' Oli knelt down next to them. 'Well, let's hope that this little girl makes a full recovery, which I'm pretty certain she will do, then hopefully, she can come live with you.'

'And us,' Tom whispered.

'What's that, Tom?' Oli cocked his head.

'Nothing, Daddy. Just hoping my Christmas wish comes true.'

Grace got to her feet and helped the children up, then they made their way out of the surgery and into the cold afternoon; the sun was already low in the sky but Grace's heart was finally soaring.

–

'If I keep eating here, I'll need new scrubs,' Oli said leaning back in his chair. 'Another absolutely delicious meal. Thank you so much.'

'You're very welcome. It's lovely to have company,' Louise replied.

'Can I help with the dishes?' Oli asked.

'Not at all!' Simon replied. 'You're our guests. You sit there and let your food go down.'

Grace helped her father to clear the table and load the dishwasher.

Oli liked eating with the Phillips family. They were warm, kind people and had been so welcoming to him and the children. Of course, he had his father and Maxine nearby, but Linda's parents had moved away to Scotland years ago and they'd never really been close anyway. And he did get lonely, so being invited to share a meal with a family and to have the chance to spend more time with Grace was something he just couldn't pass up. Besides, they'd had a wonderful day in Truro, and Amy and Tom seemed to adore Grace and her parents, so this was posi- tive all round. Grace had also encouraged Amy to speak openly to him about the cat and kittens, and that was a wonderful breakthrough. He'd suspected that Amy was holding something back and worried about her being secretive, but it seemed that Grace had the ability to draw Amy out of herself.

Good friends were hard to find and people were all so busy with their own lives, just getting through each day, so Oli was delighted to have the opportunity to have more people around his children. He knew they could never have too much love. He also knew that he would benefit from being around Grace and her parents, and if he was happier then surely that was good for his children too?

Once everything was tidy, Louise placed two large bowls of popcorn on the table.

'Popcorn?' Tom's eyes widened. 'Now?'

'Yes, sweetheart. I thought we could put a movie on.'

'Yay!' Tom held Louise's hand. 'What are we going to watch?'

'How about a Christmas movie?'

'Yay!'

'Which one, Louise?' Amy asked.

'Well, I have a few in the lounge so why don't we go on through and have a look? Come on, Simon.'

'Of course, dear.' Simon gave quick salute then followed his wife.

'Anything else need doing now?' Oli asked Grace.

She'd pulled her hair into a ponytail at the base of her neck and a few red tendrils drifted around her face. Her chin and neck were exposed and her soft white skin was enticing. He had an urge to press his lips there to taste her.

He took a step closer, then another.

'Thank you for today, Grace. We had such a great time. It's like... when we're with you and your parents, we feel relaxed and accepted. You can't knock that.'

'You can't.'

'I mean... I'm so grateful for how you dealt with Amy today. You helped her to be open with me and...' He sighed. 'I've never been very good at this stuff.'

'What stuff?' She placed her hands behind her on the counter and leaned on them.

'Talking about feelings and... hopes and dreams and all that malarkey.'

Grace laughed. 'Me neither. Well, when I was in counselling I had to open up a bit. But in the outside world, I'm not quite the same.'

'What are your hopes and dreams, Grace?'

She looked down at her feet. 'Oh... uh... talk about putting a girl on the spot.'

'You don't have any?'

'What're yours?'

'I asked first.'

She took a deep breath. 'Okay. Well... I don't want what some women my age seem to want.'

'What's that?'

'A husband, children... a four-bed semi in a nice suburb.'

'You don't?'

He'd asked her for the truth so why did her response make his heart sink?

'Well... I didn't... I mean... I'll never have children of my own.'

'Why not?'

'Because of the risks.'

'I guess there are risks, but it's like everything in life — to live is a risk.'

'Yes, but these risks are too big for me to take. I can't take a chance that I'd have a child who would have to go through what Sam did.'

'You don't like the idea of being with someone and having children?'

She met his eyes. 'Not that, no. But I never want to have my *own* babies.'

'Right. I get you.'

'A ready-made family might be different.' She offered a small smile.

'It might?'

She nodded. He stepped closer again; he was so drawn to her that it was hard to fight his feelings. He could imagine how soft her skin would be if he touched his lips to the small of her throat.

'So what do you want?'

'For the future? I honestly don't know, Oli.'

'For right now then?'

He was so close that he could smell the scent of her shampoo from her hair, a light coconut fragrance, and he could see himself reflected in her dilating pupils.

'Right now... I want to spend time with you, Amy and Tom. I want to enjoy Christmas. And I want to adopt Hope.'

He laced his fingers with hers and she sighed.

'And will you stay in Conwenna?'

'I'm certainly considering it.'

'I'd like it if you did.'

'Well, I'll consider it more then.'

'Please do. Stay here, Grace.'

He leant closer and kissed her cheek.

'Daddy!' He turned suddenly to find Amy in the doorway with her hands on her hips.

'What are you two doing? The film's about to start and Grace said I could do her makeover. Come on!'

Oli stepped backwards with a sigh and released Grace's hands.

'Better not miss the start of the film, had we?'

Grace shook her head.

'Can we talk more later?'

'I'd like that.'

'After you...'

He gestured at the doorway and Grace went through; he followed her, resisting the urge to reach out and pull her back to kiss her in the way he wanted to. Without hesitation. Without restraint. Without fear. Because around Grace, he felt that losing control wouldn't be such a bad thing after all.

Chapter 18

As they entered the lounge, Grace smiled. The room was perfectly festive, with its low lighting, the tree adorned with twinkling silver fairy lights, the warm glow from the log burner, the scent of cinnamon from the large candle burning on the mantelpiece and the warm, family atmosphere.

Rosehip Cottage now felt like a home. Because it had a family.

The only place left to sit was on the two-seater sofa. Her father was in his arm chair near the fireplace, her mother was in the middle of the three-seater sofa with Amy and Tom on either side, which left the other sofa for Grace and Oli.

She glanced at him and he winked, obviously thinking the same as she was, then she went and sat down. Oli sat at her side and she could feel his heat emanating towards her, his body a magnetic force drawing her closer.

'Are you ready now, Daddy?' Amy asked, as she lifted a hand full of popcorn to her mouth.

'Ready.'

'Grace?'

'Ready.'

'Good! Go for it then, Simon.'

Grace's father nodded, then pointed the remote control at the TV.

Christmas music filled the room along with the familiar opening scene of the latest version of *A Christmas Carol*. As the characters on screen went through their own dilemmas, Grace was only able to give the movie half of her attention. She was all too aware of Oli's leg as it gently brushed against hers, of his handsome profile that was highlighted every so often by a brightening of the TV screen and of the way his hand sat upon his muscular thigh.

Close enough to hold.

And she did want to hold him. After what she'd told him in the kitchen, she'd been worried that he might think that she didn't like children. She'd have hated for him to have misunderstood her. But he had said that he did understand how she felt. And if he understood that, then perhaps there really was hope for them…

She wondered if he was as engrossed in Ebenezer Scrooge's past as he appeared to be and dared to steal a glance at him. He met her eyes and smiled, and Grace blushed at being caught out. Then Oli discreetly slid his hand off his leg and onto the cushion next to her and she did the same so that their fingers met.

The rest of *A Christmas Carol* passed in a blur as Grace's focus was centred on the way Oli's skin felt against her own, and how gently he circled her palm with his thumb. When the children asked to stop the movie for comfort breaks, Oli withdrew his hand, but as soon as everyone was settled again, he moved it back. Grace couldn't help thinking about how good it would be if they could be open about their feelings, if she could hold his hand openly and not have to hide it. But they did it out of respect for Oli's children and for her parents, although Grace suspected that Louise and Simon had engineered the whole let's *leave the two-seater sofa free* situation.

When the final credits rolled, she sighed with disappointment, but flashed Oli a smile as he gave her hand a final squeeze.

'Who's for hot chocolate before bed?' Louise asked.

'Me!' Tom shouted.

'Yes please,' Amy said, nudging her brother.

'I meant *please*.' Tom hung his head.

'Come on then, you two, let's go and warm some milk up.'

'Oh!' Amy gasped. 'I haven't done your makeovers yet. I forgot because I was enjoying the film so much.'

'You can do them another day,' Louise said. 'We have plenty of time, Amy.'

'Thank you.' Amy smiled.

Amy and Tom followed Louise into the kitchen while Simon turned the TV off then put the DVD back into its case.

'I'll just uh… help your mother.' He gestured at the kitchen, so Grace nodded.

When they were alone, Grace's stomach flipped. They might only have minutes to talk and suddenly her mind was blank.

'What're… your plans for the next few days?'

'Well, believe it or not, I still have gifts to wrap. Nothing like leaving it to the last minute, eh? Although I'll probably do what I usually do and end up wrapping the kids' things on Christmas Eve. Or, you know, Santa will drop them off ready wrapped… I wish!'

'Do you want any help with that?' Grace asked, well aware that she wanted to see him again as soon as possible. 'I could come over tomorrow?'

Oli's expression darkened.

'What is it?'

'Tomorrow's not good for me.'

'Oh.' A pain seared through her chest. 'Okay.'

'Yes… it's um… difficult to explain. But…'

Grace put up a hand. 'Don't worry about it. You don't need to explain anything to me. I have a million things to do anyway, including trying to edit the last three chapters I've written. I just can't get the one scene right, and I never send a book to my agent until it's the best it can be. I mean, I'm far too passionate about my writing for that and…' She trailed off, realizing that she was babbling, trying to fill the silence that would otherwise fall between them, or to prevent Oli from telling her that she was a very nice person, but he just couldn't see a future for them.

But the handholding…

Perhaps he was just lonely and craving human contact. It could well be that.

Grace just really liked him and was letting herself get carried away.

Oli was staring at the tree and there was something in his eyes that she recognized. She'd seen it before, in her own reflection in the mirror. It was pain. Grief. Fear. Uncertainty. This wonderful father, caring vet, good man, had his own troubles to bear and he was doing a damned good job of it but he was also suffering silently.

She wanted to slide onto his lap, wrap her arms around him and tell him that everything would be okay, but how could she? For one, he might not want her to and, two, it would be a lie. Because Grace didn't know if everything would be okay. Life was tough, people you loved got ill and died; there was no guarantee about how long someone would be around. That terrified her and no doubt terrified Oli too.

So instead of holding him, she gently squeezed his hand.

'Oli, if you need some help with the wrapping on Christmas Eve, I'll be available to help. I'm quite good at it.'

He met her gaze and smiled, but it didn't reach his eyes.

'Thanks.' He stood up and Grace felt the cold air creep into the space where he'd just been. She shivered. Without Oli around, life would be a lot colder and duller. In such a short time she'd become so fond of him and being with him had become something she looked forward to.

'I guess I'd better get those two ready for bed. We have a big day tomorrow.'

'You do?'

He inclined his head. 'Unfortunately.'

'Right.'

'Coming to see us out?'

'I'll be there in a minute.'

Oli nodded sadly then left the room, and Grace pressed her knuckles into her cheeks.

If they had a big day, then she wanted to be a part of it, yet she had no right to ask. They were not her family, and despite Oli's apparent affection for her, he clearly wasn't ready to let her fully into his life.

A heavy sigh escaped from Grace as confusion washed over her.

It was time to get a grip on her emotions. Oli was evidently not in a place to fall in love again and Grace had to accept that.

Even if accepting it was the last thing she wanted to do.

–

Oli poured water over the coffee grains then stirred it with a spoon. He needed the caffeine after the restless night he'd had. Anniversaries could be good things but in this case, it wasn't. Linda had been dead two years today and he'd been awake most of the night thinking about what that meant.

Two whole years had passed since he'd kissed her for the last time, since he'd stroked her soft skin and said goodbye. She'd been his friend and companion, and he'd thought they'd grow old together, but instead she'd been cruelly torn from her family by a disease that ate her away. *Far too soon*. He took a mouthful of coffee and winced as it burnt his tongue, but the physical pain was preferable to the pain in his heart.

And what was he doing? Last night, he'd been sat with Grace, touching her hand and enjoying her company and that of her parents. And enjoying it far too much. Surely it was wrong of him to allow himself to fall for another woman so quickly?

What would Linda have thought if she'd known that he'd moved on in such a short space of time?

She'd have…

He covered his chest with his free hand and took a shaky breath.

He knew what she'd have said, it was the same thing she repeated to him endless times before she died.

Move on and find love again. Find another companion. Don't grieve for me for long. I want you to live and be happy. I want the children to have as much love as they can do around them. Don't hold back, Oli, you only get one life.

If it had been the other way around, Oli wondered if he'd have been as understanding. Could he have selflessly told Linda to love again? To move on and forget him?

But then she hadn't asked him to forget her, only to live on. And living on meant choosing life, not choosing to hide away from love and happiness.

He knew that. He'd just let his fears and his sadness affect him last night. And it was the pressure of today's date that had led to that.

He needed to get the children up, get them dressed, pop to the florist then head up to the cemetery that sat just beyond the village hall, overlooking the whole of Conwenna. It was a pretty cemetery, if such a thing were possible. It caught the sunlight for most of the day and the old trees there captured the ocean breezes, holding them in their branches and making the cemetery smell of brine and sunshine. There was comfort in the thought of ending up there one day, still being so close to the sea and being surrounded by the beauty of the Cornish village.

Two hours later, Oli, Amy and Tom got out of the Land Rover and walked through the cemetery gate. The children knew the way to their mother's final resting place and Oli followed them, all three of them silent as their thoughts were focused on one person. For Amy, it was difficult, Oli knew, because she had memories of her mother's love. For Tom, it was slightly different. He knew that Linda had loved him and that she'd been a good mother, but he knew that from the stories Oli and Amy told him. Oli knew that Tom's memories of her were vague and probably mainly helped along by photographs and the few video recordings they had of Linda. And by that time, she'd changed, no longer the vibrant beauty with her long blonde hair and shiny brown eyes. By then, her hair had been thin and short, her cheeks sallow and her eyes dulled by pain and fear of what was to come. Oli wished with everything he was that Tom had known his mother as she'd once been, and he tried every day to tell Tom some snippet about Linda that would keep her alive in his memory.

They reached the grave and the three of them stood in front of it. A cold wind whipped around the cemetery, shaking the bare branches of the trees and causing the empty flower pot on the adjacent graveside to whistle.

Amy glanced at him and he shook his head. 'Just the wind. Nothing to worry about.'

She nodded then leaned forwards and placed the festive wreath she'd chosen against the headstone. 'Hello, Mummy. Hope you're okay. Love you and miss you. I got you this because I know how much you liked Christmas decorations and this one has red bows, gold glitter and real holly and ivy.'

Oli took her hand as she stepped backwards and his heart cracked when he saw how she was biting her lip, determined not to cry. She'd told him on the journey there that she wanted to be happy for her mummy and not to make her sad.

Tom knelt down and placed the small white teddy bear wearing a Christmas hat on the grave. 'Hello, Mummy.

Hope you're not too cold. I got you a teddy bear to cuddle. Love you.'

He stepped back and took Oli's other hand.

'Hi Linda.' The pain in his throat made his voice croaky. 'Love you and miss you. Hope you're at peace, angel.'

'You can cry if you need to, Daddy,' Amy said as she stroked his hand.

'I know, sweetheart. Same goes for you.'

He lowered into a crouch and pulled his children into his arms. They hugged one another tight as they took turns to tell Linda about their week, about the cat and kittens and about Hope, as well as about their Christmas plans.

When they'd all finished their stories and had fallen silent, Amy pushed backwards so she could look into Oli's face. She cupped his chin and smiled through her tears.

'Daddy, Mummy wants you to be happy. You know that don't you?'

'How do you know that?'

'I just know.'

He swallowed hard.

'She wouldn't mind about Grace. She'd be glad for you and for us.'

'About Grace? What about Grace?'

'Oh come on, Daddy.'

She was so perceptive sometimes that it unnerved him. But then perhaps he hadn't been doing as good a job of hiding his feelings as he'd thought.

'You think so?'

'Definitely. Grace is a good person. She makes things feel better.'

He bit down on his bottom lip, but as hard as he tried to control his emotions, a tear escaped and trickled down his cheek. Amy caught it with her gloved finger.

'Come on, Daddy. Let's go and get warmed up.'

'Sometimes I think you're older than you are, Amy.'

'Does that mean I can have a smartphone for Christmas then? Like all my friends?'

In spite of the sadness in his chest, Oli laughed. 'I don't know if Santa has got one for you.'

'Daddy!' Amy frowned at him then rolled her eyes. 'You know I don't beli—'

Oli shook his head and nodded at Tom.

'What I meant was, I'm sure Santa can do some last minute Christmas shopping. After all, I'm going to have a cat to take photos of now.'

'Oh, Amy…' Oli sighed. 'Sometimes you're so much like your mother.'

'Well, that's something I'm proud of.' She smiled, then took Tom's hand and skipped along the path, her young mind full of Christmas and gifts, of love and the future and of living. With her cat, of course.

Oli paused and turned back to the gravestone.

'I love you Linda and I always will. I'll never forget what we had… but I need to grab happiness now, for me and for the children. I don't know if it's with Grace. It's early days and I can't be sure yet, but I hope you understand.'

And as he turned and followed Amy and Tom back to the car, he could have sworn he heard someone whisper… *I do.*

Chapter 19

Grace strolled through the village, taking deep breaths to try to ease the ache in her chest. Just last evening, she'd been cosied up next to Oli in her parents' lounge as they'd enjoyed a Christmas movie, and within such a short space of time the warm fuzzy feeling she'd been enjoying had been replaced by doubt and emptiness once more.

This morning, she felt as if she could just run away from it all, pack up and head straight back to Cardiff and continue her previous existence by immersing herself in her writing and ignoring everything else. But she knew it wouldn't be that easy. Being in Conwenna Cove and spending time with Oli and his children had awakened something inside her, something that she hadn't known was even there. It was as if she'd been sleepwalking for years, at least since Sam had died, and now she was wide awake, aware of what life could be like if she just took a chance. The problem was that she didn't know if Oli wanted to take that chance too.

If he did then what did that mean?

She bit her lip and pulled her coat tighter around her throat. But he'd told her he had something to do this morning and it quite clearly didn't involve her. That stung. It shouldn't, but it did and Grace didn't want to feel like that. Life was too short. Yet wasn't life also too short not to feel, to spend days, weeks, months and even years in a state of numbness as she had done after Sam had died?

She heard a familiar voice and looked up to see Oli, Amy and Tom standing outside Scoops and Sprinkles. Not wanting to be seen, she ducked into the nearest doorway and found herself in the Conwenna Café. She stood at the glass for a few moments, watching as Oli and his children eyed the ice creams on offer in the shop window.

And she felt lonelier than she ever had done before. Because they were there and she was not with them.

'Hey, Grace, who're you spying on?'

She jumped and turned to meet Nate's smiling face.

'Oh! What? I'm not spying.'

He leaned forwards to see who she was looking at, then nodded.

'I see.'

'See what?'

'You need a Nate special.'

'No... I don't. I'm going.'

'No, you're not. Come on.'

He took her hand and led her to a table near the counter then pulled out a chair.

'It's my break now and I think you need a friend.'

'I should go,' she said, even as she sat down.

'Take your scarf and coat off, and I'll be back soon.'

Grace had no energy to fight and nodded gratefully.

While she waited, she tried to focus on her surroundings. The lights on the tree in the corner of the café twinkled softly like randomly strewn diamonds on the thick spiky branches. Frank Sinatra crooned about Christmas from the radio on the counter, and the sounds of people enjoying the last Saturday morning before Christmas soothed her: voices, laughter and the tinkling of cutlery. Normality. Delicious aromas wafted around her: fruity, spiced mince pies, strong exotic coffees and cheese toasties made with herby breads. And everywhere she looked there were smiling faces, bags full of shopping and people just being people. Life was good, life went on.

'Here you go.' Nate was back, carrying a tray laden with food.

'I really couldn't eat all that.' Grace eyed the toasted cheese and tomato ciabattas with pale mozzarella that oozed from between the slices of bread, the steaming mini Christmas puddings in their bowls with shiny blobs of thick yellow Cornish cream, and the two large glass mugs that held hot chocolate topped with pink and white marshmallows and frothy whipped cream.

'Don't worry, it's not all for you,' Nate said as he undid his apron and hung it on the back of the chair opposite Grace. 'It's my break so I'm joining you.'

'Okay, lovely. Thank you.'

Nate sat down and handed her a plate with a ciabatta then placed a bowl with a pudding next to it and gave her some cutlery.

'Right… now you tell me why you were spying on Oli and his kids.'

Grace's mouth fell open.

'Grace, it's obvious that you've got a bit of a thing for him, so shoot! I'm a good listener.'

'I don't have a… a thing for him.'

Sinatra finished singing then Band Aid's *Do They Know It's Christmas?* rang out around the café.

Nate's piercing blue eyes twinkled.

'Yes you do, and he has one for you. I saw it the moment you met. Of course, if I'd said anything back then you'd have thought I was mad, but it's obvious that there's a spark between you. The question is… what're you going to do about it?'

'I can't… I don't…'

'Grace, I also saw you together at Carols at the Cove.'

'Oh.'

'As did most of the village.'

'Oh.'

'It's a small place and people do talk.'

'The last thing I want is to be the focus of village gossip.'

Grace bridled at the thought that she was providing the folk of Conwenna with some juicy morsels to mull over. She was used to being anonymous in a big city, of staying below the radar and it had suited her. No one had cared that she was alone and not interested in falling in love. Except for her parents and they'd known not to push her on the subject.

'Nothing malicious, Grace. We all care about Oli and his kids. No one wants to see him on his own any longer and, to be honest, he's had a few local women after him at different times but never shown a flicker of interest. He's a good catch, you know. Single father, good career, lovely kids.'

'I'm not after him because of that.'

'Of course not.' Nate sipped his hot chocolate then without meeting her eyes asked, 'What does draw you to him?'

'I can't quite believe how open you are, Nate. I mean… you've been very kind to me since I arrived but you hardly know me.'

'Grace... I like you and I do feel that I know you now. I'm an open and honest guy, sometimes to my detriment, and I just want you to know how things roll around here. People talk. They know things. It might be different to what you're used to but it's not a bad thing. This is a supportive community and if you stay here, you'll find a lot of friends.'

Grace picked up her ciabatta and nibbled at the end. 'Oh... this is good.'

'It is, right?' Nate smiled his open smile and Grace relaxed a bit. He was just being friendly and it would be good to talk about her feelings.

'Okay. Between you and me, I do really like Oli. He's a good man and I've grown very fond of him. And yes... I think he's gorgeous too... but the situation is complicated.'

'Why?'

'Is everything always straightforward for you?'

He shook his head. 'No, but I do think we sometimes put obstacles in the way of happiness when there shouldn't be any. If we really want something, it can be achieved.'

'What? Anything?'

He glanced upwards then pursed his lips. 'Well, not anything... I mean, I'll never be president of the United States or marry Mariah Carey... but lots of other things. And as for love... well, two people who want to be together should be.'

'But Oli has the children and his job and he's settled, and I have a flat and a life in Cardiff and—'

'They all sound like things that could be worked out, Grace. There's nothing there that can't be overcome. I suspect it's just fear holding you back.'

'Fear is there to prevent us from making big mistakes though, Nate. It's there to protect us, a primitive instinct that prevented us from playing in front of wild animals or jumping from clifftops.'

'Yes, but what an awful way to live. Constantly being afraid. And there aren't many wild animals around here... ones that would be dangerous, I mean. There are cliffs but thankfully they're only dangerous if you lean over the edge.'

Grace chewed her sandwich, savouring the creamy cheese and the sweet ripe tomatoes along with the crustiness of the bread. Fear was a terrible thing and she had lived her life in its shadow, terrified of losing someone she loved again. She'd had just two people to worry about in her mother and father, and that had made her feel safer than knowing that she'd opened her heart to more. More people to care about meant more people to worry about losing.

'But I don't know how he feels about me, Nate. And I don't want to push him to find out because he's got enough to deal with.'

'Like what?'

'Like what was he doing this morning? He told me he had a big day, and turned me down when I offered to go round and help him wrap the children's presents.'

Nate wiped his mouth with a napkin, his own sandwich devoured.

'Ah... I know why today's a big day.'

'You do?'

'It's the anniversary.'

'Anniversary!' Grace gasped. 'Oh no.'

'Yes, it's two years isn't it? Got to be a tough time for him.'

'Of course.'

'And two years alone with two children hasn't been easy for Oli.'

'No.'

'Why don't you have a proper talk with him? At least find out how he feels about everything, and then you'll know if there's a chance that you could make something work between you.'

Grace sipped her drink. The chocolate was silky with cream and the marshmallows slipped into her mouth, sweet and chewy.

'I suppose I could.'

'I suppose you should. It's dreadful losing loved ones, I know. I lost my father a few years back. But you have to keep moving forwards or you're just giving up. Oli deserves to fall in love again and if he's happy, Amy and Tom will be too.'

'I hope so.'

'I know so. After all, what child wants a miserable and lonely father?'

The thought of Oli being miserable and lonely made Grace want to dash out of the café, across the road and straight into Oli's arms. But she forced herself to stay where she was. This couldn't be rushed. Today was a difficult day for Oli and his children and they needed some space. She was staying until the New Year, so she'd have time to talk to Oli before she left and she'd also have time to consider what she was going to do about staying on in Conwenna long term.

Grace entered the hallway of Rosehip Cottage and dropped her bag on top of one of the remaining packing boxes, then slipped off her shoes and hung her coat on the stand. She'd enjoyed her lunch with Nate; then had strolled around the village doing some last minute Christmas shopping.

The pretty little shops had all been festive with twinkling lights, Christmas music and plenty of gifts on offer. She'd picked up a card for her parents and one for Oli and the children. It had a cat and three kittens on the front wearing red Christmas hats, and it made her think about Amy and her admission about the cats. She hoped Amy was feeling better now she knew she could home the mother cat and now that the kittens all seemed to have potential homes too.

The afternoon was dark and brought back memories of cold winter days when she was a child, when life had seemed to stretch out before her like a blank canvas just waiting to be filled. Everything had seemed so full of promise back then and even though Sam had suffered with his illness, she'd been convinced that he'd get better as he grew. But that was childhood, the unerring belief that everything would work out and that you and your loved ones were immortal. Of course, not all children enjoyed such carefree times and Amy and Tom certainly hadn't, but Grace knew that at their ages she'd clung to the belief that her parents or the doctors would be able to fix Sam and that she'd always have him around.

She entered the kitchen and found her parents kneeling down next to a large box. Someone had cut a semicircle out of the front of it and Louise was leaning in through the hole.

'Mum? Dad? What's going on?'

Louise and Simon turned around and both immediately looked guilty.

'Oh… this was going to be a surprise.' Her father smiled. 'Never mind, you can enjoy it now.'

'What's a surprise?'

'Look.' Her mother stood up then gestured at the box; Grace approached it then peered inside.

'Wow!'

A pretty black cat lay there grooming herself, while all around her the kittens played. There was a black kitten, a tortoiseshell one and a black and white one.

'They're gorgeous. But… you're not keeping them all?' She thought instantly of Amy.

Simon laughed. 'I would, but Edward and Mary have agreed to home one and we're having the other two. Then Oli has promised Amy that the mother is going to live with them, of course.'

'Yes, she's very excited about having her.' Grace nodded.

'The kittens are ready to be homed now, but we said we'd have them here over Christmas just to give them a bit longer and to get them used to a home environment.'

'A messy home environment,' Louise added. 'Your father's promised to empty the rest of the boxes in the hall this afternoon, so we'll be able to walk through it without dodging cardboard. My shins are black and blue. Besides, we don't want the kittens wandering through and getting stuck in any of them.'

Grace leaned over the box and stroked the tortoiseshell kitten. It turned and swatted her hand with a paw then lost its balance and fell over onto the thick soft blanket her parents had lined the box with.

'She's beautiful.'

'You could home her?' Louise suggested. 'If you wanted one too. And we could keep her brother.'

'I'd like to.'

'What's stopping you?'

'Well, there's Hope to consider. Besides which, Dad is clearly besotted with them all.' She smiled then felt her face fall. 'Oh Mum... I can't bear the thought of going back to that clean quiet little flat alone.'

'Come here.'

Louise pulled Grace into a hug and rocked her as she used to do when she was a child.

'Why not move to Conwenna? You can stay with us for as long as you want, then when you're ready, buy a house here. Or in a nearby town or village if you don't want to be on our doorstep.'

'I don't want to be far from you and Dad.'

'Well, stay with us then.' Louise leaned back and met Grace's eyes.

'I can't live with you forever. I'm thirty-one now and need to be independent.'

'We love having you around, Grace,' Simon said as he lifted a kitten and rubbed his thumb over its tiny head.

'What about things with Oli?' Louise asked. 'We thought... hoped that there was something happening between you.'

'Well, there is... kind of... but it's all so complicated.'

'I know, love.' Her mother kissed her forehead. 'I wish I could make it all better like I used to do. It's so difficult when your children grow up.' Her eyes widened. 'No! That's not what I meant. I mean… oh god I miss Sam so much.'

'Me too.'

And this time it was Grace who pulled her mother into a hug and held her tight.

'We all do.'

Simon wrapped his arms around his wife and daughter and they sat there, beside the box with its cat and kittens, sharing old memories of Sam, as the afternoon darkened and snowflakes drifted from the moonlit sky.

Chapter 20

Grace woke on Christmas Eve to find something soft and warm nestled against her cheek.

'Hello you.'

The cat rolled onto its back and purred as she rubbed its head.

'Where are your babies?'

As if suddenly remembering them, the cat jumped off the bed and disappeared into the hallway.

'I guess Mum and Dad will need to give you and your babies a name soon. We can't keep calling you Cat. Although ultimately, it's up to Amy to name you.'

Grace sat up and pushed her hair from her face. Christmas Eve always felt special, even though she was an adult now. It was part of the festive build up and she'd always enjoyed it, probably even more than Christmas Day.

She picked up her mobile off the bedside table and noticed that she had two messages, both from Oli. She opened the first one:

> Hi Grace, hope you're okay. Just wondering if your offer of help is still open? I haven't wrapped a thing! Oli X

The message had come through half an hour ago.

She opened the second one:

Hi, me again, look no pressure at all and I'm sure you have plenty to do. However, if you would like to come over this afternoon I have some good wine in and the children would love to see you. Oli X

Grace smiled and hugged her knees to her chest. So Oli did want her to go round to help him. The idea of spending Christmas Eve with him and the children lifted her heart and the sense of the day being special grew.

She sent a reply asking what time he needed her, then got up and pulled on her fluffy red dressing gown and stuffed her feet into her slippers. Her bedroom was chilly and when she opened the curtains, frost flowers decorated the edges of the windowpane as if someone had created a deliberate festive display.

Beyond the garden, the sea sparkled in the early morning light and everything outside was white with snow and frost. It was a perfect Christmassy morning. Hopefully, today would work out after all and perhaps her life would work out too.

She padded down the stairs and into the kitchen where she found her father frying bacon and eggs on the Aga, and her mother sitting on a cushion in front of the cardboard box with two kittens climbing over her lap.

The mother cat was twirling around Simon's legs, evidently asking for some bacon.

'Has she been fed?' Grace asked.

'Yes, your father bought her some of that top quality cat food from Oli's surgery and he's got the brand that the kittens need too for weaning.'

'She's just after this bacon,' Simon said as he placed the meat onto a plate then took it to the table. 'Not good for her though.'

'A bit of what you fancy doesn't hurt, Simon, and she has just had babies.' Louise put the kittens back in the box, then got up and took a seat at the table.

'What are your plans today, Grace?'

Grace poured tea from the pot into three mugs.

'I thought I'd visit Hope then... uh... Oli has asked if I'd like to help him with his Christmas wrapping.' At Louise's raised eyebrows, she added, 'He sent me a text this morning.'

'This morning, eh?' Simon said then looked at the clock on the wall. 'It's only seven-thirty now. Seems like someone has been thinking about Grace all night.'

'Stop it, Dad.'

'Just saying.'

'Well don't.' Grace grinned, as she helped herself to bacon and eggs.

After they'd finished eating and cleared the dishes away, Grace spent some time playing with the kittens. The tortoiseshell one came to her readily and she lifted it and pressed her face into its soft fur.

'What shall we call her?' Louise asked.

'I was thinking about something cute because she is so fluffy.'

'We'll call her Fluffy then?' Louise suggested.

'You should.'

'That's settled,' Simon said as he carried a fresh pot of tea to the table. 'Now you've named Fluffy you'll have to stick around to see plenty of her.'

Grace gazed down at the kitten that had curled up in her lap and was struggling to keep her eyes open. And she knew that she would have to see her regularly.

'What're you calling the boy?' she asked.

'We've been unable to agree on names yet.' Louise refilled their mugs.

'But I like Frank for the boy and Tilly for the girl with the white socks on.'

Grace placed her mug of tea on the floor beside her then stroked the kitten in her lap. At least the kittens would have good homes, and she knew her parents had wanted to have pets for years. With Sam's condition, they'd worried about allergies and hygiene so they resisted their urges to get a cat or dog. Opinion had been divided about the pros and cons of pets for someone with Sam's condition, but Louise and Simon had been terrified of taking any risks at all.

'We'll just have to introduce you and Hope gradually, so she doesn't frighten you. Or the other way round I suppose.'

Fluffy snuggled her face into her tail, her tiny chest went up and down as she breathed and Grace caressed her ears gently. Animals deserved to be treated well, just as humans did too.

—

Oli closed the surgery door then locked it. Christmas Eve had been busy as residents panicked about the fact that he'd be closed for two days; however, the single locum had agreed to be on call should anything arise over the Christmas period. Oli had offered to pay the locum extra for the inconvenience, but the young man had told him he was glad of the experience and that he didn't really like Christmas very much anyway. Oli could understand that – after Linda had died he had thought Christmas would never be something to enjoy again – but he had children to think of, as well as the very welcome idea of spending more time with Grace.

His stomach flipped. She'd replied to his early morning texts and agreed to come over this evening. Once the children were asleep, they could open a bottle of wine and wrap the presents then get everything ready for Christmas Day. He'd been worried that his texts would upset her, or that she'd find him a bit forward after he'd declined the offer of help the other day, but her replies had been warm and friendly.

After visiting the cemetery, Oli had thought he might feel guilty about Grace and their burgeoning friendship, but visiting Linda had had the opposite effect. Instead of feeling bad, he felt that Linda approved, that somehow she had given him a sign that he should go on with his life. Oli would always hold Linda in his heart and love her for the time they'd shared and for the beautiful children she had given him, but he also knew that he could never get her back. So he would keep her memory alive for the children and for the life they'd shared together, but he would also try to live as full a life as he could, as he knew Linda would have wanted him to.

'You all right there, Oli?' Pamela asked, as she pulled on her coat. 'You looked a million miles away.'

'I am, thank you. Just working out what I need to get done first.'

'I bet the children are excited today.'

'My father said he'd take them out, because otherwise they'd be climbing the walls at his.'

'Good plan.'

'Well, have a lovely Christmas.'

Pamela came and hugged him, her floral perfume as familiar as the fabric softener he used, then planted a kiss on his cheek.

'You're a young man, Oli, and you need to get yourself a woman now.'

'What?'

'Just think about it. Linda was an angel, but you're still alive and you deserve to be happy.'

She patted his arm. 'I'm older than you and have known you a long time, so I can say things like that. I knew Linda very well too, remember, and she'd hate the thought of you being alone for the rest of your life.'

Oli nodded. 'Well, we'll see.'

'We will. Merry Christmas, lovely.'

Oli walked Pamela to the door then let her out and closed it behind her. It felt like everyone he knew was trying to tell him the same thing. Was it because it had been two years and they thought that was long enough to spend grieving, or was it because Grace Phillips had arrived in Conwenna Cove and they saw that there was a spark between them?

He walked into the recovery room and found Hope standing up in her crate wagging her tail.

'Well, hello, girl. You want to come out?'

She lowered into a bow, a sign that she was keen to spend some time with him.

'How about you come home with me today?' Maxine had taken their other patient home with her for the evening and Simon and Louise had taken the cat and kittens, so Oli didn't have to come into the surgery on Christmas Day.

He let her out of the crate then held out his hand. She approached him cautiously then allowed him to stroke her chin.

'You're a beautiful girl and I think that at some point, someone loved you, but then it all went wrong. Let's take you through to the house and you can have a nice spot in front of the fire. As long as you promise not to eat any of the presents.'

Hope bowed again.

'I have your word on that then? Come on, sweetheart.'

He gently slipped a greyhound fleece onto her then put a harness on over it and led her from the recovery room and through the surgery to the door, then switched off the lights and went out into the cold.

–

'Come on through. There's someone here who wants to see you.' Oli led Grace through to his lounge. She gasped when she found Hope lying on a folded-up quilt near the fireplace.

'What's she doing here?'

'I didn't want to leave her in the surgery alone overnight, and thought it would give me a chance to observe her in a home environment. She might well need rehabilitation at the sanctuary, but I have a feeling from how she's been since I brought her in, that she's lived in a house before.'

'So she was someone's pet and they treated her like that?'

'Could be that she was stolen or passed on. Perhaps her owner couldn't keep her any longer.'

'There could be someone out there looking for her?'

'She's not chipped, I've already checked. We sent out emails to all other local vets and police but no one has come forward to claim her.'

'Just like the cat.'

'It's annoying how irresponsible some people are.' He frowned.

'Amy's excited about having the cat though isn't she?'

He nodded. 'They want every animal that comes in, but up to this point I've said no. We'd have no room for us if we homed every waif and stray. But if you do go ahead and home Hope, then we'll be able to see plenty of her.'

Grace smiled. 'You certainly will.'

'Amy and Tom aren't here yet. My father's dropping them off when they get back from their outing.'

'Where did they go?'

He shrugged. 'Knowing my father, here, there and everywhere. He'll have tried to wear them out today, knowing they'll be overexcited all night.'

Grace was suddenly and acutely aware, that they were, in fact, alone.

She stood up and Oli came towards her.

'Grace.'

She held up a hand and shook her head.

'Just kiss me.'

He took her hands and gently pulled her towards him then cupped her face before lowering his head. As their lips met, Grace's heart beat faster and she slid her arms around his neck.

Then there was nothing other than them. Kissing. Touching. Tasting each other as if they had waited their whole lives just to be together.

When Oli pulled away, Grace almost collapsed but he held her up, pressing her body against his.

'Grace… I want you so much.'

She stroked his cheek.

'I want you too.'

'But not just here, like this. I want you in my life. I never thought I'd love again but you… you're different. You've been through so much and you understand me. You carry your own pain. But it's also more than that. The first moment I saw you, I wanted to hold you and to make you mine.'

She gazed into his blue-green eyes, watched his pupils dilating as he roamed his gaze over every inch of her, and she felt as if she could float away.

'I've never felt like this before, Oli. This is so new to me.'

He nodded. 'I did love Linda. I really did. But this is different too. I'm not the young man I was when I met her and I've been through a lot. It changes you, shapes you and who you become. Grace, I think… in fact I know… I'm falling in love with you.'

Grace gasped.

'I don't expect you to say you feel the same. All I want is to spend Christmas with you and to enjoy your company and for Amy and Tom to spend time with you too. They think a lot of you. Give us a chance to show you how life could be if you stayed in Conwenna.'

'Of course. I mean… yes please.'

She reached up and slid her hand behind his head then pulled him towards her, keen to taste him again and to enjoy the heat that he sent flooding through her body. He lifted her into his arms as easily as if she weighed nothing more than Fluffy the kitten, and carried her to the sofa and knelt beside her.

'What now?' she asked.

'Now...' There was a knock at the door and he winced. 'Now the children are home.'

Grace quickly sat up and straightened her black dress.

'I'm so sorry.' Oli shook his head.

'It's fine.' She gave him a quick kiss then he went out into the hallway, leaving Grace smiling to herself.

Oli came as part of a package and she knew that. So the children arriving at that moment wasn't a bad thing; it was probably how life would be. And she knew that she didn't just want Oli, she wanted his children too and anything else that came with him. She would happily take on his grief, accept the life he lived before her arrival, love and care for his children and respect his memories, because no one came through life completely unscathed. And being with someone was about loving them and everything that made them who they were.

Grace realized as she sat on the sofa, gazing at Hope where she lay on her comfy quilt in front of the fire, that she really did want to give this a chance with Oli, Amy and Tom. And she was prepared, finally, to take a chance on loving them all.

Chapter 21

'That's the last one,' Oli said as he pressed down on the Sellotape then slipped the small gift into Tom's stocking.

'Do you think they're sleeping now?' Grace asked as she pointed at the ceiling.

'I doubt it but I'll check.'

He left the kitchen and tiptoed up the stairs.

Grace held her breath and listened. Amy and Tom had been under strict instructions to remain upstairs, even if they heard an army come marching through the cottage.

A floorboard above her head creaked and she heard a yelp.

Hope raised her head from where she was lying on the quilt near the Aga. They'd brought her out to the kitchen with them, because Oli said he didn't know if she'd try to climb the stairs and he didn't want her disturbing the children. He also wanted to keep an eye on her in case she needed the toilet.

'It's okay, girl. He'll be back soon.'

Hope lowered her head again and blinked knowingly.

'I'm sure you understand me, don't you?'

Grace blew a kiss to the greyhound just as Oli reappeared in the doorway.

'Surprisingly, both sound asleep. I even waited to see if Amy was pretending but nope. Then I stepped on a Lego brick and it really hurt, but my yelp didn't wake them. My father must have worn them both out.'

Grace snorted before she could stop herself. 'Lego can be dangerous stuff. Perhaps Tom left it there to catch Santa out.'

'I wouldn't be at all surprised.'

When Paul had arrived with the children that afternoon, and found Grace there already, his eyes had lit up. Oli had explained that Grace had come to see Hope and that she was going to help him with festive preparations, but Paul's smile had suggested that he thought otherwise.

'Okay, let's get the presents piled up in the lounge then I have a little surprise.'

'What is it?'

Oli tapped his nose. 'You'll have to wait and see.'

They carried the two stockings and the gifts in their different wrapping paper into the lounge then set them out in two separate piles.

'I'll take the stockings up later when I go to bed. Now, you take a seat.'

'No, let me help you.'

'Absolutely not. Stay there.'

Oli disappeared then returned with Hope and her quilt and settled her in front of the fire. Grace watched as Hope stretched out then let out a long satisfied groan. She giggled. That greyhound noise would never cease to amuse her.

Oli entered the room carrying a tray.

'Close your eyes.'

'What?'

'Grace, please, close them.'

She did.

'Now you can open them.'

On the coffee table in front of the sofa was a bottle of champagne and two crystal flutes. Next to them was a plate of small circular crackers piled high with smoked salmon, cream cheese and a bowl of what appeared to be a rich dark chocolate mousse.

'Oli... how wonderful.'

'You're wonderful and you deserve to be spoilt.'

'It's just perfect.'

'Good. And... if you're wondering, because I know it must be difficult sometimes, the flutes are brand new. I bought them recently, hoping you'd come here for champagne at some point.'

'I hadn't wondered that, but, thank you.'

Oli popped the cork then filled their glasses. He handed one to Grace.

'Merry Christmas, Grace. May this be your first of many at Conwenna Cove.'

They clinked glasses.

'I hope so.'

Grace sipped her champagne, savouring the crisp finish and the clean, pure flavour.

'It's delicious.'

Oli nodded.

'Is everything ready for tomorrow?'

'Yes, I think so.'

'And what are you three doing for lunch?'

'My father and Maxine are meant to be coming here. Would you like to...' He leant forwards and put his glass on the table. 'How do you feel about Christmas dinner?'

'In what way?'

'Well, do you want to spend it with your parents or would you like to join us?'

'Oli, I would love to join you, but it's my parents' first Christmas here and I think I should be with them.'

'Of course. I understand that.'

'And you need to be with your family.'

He nodded, then ran a hand through his hair. 'Silly, right, but I hate the thought of not being with you.'

'It's not silly, it's lovely, and I would love to be with you too, but we can get together later on tomorrow.'

'This is all quite difficult isn't it?' He took her hand.

'It's not a straightforward situation, but it's not a bad one either.'

He gently stroked her fingers in turn then ran his thumb over her palm.

'What's wrong, Oli?'

'I want to be with you but I feel... a bit guilty too.'

She wriggled closer to him on the sofa. 'I'm sure that's probably natural when you lose a partner.'

'I do know that Linda would want me to live life to the full. She told me as much. But even so, it's like I'm here living and she's cold in the ground.' He shook his head. 'God, Grace you don't need this. I just wanted to explain to you. I want to be with you, but I have to make sure that you want the kids too.'

Grace took a deep breath then released it slowly.

'You, Amy and Tom come as a package deal and I wouldn't want it any other way.'

He reached for his champagne again.

'Well, here's to the future and whatever it may bring.'

They both drank from their glasses.

'Now, let's eat that salmon. I'd hate for it to go to waste.'

They sat and ate in silence as festive images flickered across the TV screen and Hope eyed them from her quilt. Grace and Oli handed her some small pieces of salmon and she accepted them gently, licking her lips in appreciation.

'We could get used to this Hope, couldn't we?'

'I could get used to this.' Oli stroked her cheek. 'I'd love to spoil you both on a frequent basis.'

When they'd finished the crackers, Oli lifted the champagne bottle. 'More?'

'I probably shouldn't. I'm already a bit lightheaded and if it's okay with you, I'd like to come back early in the morning and to see the children opening their presents.'

'You could always stay?'

'I could but I did stay recently... by accident... and if I stay again, won't the children get confused?'

'Confused? They might do, I guess but they do like having you around.'

'Well, I'll go home now and come back early shall I?'

'Okay. Great.'

Grace rubbed Hope's chin then gave her a kiss on the head before going out to the hallway and pulling on her coat and hat. She stuffed her feet into her boots then picked up her gloves.

'I'll see you in the morning, then.'

'Grace... hold on.'

Oli went to the chest of drawers, opened the top one and took something out then he returned to Grace.

'Take this.' He held out a key.

Grace stared at it. 'You're giving me a... key?'

'Yes.'

'Oh... Oli... uh... Wow! That's such a big step.'

'It is. But Grace…' He rubbed his eyes with the heels of his hands. 'Look, I realize how it looks but I was only giving you the key so you could get in in the morning.'

Grace slapped a hand to her forehead. 'I'm such an idiot.'

He stepped backward then scuffed his foot on the rug. 'No you're not. I mean… I thought I was giving it to you for that but perhaps, deep down, I was hoping you'd keep it after tomorrow.'

'After tomorrow? So you did mean…' She bit her lip as dozens of thoughts raced through her mind. 'I will have to go back to Cardiff in January, but then once I've sorted everything out—'

A floorboard on the landing creaked and they both froze, staring up into the darkness as if they'd been caught discussing something they shouldn't. A few moments later, the chain flushed and there was the sound of the tap running. Oli and Grace stood still, waiting for whichever child it was to return to bed. When they heard Tom returning to his room, they both released the breaths they'd been holding.

'I was going to say that I will be back and that I will definitely use this key. As long as you want me to have it.'

'I really do.'

He leant past her and opened the front door so she stepped out into the cold darkness.

'Merry Christmas, Grace.'

'I'll see you tomorrow?' she asked, her heart thudding as she didn't want to leave him.

'Yes. Looking forward to it. I'll watch you along the path now and be careful because it'll be icy.'

Grace turned then and walked away, an ache growing in her chest because she had to leave him. She'd see him again in the morning and that was something to look forward to. She just felt like an idiot for how she'd reacted about the key and hoped that she hadn't hurt Oli's feelings at all.

As she trudged back to Rosehip Cottage, a cold wind whipped around her legs and made her unsteady on the frosty ground. Then, as if the heavens had suddenly opened, snowflakes came swirling down, thick and soft, and soon the ground behind her was covered in white, as Christmas Eve dwindled and made way for Christmas Day.

Chapter 22

There was only one thing to do when she knew she'd be unable to sleep.

Write.

Grace needed to lose herself in a fictional world.

She quietly let herself into Rosehip Cottage – because her parents were evidently already in bed – made a large mug of tea, carried it upstairs to her bedroom and switched her laptop on. She changed into her fleecy pyjamas, pulled on a comfy but stretched old sweater, and climbed into bed.

After selecting some music on her laptop, she plugged in her earphones and began to type.

Grace picked up her tea to find it was cold. She checked her mobile and found that over an hour had passed. It was like that when she was writing, time lost all meaning and she forgot to eat or drink when she was immersed in a story. Her phone buzzed and when she checked the screen, she saw that she had five missed calls from Oli within the last ten minutes. She tugged the earphones out and checked her messages. Oli again, asking her to call him: ASAP.

What did he want?

Just then there was a pounding on the door that echoed through the hallway. Grace's heart leapt into her throat.

Something was wrong, and she had a terrible feeling that it either involved the children or Hope.

She hurried down the stairs, followed by Simon's shouts to be careful and let him answer the door first. Grace switched on the porch light, then flung the door open. She knew who it would be.

'Grace!'

In the glow from the porch light, his face was ashen, his eyes dark hollows, his jaw set as if he was in great pain.

'Oli, what is it?'

'I can't stay... I have to get back... I have Amy in the car but she's asleep. I carried her out of bed, but Hope is still in the cottage and I don't want her left alone. She'll panic.'

Louise and Simon appeared beside Grace.

'Oli, what's wrong?' Louise asked as she pulled her dressing gown around her.

'It's Tom. He's missing.'

'No!' Grace's panic rose like acid in her throat. 'How... why... when?'

'Not long, I don't think, but I need to look for him. I phoned my father and he's on his way but I have to go look for my little boy.'

'Simon and I will take Amy back to yours, Oli,' Louise said. 'You and Grace go and find Tom.'

Oli nodded, clearly too distressed for politeness or formalities. Simon followed him out to his car and carried the drowsy Amy into Rosehip Cottage. Oli handed his house keys to Louise while Grace raced upstairs and quickly dressed, then came back down, pulled her boots and coat on and tugged a hat over her hair.

As Grace hurried out to Oli's Land Rover, she asked, 'Where might he have gone?'

'I'm not sure. I searched the garden and the surgery car park but he wasn't there. I couldn't find any tracks because the snow is so heavy.' He started the engine then negotiated the vehicle out of the driveway and onto the main road.

'Did he take anything with him?'

'Yes...' Oli increased the speed of the windscreen wipers, but even then the snow was falling so heavy that visibility was poor. 'He took his little school rucksack, his pen torch that he always keeps by his bedside, his coat, hat and gloves. He never goes out alone but after you left, I was putting the rubbish out the back and he must have let himself out. I didn't hear the door but I was so lost in my thoughts. Grace I could lose my son because I was so wrapped up in thinking about you and me. How irresponsible am I to allow myself to become so self-absorbed?' He glanced at her, and she winced at the pain in his eyes that was highlighted by the glare of the headlights on the snow.

'Oli, you're not at all self-absorbed. You're the least selfish person I know and you always put the children first. This isn't your fault. Now don't worry... we'll find him.'

She gripped the seat, as the vehicle trundled up the lane, trying to sound far more certain than she felt. Oli couldn't lose Tom and neither could she. The adorable little boy, with his blond hair, sweet smile and his trusting soft brown eyes, was such an angel and the thought of any harm coming to him would break her too.

'Oli... why do you think he went?'

'I have no idea. Unless…' He thumped the steering wheel. 'He must have heard us talking. When he went to the toilet. He's very fond of you and perhaps he thought we were arguing when you said you had to return to Cardiff.'

'Poor Tom.'

Grace rubbed her chest where the pain was growing by the minute.

'I phoned my father and Maxine is ringing around the village, so I said I'd drive around to see if I could spot him. It's freezing out there and that little torch of his won't help him to see much.'

'He'll be okay.'

Grace hoped that if she repeated the words that they'd be true.

'I couldn't cope if I lost him or Amy, Grace. It would finish me off.'

'You won't lose him, Oli.' Grace leaned over and squeezed his arm.

A buzzing sounded from within the vehicle and Grace pulled her mobile from her pocket. 'It's not mine.'

Oli handed her his mobile and she swiped the screen to answer it.

'Hello?'

A deep voice on the other end asked her to switch the speakerphone on.

'Oli?'

'Yes… I'm here, Dad.'

'I've tried everyone we know and no one's seen him but the village is setting up a search party as we speak.'

'That's great.'

'Oh… hold on… Maxine is waving at me.'

243

Oli and Grace listened as Maxine spoke urgently in the background.

'Oli? You hear that?'

'Not really, Dad.'

'Neil Burton rang. He tried your mobile but couldn't get through. He was checking all his outbuildings, making sure the animals were settled with this snow coming in and he said one of his dogs was fussing around outside the old stable in the field nearest to the woods.'

'A stable?'

'Yes. He's investigating as we speak but might be worth a look? I'll keep trying here.'

'Thanks, Dad!' Oli glanced at Grace. 'Let's get up there.'

The Land Rover's four-wheel drive carried them through the snow and soon they arrived at Foxglove Farm. Oli jumped out to open the gate then drove them in before closing the gate behind them.

He drove along the dirt path that was barely visible now and around to the field near the woods that bordered the farm.

Neil Burton was there already, his own Land Rover parked up so the headlights shone on the barn. His collie was sat in front of the barn barking and Neil waved Oli and Grace forward. Oli jumped out without even taking the key from the ignition.

'Oli, you might want to take a look in there.'

Oli paused. 'Is he…'

'He's okay, but I didn't want to startle him. He's snuggled up in the straw next to the donkeys. Soft old girls they are and he's at the rear of their stable.'

'He must have marched up here to get here so quickly.' Oli looked at Grace. 'He's only got little legs.'

'Probably got lost, Oli, and ended up cutting through the woods by Mary's place then across the field. Any idea where he was heading?' Neil asked.

'Out of the village it seems.' Oli shook his head. 'I'll go and speak to him.'

Grace nodded.

'Come with me?'

Oli held out his hand and she took it, then they went into the stable together.

Inside, it was warm and dry. The smells of hay and animals were strong but not unpleasant. Neil had hung an LED lantern from a beam and it gave the stable a warm golden glow.

They spoke softly to the two donkeys, who stamped their feet and watched them curiously as they went to the very back of the stable where Tom was curled up in the straw. His face was relaxed, his skin the colour of peaches and cream. Grace was so relieved to see him that she had to stop herself gathering him up in her arms and hugging him tight.

Oli knelt down in the straw.

'Tom?'

The little boy's eyelashes fluttered.

'Tom? It's Daddy.'

Tom blinked and sat up then peered around him.

'Daddy? How did you get here?'

'You ran away, Tom. We came looking for you.'

Tom peered at Grace.

'Grace, you didn't leave.'

'No, of course not. Why would I?'

'I heard you say to Daddy that you were going away.'

He rubbed his eyes and yawned.

'Tom, were you going to leave me and Amy?' Oli asked.

'No, Daddy, but I was going to see if I could find Santa tonight to ask him to make my wish come true. He said he would try, so I wanted to remind him. You said he never comes to the house when we're still awake, so I thought I'd go and look for him.'

'You must never ever wander off like that, Tom. If you're worried you must speak to me and I'll do what I can to help you. But you could have...' Oli's voice cracked and he hung his head. Grace rubbed his back gently.

'What your daddy means, Tom, is that you could have been hurt. It's dangerous for a little boy to be out on his own.'

Tom nodded.

'But you're okay, so you must just promise never to run off again.'

'Are you staying now, Grace?' His big brown eyes held hers and her heart melted.

'Yes, I'm staying, Tom.' She opened her arms, and he got up and ran into them. She hugged him tight and he pressed his soft cheek against hers, and she knew in that moment that she meant what she'd said.

She would stay in Conwenna Cove. Whatever happened between her and Oli, she would make a life in the pretty Cornish village and she would be here for Tom and for Amy, for as long as they needed her. She and Oli had been worried about Amy, but it seemed that Tom was going through his own emotional journey too. He'd seemed so accepting of Grace and neither she nor

Oli had thought that Tom might also be afraid of losing her. So afraid that he'd run off in the night alone, looking for Santa so he could ask him to grant his Christmas wish.

'I'll be here, Tom. I'm not just your daddy's friend, I'm your friend too.'

'And Amy's?'

'Yes, and Amy's.'

'Then my Christmas wish has almost come true.' Tom leaned back and smiled at her, his tiny white teeth glinting in the light from the lantern.

Grace felt a hand on her back and she turned to find Oli gazing at her, his eyes shining, his expression one of hope. She shuffled around so that Tom was closer to Oli then he wrapped his arms around them both and they stayed that way for some time.

Holding on. Tight. Together.

Chapter 23

Back at Oli's cottage, after everyone else had gone, Amy and Tom were tucked up safely in bed. Grace was in the lounge sitting on the floor next to Hope, who sighed at intervals to express her pleasure because Grace was stroking her belly.

Oli appeared in the doorway.

'It was really kind of your parents to invite us all for lunch tomorrow, including my father and Maxine.'

'It will be lovely to have everyone together.'

'It's a good thing too. Seeing as how I don't have anything to cook now.'

'What?'

He held up an empty foil tray.

'After you left, I got the turkey crown out of the fridge to prepare it for tomorrow, but when I checked on the children and found Tom gone, I forgot about it.'

'Where did it go?' Grace frowned.

Oli pointed at Hope, who rubbed a paw over her face.

'No! She couldn't have eaten a whole crown of turkey?'

Oli nodded. 'You'd be surprised what greyhounds can put away.'

'But it was raw, wasn't it?'

He nodded, again. 'Doesn't bother them. Raw meat is more natural for them anyway.'

'Oh, Hope. And there we were thinking you needed help going out to the toilet.'

Oli laughed. 'She's obviously making better progress than we thought. It's my fault for leaving the meat out.'

Grace ran her hand over Hope's belly. 'I thought it felt full, you greedy girl.'

Hope licked her lips.

'Well, you can have a proper Christmas dinner tomorrow, Hope. One of my Dad's specials.'

Hope let out a long groan.

'I suppose I should go.' Grace peered at the window where the curtains were open and where snowflakes still drifted down from the sky, illuminated by the silvery moonlight.

'Don't leave. You'd just as well stay now,' Oli said.

'Okay then. Your sofa is quite comfy. Can I go and check on Tom before I go to sleep?'

'Of course. I'll come with you.'

Upstairs, they sneaked into Tom's room and found him fast asleep. In the gentle glow from his nightlight, Grace could see his eyelids flickering as he dreamt.

'He's so peaceful now,' she whispered.

'He just wanted to know you'd stay in Conwenna.'

Grace nodded then she sat on the floor next to the bed, and watched as Tom's chest moved up and down.

'I used to do that all the time when they were babies,' Oli said. 'Just to know they were okay.'

'I would have been the same if I'd had children of my own.'

'Grace...'

She reached out and ran a hand down Oli's cheek. 'Don't worry about anything now. It's late and we're tired.

Let's enjoy Christmas and leave the more serious talks for later.'

'Okay. But you are staying?'

'I'll need to go back to Cardiff and arrange to have my belongings moved to Conwenna, but yes… I'll be here.'

He leant forwards and kissed her forehead, then pulled her into his arms and hugged her tight. And in that moment, she knew that she was exactly where she wanted to be and she had no intention of going anywhere. Ever.

—

'Wake up! Wake up!'

Grace was jolted from sleep by shouting and the sound of footsteps thundering around her. She opened her eyes and met Oli's. He looked as exhausted and confused as she felt.

She pushed herself upwards and realized that she was on Tom's bedroom floor. She'd fallen asleep there next to Oli, but judging from the fact that there was only pale grey light filtering through the curtains into the bedroom, they hadn't been asleep for long. Her whole body ached from lying on the floorboards and she was cold and stiff.

'Morning,' Oli said as he yawned and stretched.

'Is it?' Grace smiled. 'I'm not sure.'

'Grace… Come on, let's go and see if Santa's been!' Tom tugged at her hand.

'Tom, hold on!' Oli shook his head. 'Let Grace come round a bit.'

'Morning.' Amy danced into the room. 'It's Christmas!'

'Come on,' Grace said to Oli. 'I don't think they can wait.'

'I think you're right.'

They got up and went down stairs behind the children. At the lounge doorway, Tom paused. He turned to Grace and gave her a big smile.

'I'm so excited.'

'I know.'

Amy and Tom rushed into the lounge, and Grace and Oli followed them. Grace's own stomach was tight with excitement; Tom's enthusiasm was infectious.

Oli pulled Grace onto the sofa, and they sat and watched as Amy and Tom tore through the wrapping paper on their piles of gifts. Tom was so excited that he was trembling.

Everything that he opened, he held it up for Grace and his father to see, and they oohed and aahhed appropriately. When the lounge was a mess of Christmas paper and envelopes, and Hope was gazing at Grace in a way that suggested she was hungry, Oli went and grabbed some bin bags and started to tidy up.

Grace fed Hope then let her out into the garden. As the greyhound wandered around, Grace stood at the French doors watching her. Everything outside was white, from the grass to the path, to the shed and the trees behind, and tiny paw prints showed where Hope had been. Although the snow had stopped falling, the morning had the muffled effect that came with heavy snowfall. She breathed deeply and enjoyed the sensation of the cold air as it filled her lungs; the smell of freshly fallen snow that always seemed so clean and crisp, as if everything had been cleansed.

'Time for a special festive breakfast, Grace?' Oli was right behind her, his breath warm as it tickled the back of her neck.

'What have you got in mind?' She turned and met his eyes.

'Well, what I have in mind is impossible right now...' he winked at her, 'but smoked salmon and scrambled eggs will have to do.'

'I guess it'll come a close second.' She leant forwards and gently kissed him.

They sat at the table twenty minutes later, and Oli popped the cork on a bottle of champagne while Grace poured fresh orange juice into the children's glasses. Then they tucked into the tender salmon and fluffy yellow eggs that Oli had prepared.

As the children chattered about their gifts and their plans for the holidays and Oli filled her glass as soon as it was empty, Grace's chest filled with happiness. There had been ups and downs over the past few weeks, but meeting Oli and his children had been the best thing that had happened to her in ages. Yes, it was scary, and yes, it was hard to let go of her fears and to let them all into her heart, but it also felt so damned good.

For the first time in years, Grace was actually living, not just existing as she had come to believe was okay. Looking back, it hadn't been enough, but after losing Sam, she hadn't wanted to feel such intense agonizing loss again. But by denying herself the right to feel, she had denied herself the right to a full and colourful life with all the joy that came from caring about other people.

After breakfast, they all showered and dressed – Oli and the children in smart Christmas outfits and Grace in the clothes she'd worn the previous evening. But she knew she could change when she got back to Rosehip Cottage.

They wrapped up warm in coats, hats and gloves. Grace put Hope's new warm winter fleece on her that Oli had bought for the greyhound at Amy's instruction. She'd seen it on Amazon and insisted that he ordered it the previous week and he'd agreed that it was a good idea.

Then they trudged through the snow to Louise and Simon's house, their breath like smoke in the air and their noses tingling with the cold. Grace led Hope along the least snowy places so her legs wouldn't get too chilly. She'd already sent a text ahead to tell her mother to get a big fluffy towel ready to dry Hope's feet when they arrived.

Louise opened the door as they walked along the driveway and ushered them inside. The house smelt of roasting turkey, potatoes and all sorts of delicious side dishes, and when they entered the kitchen, Simon pressed glasses of champagne into their hands.

"We've already had a bottle with breakfast,' Grace told her father, but he shook his head.

'It's Christmas Day, Grace. And we've plenty to celebrate this year.'

Amy and Tom knelt by the box in the corner and played with the kittens while their mother wound herself around Simon's legs, almost tripping him up on several occasions. Simon refused all offers of help, so Grace was able to enjoy sitting with Oli and her mother and watching as Hope lay down next to the children.

'She seems okay with the cats.'

Oli nodded. 'Might well have lived with some before. I was a bit apprehensive but she did have time to get used to being in the same room as them at the surgery, so they're not completely strange to her. But, yes, I do think that she's lived with other animals. We should keep an eye on her when she's around the kittens but from what I've seen so far, there's no need to worry.'

'She only likes turkey crowns.' Grace giggled.

'Yes...' Oli shook his head. 'That'll teach me not to leave food where she can reach it.'

'Well, she can have some of your father's cooking,' Louise said, 'and I'm sure that'll stop her feeling the need to scrounge.'

'I wouldn't be so sure about that.' Oli raised an eyebrow. 'It's learnt behaviour and goes back to how they grow up. If she wasn't fed enough or had to search for her own food, then she's in the habit and it could take a while for that to change. If it ever will.'

'Oh, poor Hope.' Grace shook her head. 'I hate to think of her suffering.'

'That part of her life is over, Grace. Everything is going to be much better for her from now on.'

When Paul and Maxine arrived, Simon gave them flutes of champagne too. Christmas music filled the house, blaring from the TV in the lounge and the radio in the kitchen, and even better was the laughter from the adults and the children. Grace thought she might burst from smiling so much. It was wonderful to have so many people around on Christmas Day, and she had to admit that the children made it extra special.

Dinner was a delightful affair, with Simon insisting that they all pulled crackers and wore the party hats, then Amy and Tom told the cheesy jokes that came from the crackers. They tucked into the piles of succulent turkey, fluffy roast potatoes, cauliflower and broccoli cheese, buttered carrots and creamy mashed swede and parsnip. Dessert was homemade Christmas pudding drenched in fine French brandy or hazelnut chocolate torte with thick clotted cream.

'Simon and Louise, thank you so much for yet another fantastic dinner.' Oli rubbed his full stomach.

'It's our pleasure again,' Simon said, waving off the compliment.

'It really was delicious.' Paul raised his glass. 'We owe the chef a toast.'

'To Simon, but also to Louise and Grace,' Maxine said as she raised her glass. 'Welcome to Conwenna.'

'Cheers!' was repeated around the table then glasses were topped up again.

'Shall we go through to the lounge and open the rest of the presents now?' Louise asked.

'More presents?' Tom's eyes widened.

'Yes, Tom. You didn't think we wouldn't have anything for you did you?'

'Amy did you hear that?'

'Yes, Tom, of course I did. Thank you, Louise and Simon, it's very kind of you.'

'Do you want some help tidying up?' Oli asked.

'Not yet. Leave it until later. I don't know about you, but I'm a bit full for dish duty yet.' Simon patted his shirt front.

They got up and made their way through to the lounge. Louise turned up the TV and Christmas hits filled the room. The fire was already lit and it filled the room with a comfortable warmth, fragranced with pine and rosemary. Around the fireplace, Louise had hung holly and mistletoe, and Tom went over and pointed at it.

'What's this?'

'Holly,' Grace said.

'No, not that one… this.' He pointed again.

'That's mistletoe,' Louise replied. 'It's traditional to kiss under it.'

Tom frowned then his expression changed and he pulled a sprig of mistletoe from the rest.

'Tom! Don't ruin Louise's decorations.' Oli shook his head.

'It's all right, Oli. He can take some.' Louise sank onto one of the sofas and smiled at Tom.

Grace gulped as she saw Tom approaching her and Oli where they were sitting on the sofa. He had mischief in his eyes and his tongue was poking from the corner of his mouth as he concentrated.

'Daddy…'

'Yes, Tom.'

'Now you have to kiss Grace.'

'Sorry?'

'Kiss Grace.'

'Oh… Tom, don't be silly. It's an old myth that's all.'

Tom shook his head. 'Louise said.'

Oli turned to Grace as Tom raised the mistletoe over their heads, his small arm stretched as far as it would go.

'Kiss! Kiss! Kiss!' Tom shouted, then Amy joined in, 'Kiss! Kiss! Kiss!'

Oli leant closer to Grace. 'I guess we don't have a choice.'

'I'd hate to go against tradition.'

She moved closer to Oli and he slid his hand around the back of her neck then lowered his mouth to meet hers. His lips were soft and tasted of champagne and his breath was warm against her skin.

When they parted, Grace had to blink rapidly to focus again. The effect of Oli's kiss was overwhelming.

'There, that's better,' Tom said as he put the mistletoe on the table. 'Now Daddy and Grace will get married and she can live with us.'

He skipped over to the Christmas tree where Louise was waiting and sat down on the floor there with Amy.

Oli took hold of Grace's hand and squeezed it. 'I've heard worse plans, you know.'

'Really?'

He shrugged. 'It's something to think about anyway.'

Grace took a deep breath and tried to compose herself. Oli was actually suggesting that they consider getting married and become a family. It was almost too good to believe. But he'd said it and his children seemed comfortable with the idea, and she was staying in Conwenna now.

Could it really happen?

–

Amy and Tom opened the gifts from Louise and Simon, and thanked them effusively for every one. Then it was time for the gifts from Grace.

Amy opened the scarf with the stars on it and immediately wrapped it around her neck. Grace had also picked up a small bottle of perfume for Amy and some lip gloss, and Amy sprayed herself with the perfume then slicked on some of the peach gloss.

'It suits you, Amy,' Grace said.

'Thank you, Grace, I love them.'

Tom held his gift up and turned it over in his hands.

'Aren't you going to open it?' Oli asked him.

'I want to, Daddy, but I'm nervous.'

'Why are you nervous? You love opening presents.'

'I do but… I made a wish on the cake at Amy's birthday and I asked Santa for the same wish. If I open this then perhaps my wish won't come true and Grace won't be my new mummy.' His eyes widened. 'Ooops.'

Grace glanced at Oli but he was smiling.

'Is that what you wished for, Tom?'

The little boy nodded. 'But I'm not supposed to say anything.'

'It's okay. I'm sure no one knows. Now open your gift from Grace.'

Tom nodded then unwrapped the box containing the castle.

'Wow! Just what I always wanted.'

'I'm so glad you like it.' Grace smiled.

'Will you build it with me?'

'Of course. It'll give us something to do over the holidays.'

'Look, Amy, we can play with this… and there's animals to go inside it.'

'You've made one little boy and girl very happy indeed.' Oli held her gaze. 'And you make me very happy too.'

'I'm glad. This has been a lovely Christmas… well, except for Tom going missing and that worked out all right in the end, so I need to thank you too.'

'This is for you, Grace.' Louise handed her a present from under the tree.

'There's one there for Oli too, Mum.'

'Yes, here it is.' Louise handed Oli the gift.

'Bet you can't guess what it is.' Grace pointed at the bottle-shaped gift.

'No idea…' Oli frowned. He tore away the wrapping paper. 'Mead, eh? Thank you, Grace. Never had this, but heard it's good with cheese.'

'That's what it says on the bottle.'

'Well, you'll have to promise to enjoy it with me.'

'Okay.'

'Now open yours.'

Grace carefully unwrapped the small box then lifted the lid. Inside was a small silver charm in the shape of a figure eight.

'It's the eternity symbol,' Oli explained. 'Just so that you remember that a part of you will always be in Conwenna Cove and it will also always be with you.'

She ran her finger over the charm. 'It's beautiful.'

'You can read more into its significance if you wish,' Oli whispered. 'I'd like you to. And there's something here to go with it.'

He gave her another small box.

'Oli, you shouldn't have.'

'I wanted to. Besides, when you open it you'll understand.'

Inside was a silver charm bracelet.

'You need a charm bracelet to put the charms on.'

'I have one for you too!' Tom jumped up and ran over to her.

'Tom, it's supposed to be secret.' Amy shook her head.

'Not now it's not.'

Tom handed Grace a box and when she lifted the lid, inside was a small silver greyhound.

'So you can always remember Hope and how she chose you.' Tom grinned.

'Here you are, Grace.' Amy passed her a box. 'This one is because you're my friend.'

'Thank you.' Grace opened the box and found a silver heart with *friends forever* engraved on it. 'Oh…' Her vision blurred and she covered her face with her hands.

'Don't be sad, Grace, it's a happy time.' Tom pulled her hands away from her face.

'Right, now that's all the gifts exchanged, shall we play some games?' Simon asked.

'Yes please!' Tom jumped up and down on the spot causing everyone to laugh.

Oli took the charm bracelet from Grace then fixed the charms on it and fastened it around her wrist.

'I'll never take this off.'

'Well… you might want to when you shower, but apart from that, don't. It links us all together.'

He glanced at the children, but they were helping Louise and Simon to get the boxes of games out of a cupboard in the corner, so he quickly kissed Grace's cheek.

'Merry Christmas, Grace.'

Chapter 24

'Are you ready for this?' Grace asked her mum and dad for the fiftieth time that morning.

'Yes, Grace. I'm ready.' Louise nodded, but her face was pale and she had shadows under her eyes as if she hadn't slept a wink.

'Dad?'

Simon wrapped an arm around his wife.

'It's time, Grace. We moved here to make the most of life and this is something we've needed to do for a long while, but the time just never seemed quite right. I'm sure Sam would want this.'

Grace nodded. 'Come on then.'

She pulled on her coat and hat, slid her hands into her gloves then stuffed her feet into her boots. When she opened the front door, an icy wind whipped in around their legs.

'Hope?' she called and the greyhound appeared in the hallway. 'You coming?'

The dog jogged to her side, already wrapped up warm in the colourful fleece Oli had bought her with its matching snood from Maxine.

They set out down the driveway then walked to the cliffs overlooking the cove. It was a bright morning and the sun was visible behind the cloud covering, a white-hot

261

ball shielded by a fluffy screen. They made their way carefully down the path to the cove, Grace keeping a tight hold on Hope's lead, and Simon holding onto his wife.

When they reached the sand it was deserted. The tide was on its way out so they walked right up to where the waves gently lapped the shore.

'Okay, girls.' Simon slid an arm around each of them. 'Let's say goodbye to our boy.'

Louise was holding the urn containing Sam's ashes close to her chest. She raised it and kissed it gently, then handed it to Simon. 'You do it.'

'Sam, we loved you and we still love you. We will always love you. But keeping you in this... urn... isn't what you'd have wanted. Today we're releasing you, so you can roam the seas, travel to new places and see all the things you never had a chance to see when you were alive.'

Louise grabbed Grace's hand.

'Goodbye my boy,' Simon said, his voice breaking on the final word.

'Goodbye, Sam,' Grace said, as her father gently lowered the urn and scattered her brother's ashes onto the water.

They watched silently, as the waves carried Sam away, then Grace opened her arms as her mother broke down.

'He's at peace now, Mum, and he'll be all around us. In the water, the air, the trees, the grass, the sand...' Her own throat ached with the effort of holding her tears back. Next to her Hope whined, clearly concerned, so Grace gave her a gentle stroke.

'That was difficult but also kind of liberating. Sam would have been glad to set off like that. Just think of all the places he'll go now.'

Simon hugged his wife until she stopped crying.

'Shall we go and get a warm drink?' he asked.

'I'll catch you up,' Grace said. 'Take Hope with you so she doesn't get too cold.'

Simon took Hope's lead and Grace kissed her head then turned back to the waves as her parents walked away. She needed a moment to catch her breath, to process what they'd just done and to let go of the pain in her heart.

The past week had been wonderful. She'd spent it with Oli and the children, as well as with her parents. They'd played games, eaten lots of delicious meals and she'd got to know Amy and Tom even better. Hope was recovering well, and the antibiotics and good food she'd been given had aided her progress. She was like Grace's shadow, following her around and even sleeping in her room, and Grace already loved the dog, just as she loved Oli and his children.

Her parents had discussed scattering Sam's ashes on New Year's Eve as a way of starting the new year afresh. They hadn't wanted to leave him in Cardiff and had kept his ashes all this time, waiting until they found the right place to let him go. The cove was perfect and Grace knew he'd have been happy to drift away on the sea. He'd always wanted to travel, but had known his parents were terrified of the impact it could have on his health, so he'd kept his dreams between him and Grace. She knew Louise and Simon had regrets about how they'd handled Sam's care, and they'd shared their sadness with her and their suspicions that they'd held their son back because of their own fears. Grace had tried to comfort them by telling them Sam had been an adult and he could have gone away if he'd chosen to do so. But he hadn't, because he'd loved them and wanted to be with them for as long as he could. Travelling could have been a good thing for him, but Grace kept these thoughts to herself. Hindsight could lead to more pain and she didn't want her parents to suffer any more than they already had. Sam had loved them and they had loved him and that was all that really mattered in the end.

'Grace?'

She turned to find Oli standing beside her.

'How are you feeling?'

She sniffed. 'It's a strange one, that's for sure. But I'm glad they've let him go now and I know he would be too.'

Oli took her hand and raised it to his lips then slipped her glove down and kissed her palm. His tenderness sent shivers of delight throughout her body and warmed her right through.

'Oli… will you tell me how you're feeling?'

He nodded. 'Meeting you a few weeks ago was a shock. I never expected to ever find a woman I could want to be with again. I grieved so hard for Linda and it was something I thought I'd never get over. Then I saw you in the café that day with your bright red hair and lively eyes, your cute freckles and gorgeous curves and you just took my breath away.'

She smiled at his compliments.

'Then I got to know you and I realized that I'd been completely shut down. You started to open me up, to get to me, and in spite of my fears about the children and whether it was too soon for us to be together, I couldn't help myself. I just wanted to be with you. You're wonderful, Grace, and I love you.'

'You love me?'

'I've almost said as much, haven't I? It's just the words sometimes seem inadequate for what I'm actually feeling. But I do. I love you Grace and I want to spend the rest of my life with you. So stay in Conwenna with Hope, Amy and Tom and me. The thought of life without you now is too bleak to contemplate.'

She nodded, taking in the way his eyes roamed her face and how good his fingers felt laced between hers.

'What about Linda, though? I'd hate for you to turn around in a few months' time and compare me to her. I've thought a lot about this over the past week. She'll always be perfect in your eyes and in the children's, and I can't compete with a… a dead woman.'

'There's no competition here at all, Grace. I loved Linda but she wasn't perfect. No one is. Amy has memories and I'll always do my best to keep them alive for her. As for Tom, he was a lot younger, but I will do what I can to help him remember her too, because that's my duty as their father. Linda will always be their mum. She loved them deeply and I don't want them to forget that. I won't let them forget that. But we have a future ahead of us and my children are crazy about you. Amy and Tom want and need you around now, Grace. Amy hasn't taken off that scarf you bought her and I even found it on her pillow next to her last night.'

Grace blinked hard. 'That's so sweet. I love them too.'

'I'm not saying that life with two children will be easy, because it certainly won't, but I promise there'll be many good times and that we'll have fun. We'll have ups and downs, but isn't that called living?'

Grace nodded. 'I want ups and downs. I don't want to live without feeling any more, Oli.'

'So stay. Live with us. See what the future brings.'

'I will.'

'Are you sad at the thought of… leaving anyone behind in Cardiff?'

'There is no one.'

'No friends?'

She shook her head. 'Growing up, I focused on my family. Sam was often unwell and I spent as much time as possible with him, reading to him, playing cards with him and watching movies with him. We'd talk for hours. He was my brother, but he was also my best friend. I know lots of siblings don't get on but we did. Whether it was because we knew he wouldn't have long or not, I don't know, but we were so close.'

'He was lucky to have you.'

'Sometimes I get angry, you know? At Cystic Fibrosis. My parents do too and they've carried so much guilt about it. They were both carriers and after they had Sam and he was diagnosed, they decided not to have another child in case it happened again. They loved and adored Sam but were terrified of losing him. Then I came along in spite of their decision.'

'As if you were meant to exist.'

'That's what Sam always said. I made my own way into the world despite everything that should have prevented it.'

'So you could have been ill too?'

'Yes. There was a one in four chance. But I was clear. I could be a carrier, which is why I'll never have children, but I don't actually have it.'

'Did you feel guilty about that?'

'Every day of my life. It seemed so unfair that Sam had it and I didn't.'

'Did he ever say that?'

'Once. Not to me but to my mum and I overheard him. He was feeling particularly poorly on his sixteenth birthday and he said that life was cruel. He asked her why it was him who was ill, and why he couldn't have just one day where he didn't have to suffer. But as far as I know, he never said it again. He'd have known how much that would have hurt them and how bad they felt anyway.'

'That's a lot for you to carry around with you, especially when you were growing up.'

'But I always felt that I could carry it because I wasn't the one who was suffering. I didn't feel sorry for myself because that would have been awful... how could I pity myself when my brother was the one who was ill?'

'I felt guilty after Linda was diagnosed with cancer. She was pregnant and I asked myself a million times why it couldn't have been me. I could have started treatment right away and she could have lived. But she refused treatment, in spite of my encouragement. She wouldn't risk the baby. I pressed her, said that we could have more children and I'd never be able to replace her, but she refused. And now... when I look at Tom, I'm so glad. I can't believe I ever suggested that he wasn't as important as her because those children are my world.'

'Oli, we've both carried guilt and grief around for so long.'

'The counselling helped a bit, but letting go is hard.'

'It is harder to forgive yourself than it is to forgive someone else. But really, neither of us is to blame.'

He shook his head.

'You know… Sam could have had a transplant but he refused it. He said he was tired of fighting, and couldn't bear to go through all that if it just ended up with him not getting any better. I tried to persuade him to have the operation when a donor came up but he wouldn't even consider it.'

'So, he was as stubborn as Linda in that respect.'

'Yes, even though it was for different reasons.'

'Did you ever… fall in love then?'

'No. There was a guy… a while back. I'd known him from school and we went on a few dates but I couldn't really get into it, if that makes sense? I mean… I had a few… flings, but never anything serious because I was terrified that they'd want more. And I couldn't give them more.'

'And that guy?'

'He proposed. Said he'd always fancied me and wanted to approach me. Although I think he was lying, because I didn't remember him paying me any attention in school. To be honest, I think he liked the fact that I was an author and he fancied himself as a kept man.'

'So he proposed?'

'It was ridiculous. We'd been on about six dates, then he took me to a restaurant and pulled out a ring.'

Oli grimaced.

'I know. He gave me this spiel about how he adored me and how I was his perfect woman and blah blah…'

'Right. So proposals turn you off.'

'His did because I'm sure he was just after my money. He cottoned onto the fact that I was earning and he wasn't. I think he saw me as a vulnerable woman who'd make a great meal ticket.'

'Give me his address and I'll go round there.'

Grace laughed. 'He's really not worth it. Besides, two weeks later he was with another woman, so I don't think I broke his heart.'

'I can't stand to think of anyone coming after you like that.'

'He was harmless enough. My parents were a bit disappointed as they hoped he might be the one, but they didn't know him very well, and if they had, they'd have warned me off him.'

'So he bit the dust then?'

'Yes. I walked right out of that restaurant and didn't look back.'

Grace moved closer to him and wrapped her arms around his waist.

'Oli… I love you.'

He lowered his head and kissed her gently.

Two seagulls screeched overhead and a boat out on the water honked its horn. The sea breeze washed over them, sharp and briny, a reminder of where they were, and Grace's heart soared.

'I also love it here.'

'I love having you here.'

'Well, in that case, I'm never going to leave.'

Oli lifted her up then and squeezed her so tight, she gasped.

'Good. Because, Grace Phillips, I'm never letting you go.'

Epilogue

Grace finished typing a sentence, saved the document then closed it. She stood up and stretched. Another book was finished and ready for Louise to check before she sent it to her agent.

There was an enormous sense of satisfaction from finishing a book, even when she knew it would need to go through several rounds of edits and copyedits. It was like the first rung on a ladder, a step in the right direction, and Grace knew that she could enjoy the summer holidays with her family without worrying about meeting her September deadline.

She looked around her writing room and smiled. Oli had enlisted Simon's help to build Grace a writing space in the pretty cottage garden. It was, essentially, a wooden summer house, with its circular floor and French doors that overlooked the garden, but they'd built floor to ceiling shelves inside it to cover the walls, bought a beautiful antique writing desk complete with a comfortable chair, and even added a squishy sofa, so that Grace could read if she tired of writing and wanted some peace and quiet. Of course, the sofa was occupied most of the time by Hope – as it was now – the faithful greyhound was never far from Grace's side.

Hope had made a good recovery and had turned out to be the sweetest, most gentle hound. Oli had cautioned that she might need some rehabilitation, but Hope had responded so well to living with Grace and her parents, that Neil and Elena had said it wouldn't make sense to take her back to the sanctuary. Besides, Oli was experienced with rescue dogs and he was on hand for any issues they might face with Hope, but none had arisen. She still occasionally stole food from the kitchen, even though she was well fed, but they all learnt to accept that it was a throwback to the life she'd lived before. And she was a friendly, happy dog. Hope needed to know exactly where Grace was at all times, but Grace knew that she wouldn't want to leave Hope for an extended period of time anyway. She also knew that her parents would be happy to dog sit, so Hope would never be left completely alone and they wouldn't need to worry over separation anxiety, as it seemed that Simon was her second favourite person.

The doors to the summer house were wide open and the summer breeze filled the space, carrying the beautiful scents of the roses that climbed the exterior of the summer house, as well as the sweetness of the honeysuckle that grew on the pergola just outside the cottage. Everything was in full bloom: Grace and Oli had worked hard that spring to create a garden that they could enjoy together. They'd also bought some new furniture for the cottage that they'd chosen together, and put everything of Linda's that the children had wanted to keep into a local storage facility. It was important, they'd agreed, that Amy and Tom keep everything of Linda's that they wanted to, and even though Tom was still a bit young, they'd put some things aside for him just in case.

Grace had moved in with them in the spring. She'd stayed at the cottage a few times a week, while they all got to know one another properly, and soon it had seemed the natural next step for Grace to move in. She'd returned to Cardiff twice with her parents to collect her belongings and to sign off on her rental flat, but she'd been so glad that she wasn't going back there to stay permanently. Her old flat in the Welsh capital seemed so small and clinical, not at all like the cottages in Conwenna Cove that were full of character and life. She knew that if she'd returned to Cardiff to live, she'd have spent her life wondering *what if* . . . and that thought was unbearable when she now knew how much she could have. It wasn't that she didn't like the Welsh city, because she did and she'd always have fond memories of her childhood there, growing up with Sam, but she had nothing left there any more; her life was in Conwenna Cove, with Oli, Amy, Tom and Hope. As well as her parents who were thoroughly enjoying their time in the pretty coastal village.

Grace knew that being in Cornwall had helped her and her parents to heal. Letting go of Sam on New Year's Eve had been a big step for all of them, and she felt that he was finally at peace too. Knowing that he'd been sitting in that urn had unsettled her for a long time, but the thought that he was free, that his atoms were out on the sea carrying him to foreign climes, comforted her. He was being absorbed by the world around them and that meant that he'd always be close. And, of course, she'd always carry him in her heart.

She walked out into the garden and Hope leapt off the sofa and followed her.

'I guess the rest of the day is ours to do with as we please, Hope.'

The greyhound dropped into a bow, wagging her tail in wide arcs.

'Are you done now, Grace?'

Tom ran into the garden and stopped right in front of her.

'Yes, Tom, all done.'

'Can we go to the beach?'

She looked down at him and took in his big happy smile and warm brown eyes. Her little boy.

'Yes, Tom, we can. Have you got sun cream on?'

'Yes! Daddy covered me in so much that I was white.' He shivered and Grace smiled. Tom hated having sun cream on, to the extent that they sometimes had to pin him down and cover him with it as he wriggled and squirmed. It always ended up with them all laughing and covered in the sticky white sunblock.

'It's all rubbed in around your ears and the back of your neck?' Grace peered around him to check.

'Yes.'

'Promise?'

'Promise.'

'Okay, well grab your cap and your sunglasses and I'll go and get ready.'

Grace and Hope went into the cottage and she headed upstairs to change while Amy made sure that Hope had a drink.

'There you are!' Oli met Grace at the bedroom door and swept her into a hug. 'Book all done?'

'Yes. Such a relief. So now I'm all yours.'

'Hmmm. I like the sound of that.'

He kissed her softly and she melted against him.

'Hey, stop it. We have to get ready.'

'I've packed everything we need including the picnic, so you get you bathers on and we're good to go.'

Ten minutes later, Grace padded down the stairs to find her family waiting in the hallway, the three of them wearing baseball caps and sunglasses while Hope wore a bright pink bandana around her neck.

'Grace did you put sun cream on?' Tom asked, as he gazed up at her.

'I did.'

'And where's your hat?'

'On the peg.'

She reached for the floppy straw hat and put it on. 'Don't worry, Tom, I'm taking no chances.' As a redhead, she always covered herself in sunblock and wore a hat and glasses to protect herself from the sun.

'Have you got your swimming costume on?' Tom asked.

'Yes, it's under my dress.'

'Yay!'

Grace laughed. She'd always been a bit self-conscious about her body but having children was a great leveller. For one, she wanted Amy to grow up happy with herself and who she was, so Grace had to be a good role model. Secondly, there was Tom, with his infectious enthusiasm for life that meant that Grace had to take part in everything, and that included swimming in the sea. Then, of course, there was Oli's constant reassurance that he loved her and her figure, and that he found her incredibly beautiful. If he thought she was so lovely, then that was all that mattered. The combination had meant that she now lived life to the full, unhindered by self-consciousness, or by society's projections of female perfection. She had a family and she was loved for who she was. And that was something so precious that she never ever forgot to revel in it.

They headed out of the front garden and walked down to the cove, carefully negotiating their way down the path to the sand. When they got there, Simon and Louise were already all set up near the rock pools, with deck chairs, blankets and a barbecue smoking away. They also had a large cooler that Grace suspected contained food for the barbecue and plenty of drinks.

The sun was high in the sky, so she helped Oli to set up the two sun umbrellas they'd brought with them, then they did a quick top-up of the children's sun cream.

'Can I go in the sea, Daddy?' Tom asked.

'You certainly can. I'll come too. Grace?'

She looked at her parents who nodded. 'If Mum and Dad don't need any help?'

'Food won't be ready for a while so you go on, love,' Louise said.

'Amy, are you coming in?'

'Yes!' Amy stripped off her shorts and t-shirt and took Tom's hand while Grace removed her sundress and hat.

'Hope, are you coming in?' Grace asked the dog, but Hope was taking a lot of interest in what Simon was placing on the mini barbecue. 'I guess not. Keep an eye on her, Dad?'

'Of course. And I promise not to give her any sausages. Right, Hope?' He gave the dog an exaggerated wink.

'Come on, then.' Grace took Oli's hand and they ran down to the sea with the children.

As she stood at the water's edge and it lapped at her toes, she breathed deeply. The cove was so beautiful with its soft white sand surrounded by craggy grey cliffs. The waves lapped at the shore and seagulls cried overhead, while from all around her came the sounds of people enjoying their day. It wasn't yet high summer, so Conwenna hadn't been overrun with tourists, and even in peak season the cove always stayed quieter than other beaches along the coastline, as if it was a secret belonging to the locals. It meant that Grace and her family had enjoyed many days there together, in spring when the weather still called for layers and sometimes waterproofs and now in the heat of July, when a dip in the cooling water was very welcome.

Tom ran into the water first then Amy followed, and they both gasped as the cold water covered them.

'You're next.' Grace gave Oli a playful push.

'Oh, really?' Oli raised his eyebrows. 'I'm not going in alone.'

He turned and held out his arms.

'Come on.'

'No. I need to get acclimatized to it first. See.' She dipped her toes in the water and goosebumps rose all over her body.

'It's better to do it in one go. You know that by now.'

Oli shook his head then dived at her and scooped her up.

'Put me down!' Grace kicked her legs.

'Go on, Daddy, throw her in!' Tom shouted.

'No! Please don't, Oli.' Grace clung to his neck.

'No, Tom, I'm not that mean.' Oli kissed Grace's cheek. 'But we are going in.'

He lunged forwards and carried them both into the water until it reached his chest and covered Grace's body too.

'It's freezing!'

'You'll soon warm up.'

He gently released her and she swam around for a bit until her skin grew used to the water and it was refreshing rather than shocking. They played with the children, splashing one another and taking it in turns to help Tom to float on his back. He could already swim quite well, but Oli was keen for him to become more confident. He said it was important with them living so close to the sea,

'Are you hungry yet?' Oli asked Grace after they'd been in the water for about twenty minutes.

'Starving.'

'Kids, let's go and see what Simon's got for lunch shall we?'

They headed up the beach and towelled off, then eyed the amazing spread that Simon and Louise had prepared. There were warming, spiced Cajun chicken breasts, harissa sardines, whitefish lemongrass skewers, halloumi and mixed pepper pitta breads and a large wild rice and mixed bean salad. Grace ate enthusiastically; her appetite for good food enhanced by her swim and by the lovely fresh air of the cove. The children drank rose lemonade with their food, and Simon pulled out a bottle of pink champagne for the adults.

'What's the occasion, Dad?' Grace asked as she held out the plastic champagne flutes.

'Oh, you know, every day is an occasion, Grace.'

When their glasses were full, Oli raised his in a toast.

'This summer has been perfect so far and I just want to thank you all. My wonderful children, for being the light of my life, Simon and Louise for making our family even bigger and happier – and, of course, for all the fabulous food you make – and Grace…' He paused and gazed at her. His skin was golden after weeks of being outdoors, even when he'd been coated in sun cream, and he had a spattering of light brown freckles over his nose and cheeks. The bright blue-green of his eyes was enhanced by his tan and Grace knew she'd never tire of looking into them and wondering at how lucky she was. 'Thank you for making us all so happy. You are a wonderful woman and I love you so much.'

'Let's go over to the rock pools, Daddy!' Tom blurted.

Oli glanced at him, and Grace thought she saw something warning in his expression.

'Right now, Tom?'

'Yes, Daddy, I think we should too.' Amy nodded.

'Okay then…' Oli held out his hand.

Grace went to put her champagne down but Oli said, 'Bring it. It'll be fine.'

They got up and strolled to the rock pools. Tom gestured at one and called Grace over. When she got there, she peered into the water of the pool with Tom, their heads so close she could smell the salt and sun cream combination on his skin.

'What're we looking for?' she asked.

Tom shrugged. 'Um… anything.' He glanced behind her and as she went to turn around, he grabbed her arm. 'No, Grace, look into this one.'

'Oh… okay.' She knew in that moment that something was going on, but she didn't want to spoil the surprise. Whatever it was that her little family had concocted now. They were always doing lovely things for her, like the time when Amy and Oli had gone out shopping and returned with a beautiful new throw for the sofa in her writing room, and the times when Tom and Oli had made her breakfast in bed because she'd been writing late into the night. They were always doing things to show her how much they loved and cared about her.

'Tom!' Oli called, then beckoned them towards a rock pool further along.

'Come on, Grace.' Tom took her hand and led her towards his father and his sister.

'Grace…' Oli smiled at her, 'look in this pool.'

'Yes, Grace, there's something in there.'

She looked from Oli to Amy, then to Tom; they were all smiling.

When she leant forwards and peered into the water, she saw the same as she had in the last rock pool: some slimy rocks, a few small transparent fish that darted from one side to the other and some seaweed. But there was something else in there too. Something sparkly and silver.

She met Oli's eyes.

'I've wracked my brains about how to do this and with the children's help, I decided upon this way.'

Grace stared at the diamond ring.

'You mean you're…' Her throat ached as the reality of what was happening washed over her.

'Yes, Grace. If you'll have us, that is. We three love you so much, and we want to keep you forever. So will you marry me? Or should I say us?'

Grace reached into the water and lifted the ring. The large square diamond glistened in the sunlight. 'It's perfect.'

'Like you.'

Grace held the ring up.

'Are you sure about this?'

'More certain than I've ever been about anything.'

'Come on, Grace, say yes!' Tom clapped his hands.

'I can't think of anything I want more than to be with you all forever. I love you three so much too.'

Oli took the ring from her, then slid it onto her finger.

'Grace, I promise to love you and cherish you for the rest of my life.'

'And I promise to love and cherish you, Amy and Tom for the rest of mine.'

'Give her a kiss, Daddy.' Amy nudged her father.

Oli opened his arms and Grace moved closer to him. It wasn't how she'd thought this might happen, caked in sun cream and sand with her hair tangled from the sea and the wind, and the salt drying on her skin. But it was absolutely perfect.

'What did she say?' Simon called from their picnic spot.

'Let's go and show your parents.'

They returned to Louise and Simon.

'Mum and Dad, I take it you were in on this?'

'I asked your father's permission.'

'Permission?' Grace laughed.

'Well, you know, I ran the idea past him and he was quite happy with it. Your mother too.'

'Let me see!' Louise held out her hand and Grace showed her the ring that fitted perfectly. 'Oh, it's gorgeous. Congratulations both!'

'This calls for more champagne.' Simon topped up their glasses. 'And I have something special for dessert.'

After they'd eaten the melt-in-the-mouth strawberry meringues with soft white ice cream from Foxglove Farm, they all sat under the umbrellas enjoying the afternoon. Amy and Tom worked at a word search in a bumper book that Grace had bought for them and that had proved very popular, even in this day of technology. She knew it was also good for their spelling and vocabulary, but hadn't let on that it was an educational prop too.

Simon and Louise were both reading, Louise had her e-reader and was going through the first draft of Grace's latest book, which she'd emailed to her mother earlier, and Simon was reading the latest psychological thriller that had hit the top of the charts that summer.

Grace was leaning on Oli as they finished their champagne. His skin was warm next to hers and his scent was one of summer at the beach. Sea salt, sun cream, and his own delicious smell, the one that always made Grace's stomach flip. Next to her, Hope was roaching on the picnic blanket, her tongue lolling from her mouth and her legs in the air.

'Oli...'

'Yes?'

'Thank you for making me so happy. I have more than I could ever have imagined.'

'You've made us happy too. Not many women would want to take on a widower with two children.'

'Well, I'm not sure about that because you, Amy and Tom are amazing. But for me, this is perfect. I never thought I'd have a family of my own.'

'I never thought I'd be happy again.'

'I love you, Oli.'

'And I love you.'

Happiness flowed through Grace and she gazed at the beautiful engagement ring on her left hand.

'One more thing.' Oli sat up and took her hand, his expression turning serious.

'Yes?'

'Would you be happy to adopt the children? You know, to make things more official.'

'Really?'

He nodded. 'It's the right thing to do for us and for them. I know they'd be delighted and it would make things more secure for them too.'

'That would be amazing.' Her vision blurred and her heart swelled so much she thought it might burst.

And as the seagulls swooped into the sea, the waves lapped at the shore, and her family sat around her, with her husband-to-be at her side, Grace knew that she was very lucky.

Some days, she couldn't believe that her life had changed so dramatically. It was so very different to the one she'd been living for all those years. Now she was happy, fulfilled and loved.

Now she had the perfect life.

And it had all come about because of one very special Christmas at Conwenna Cove.

Acknowledgements

My thanks go to the following:

My husband and children, for your wonderful support. I love you and you are my world. XXX

My three writing buddies: Spike, Freya and Zelda. You provide me with laughs, love and inspiration.

The fabulous team at Canelo, for helping me to develop the Conwenna Cove series. I am always grateful for your enthusiasm, your kindness and your patience, especially when I bombard you with emails and ask numerous questions. In particular, thanks to Louise Cullen, for your dedication and hard work on my books, as well as the lovely things you say about my stories and my characters. You understand what I'm trying to do, but you help me do it better!

My agent Amanda Preston. Thank you for your support over recent months. I am excited about working with you on future books!

My author friends. Your support is always appreciated.

The blogging community, because you are amazing!

My readers who come back for more. I love you guys!

And special thanks go to Greyhound Rescue Wales and its supporters.